CLASH OF BEASTS

A GOING WILD NOVEL

Also by Lisa McMann

Going Wild

Going Wild #2: Predator vs. Prey

LISA McMANN

A **GOING** *WILD* NOVEL

HARPER

An Imprint of HarperCollins*Publishers*

Library of Congress Control Number: 2018945996

ISBN 978-0-06-233720-7 (trade bdg.)

Typography by Sarah Creech

18 19 20 21 22 CG/LSCH 10 9 8 7 6 5 4 3 2 1

❖

First Edition

To the real Yolanda, and to Gigi and Lexi, who call her Abu

CHAPTER 1

The New Recruit

It was the middle of May and school was out in Navarro Junction, but that fact barely registered with Kelly Parker. She'd made a risky decision to leave her old life after the spring-break disaster and join Dr. Victor Gray and his soldiers. She sat in the backseat of the white van as they sped along the California freeway, thinking about how much her life had changed in the past few weeks and trying not to feel anxious about the important task she was about to attempt. Trying not to think about everything that had gone wrong yesterday on her first mission . . . at SeaWorld.

Kelly wasn't used to failing. But she hadn't anticipated how many problems she'd have using two of her device's animal abilities at once. Remembering what had happened messed with Kelly's head a little as she prepared for today's challenge, but she couldn't seem to stop. She knew how much concentration it took to manipulate her camouflage power to create its hypnotic effect—she should have foreseen the issue. And she should have objected to that kind of mission until she believed without any doubt that she could succeed. She ought to have told Dr. Gray that for her first task, maybe it would be better to go after DNA that *didn't* involve dangerous water animals, or require her to use her dolphin swimming ability while simultaneously trying to use her cuttlefish hypnosis ability.

Kelly's face flushed in frustration and embarrassment. She had never enjoyed swimming, but she liked it even less now. She glanced up at Miko and Dr. Gray, who were in the front seat having a quiet conversation. Kelly hoped it wasn't about what a failure she'd been.

"Stop it," Kelly chided herself under her breath. An accomplished actor, soccer player, and student, she'd never gotten good at any of those things by being negative. This was a challenge, and her competitive nature kicked in as usual. Today was a new day, and despite a few unsettling doubts after the SeaWorld incident, Kelly was feeling reasonably confident about *this* task. Because today they were visiting Safari Park, part of the San Diego Zoo, and staying far away from water. It was Kelly's time to shine and prove to Dr. Gray that she could handle her abilities. And hopefully help erase yesterday from his mind.

They parked. All three got out of the van and started toward the entrance.

Beneath her clothes, Kelly wore her new camo-friendly bodysuit, which worked with her cuttlefish camouflage and allowed her entire body to fully blend into the environment whenever she needed or wanted to. Luckily, while the Mark Four's animal abilities altered her body slightly whenever she was using them, it never permanently changed her appearance, like the Mark

One had done to Miko and the rest of Dr. Gray's soldiers. Kelly looked like an average almost–seventh grader visiting the zoo. *Above average*, she thought to herself with a smile.

Kelly's long blond hair was slicked back and secured at her neck. She walked assuredly alongside Dr. Gray, who was dressed like a civilian in jeans and a T-shirt instead of his usual lab coat. Miko was wearing her black bodysuit as usual, but with a shirt thrown over it as a disguise. And for the first time in public, at Kelly's urging, Miko had daringly left her mask off, though she kept it with her in a bag in case she needed it. Instead, she wore a floppy sun hat to cover the fur that had taken the place of her human hair. The hat brim conveniently cast shadows over her slightly altered facial structure. She kept her bodysuit zipped up tight to cover the fur on her chin and neck. As a chimpanzee-human hybrid, Miko didn't have much facial fur to draw attention to her like the others, but she still seemed a little nervous to be without the mask she'd worn in public for years. Although she was clearly happy, too. She bounced around the other two and ducked behind them when zoo visitors approached. And with the oversize hat, no one really seemed to notice her. People at the zoo were looking at the animals in their habitats and cages, not at other people . . . or at hybrids who could pass as an ordinary person.

Once inside the Safari Park gates, the three squinted at the tall sign with arrows indicating the different parts of the zoo. "Condor Ridge," said Miko, pointing at an arrow. "That's the place we need. This way." She bounded in that direction and almost hopped up to grab a tree branch along the walking path but stopped herself before too many people noticed her extreme enthusiasm. She slowed down and waited, bouncing on the balls of her feet, for Kelly and Dr. Gray to catch up. Kelly could tell Miko was trying to subdue her excitement, but her antics were drawing a bit of unwanted attention. The chimp woman looked guiltily at Dr. Gray and pulled her hat down farther over her eyes.

Dr. Gray frowned but didn't reprimand her. He was eager for this visit, too. In the past, when working for Talos Global with the other biologists, he'd had a large variety of animal DNA available to him whenever he'd needed it, without having to step foot outside the lab. Now all he had were the samples he'd already used on his soldiers over the years. To expand the collection, he and his soldiers had to gather the DNA the old-fashioned way, directly from the animals themselves, and they weren't always easy to get. Over the past few weeks all he'd successfully gotten was a porcupine quill, which he had been planning to use for Braun's upgrade. Plus a few other bits of animal DNA that he wanted for his own mysterious purposes.

But there had been some failed attempts at collecting the important samples . . . like yesterday. He was angry at himself for expecting too much of the girl—he should have known better than to have her go for the shark right off the bat. But he'd let his excitement and Kelly's self-assuredness get in the way of his better judgment. And, to be truthful, he was in a hurry. Without Zed to help him anymore, he needed every willing soldier he could find. Even the kid.

Hopefully, today would be far easier for Kelly and she'd be able to procure new samples for Dr. Gray to use in his experiments. With any success, Miko would soon be a living, breathing chimera of sorts, having her DNA mixed with a second animal and bringing Dr. Gray one step closer to his ultimate goal. The three continued the lengthy walk up the path to the condor enclosure, all thinking about different aspects of the job before them.

Miko spied a pair of the birds sitting a distance apart on a large rock inside the exhibit. She drew up against the enclosure and grimaced. "Their faces are so *uuug-ly*," she muttered. "They're even grosser in person. I really hope that part doesn't transfer to me."

"I guess we'll find out eventually if it does," said Dr. Gray lightly.

Miko's eyes bugged out. She turned to Dr. Gray, hoping he was teasing, but it was hard to tell. The soldiers hadn't seen him in a good mood in a while. Not since before the other scientists— the real bad guys, according to Dr. Gray—had come along and started ruining things. Gray continued to feel uneasy about the other Project Chimera scientists, so things had remained tense.

Kelly wasn't paying attention to Miko and Dr. Gray's discussion. She had other things on her mind, like clearing her thoughts to focus. Not messing up. And most important, trying to find the saw a sign for an ocelot. She wasn't quite sure what an ocelot was, though from its picture, it looked like a cat-type creature. She hoped it wouldn't attack her while she was busy with the condor. Kelly's hands began to sweat, and she wiped them on her clothes and then ditched those for her suit. "You didn't mention there were other animals in this section," she muttered to Miko.

"I didn't know," said Miko. "Sorry. But they seem . . . friendly."

"The sign says ocelots are carnivores," Kelly said, "and I am made of meat." She was annoyed but there was nothing she could do about it. She searched the area for a zoo worker. Finally, she spied one carrying a bucket and walking toward what looked like the entrance to the habitat. "You two stay here," Kelly said in a low voice to Dr. Gray and Miko. "Let me do all the talking."

Dr. Gray put a hand on Kelly's shoulder, like Coach Candy, Kelly's soccer coach, used to do sometimes during a pep talk. "Just remain calm and don't panic," he told her. "You only have to use one ability this time. You shouldn't have any problems."

Kelly grimaced. "I'm fine. Please . . . can you stop talking about . . . that? I'll show you I can do this better than anyone." She was one of the few people who didn't seem to walk on eggshells around the doctor, and so far she'd been able to get away with telling him what she thought, at least when it came to her abilities. Maybe it was because her device had been made by a different scientist. Or perhaps it was because Kelly could do something unique that would really help Dr. Gray collect DNA faster—because things had been going agonizingly slowly until recently. They'd had to move the lab for the umpteenth time. Then Dr. Gray had struggled for weeks trying to repair the machine that he'd forced the other scientists to make, which had been smashed to pieces when Charlie and her friends broke in and rescued them.

Whatever the reason, the man didn't argue with Kelly and stayed back with Miko.

Walking down to where the zoo worker was, Kelly clicked her bracelet to activate the cuttlefish camouflage. With each step her body slowly changed to green and brown, blending into the wood wall structure and foliage that lined the path to the enclosure. Nimbly she hopped over the chained-off area near the entrance to the habitat and concentrated for a moment until she could feel heat rise to her face and her skin begin to pulse. Then she beckoned to the zoo worker. "Excuse me," Kelly called out.

The woman looked up and almost didn't see her at first. Then she frowned and started toward her. "You can't be in here."

Soft waves of blue and white light rippled over Kelly's face, moving in a steady, mesmerizing pattern and growing stronger with each wave as the woman approached.

"This area is off-limits to park visitors," the worker said, looking startled at Kelly's strange appearance. "I'm sorry, miss. Are you . . ." The woman's face slackened, and she fell silent for a moment. "Are you lost?" She didn't move or look away.

"No, I'm not lost." Kelly smiled disarmingly as the woman stared at her. "I need to see the condors. I'm sure you understand."

The woman blinked a few times. The handle she was holding slipped from her fingers and the bucket clattered to the ground, unnoticed. She seemed to try to form words to object to Kelly's request, but was having trouble. "No, I . . . ," she said softly, "I can't. . . ."

"Yes, you can," said Kelly in a soothing voice. "I need to see the condors now." The light show on her face continued. "Just unlock the door and take me inside."

The woman hesitated, but Kelly stood confidently. A moment later the worker was fumbling for her keys, looking bewildered, but doing what was asked. Finally she opened the door.

Kelly kept the waves of light pulsing over her skin as she went in after the woman. She looked around cautiously for the nearest condor, wanting to stay as close as possible to the exit in case anything unexpected happened. She located the ones they'd seen resting on the rocks nearby, and approached one of the huge birds. As she drew near, the zoo worker followed. Kelly gazed in awe at the condor's size. The bird turned its ugly pink head and stared at her, but stayed where it was. Kelly, still pulsing, glanced around her. Out of the corner of her eye she noticed one of the horned sheepy-goat things about thirty yards away. She didn't focus on it, knowing she needed to keep her concentration. She turned back to the condor, which seemed to be entranced by her now, too. "Hi, bird," she said. "This will only hurt for a few seconds." Slowly she reached out, cringed, then gripped a couple of feathers. They were bigger and coarser than she'd imagined. Quickly she yanked them from the condor's wing and backed up a few steps.

The condor hissed and rose, spreading its dark wings wide and showing a stripe of white underneath. Each wing was longer than she was tall—the span was *enormous*. Kelly felt her heart pounding. She reminded herself that her research said condors don't attack prey. Then she saw the sheepy-goat coming closer. She had a moment of panic and clicked her device to deploy her platypus spikes on her heels, just in case it charged. Thankfully the condor settled again, and the horned creature got distracted by something in the dirt and stopped to eat it.

Kelly blew out a deep breath. She slipped the feathers into a clear plastic pouch and put it in her waist pack. Slowly she turned away, checking to see how many of the zoo visitors had noticed her. She might have to do some mind control on the way out, too. Miko was still standing by the cage but not looking straight at Kelly for fear of being hypnotized. The chimp woman's fingers curled around the railing, as if it was all she could do not to climb up the cage and start swinging on the enclosure netting.

Kelly kept the pulsing going. She reached the door with the zoo worker walking complacently alongside her. "Thank you," Kelly said as she went out. "You'll forget about me in a minute. Okay?"

The woman looked troubled, but nodded. "Okay," she said.

Kelly smiled, then began walking toward the crowds. She broke her concentration and let the hypnotic pulses fade. Her body returned to its nearly invisible camouflage state as she blended into the rocky background. She clicked off her platypus spikes. Then she clicked off the cuttlefish ability. Kelly appeared to emerge from the wall looking quite normal again. A few people close by watched her with puzzled looks, but they didn't do or say anything—they'd been close enough to have fallen under the mesmerizing spell too. Kelly rejoined her companions and handed the plastic pouch to Dr. Gray, who swiftly slid it into his pocket.

"Well done," the scientist quietly praised, though he was glancing around carefully and turning to leave. "That went smoothly."

"I told you I could do it."

"Yes, you did. I'm thrilled. A definite success."

"That was great, Kelly," said Miko. "You were such a pro."

"Thanks," said Kelly, puffing up from the praise as they moved swiftly away from the attraction. "I've gotten really good at hypnotizing," she said, impassioned. Now that she'd succeeded, she felt a sudden need to explain what had gone wrong yesterday. "You see, I just hadn't ever had a chance to practice swimming and hypnotizing at once. I guess . . . I thought I could do it."

"This mission was a much better one to start with," said Dr. Gray.

"Yeah," said Kelly. "At least it wasn't in a shark-infested pool this time, right?" She fell in step with Dr. Gray, feeling a fresh surge of confidence now that she'd managed this task without a hitch.

"The setting today was much improved," agreed Dr. Gray, and Miko nodded behind them.

Relieved, Kelly glanced at Dr. Gray a bit sheepishly. "Look," she said, "I'm sorry we got kicked out of SeaWorld before we could go in search of that jellyfish you're looking for. Hopefully Cyke and Prowl are having better luck finding it today." Cyke, a horse hybrid, and Prowl, a leopard hybrid, were two of Dr. Gray's other prized soldiers. "This job was a cinch compared to the shark incident."

"It's not your fault," said Dr. Gray, beginning to sound a bit impatient. "I made a mistake in judgment yesterday. I should have had you start with this, clearly the easier job. But I was overeager for the shark DNA. I've wanted to experiment with it for so long, but hadn't been able to obtain a sample until you came along— the Mark Four's abilities are perfect for that kind of predator." He frowned. "I let my eagerness overrule my hesitations."

"Besides," Miko added, "nobody thought that you'd actually need to go *into* the pool, you know."

Dr. Gray grimaced and shook his head, like the whole thing had been a cluster of mishaps and mistakes. "Just forget about it. We'll try again at another aquarium when you're ready, Kelly. For now, with what you've accomplished, Miko will soon be able to get her condor wings. And . . . ," he said, pressing his lips into a small smirk, "her pink bald head."

"Ugh, no!" said Miko, hopping along, but it was clear she enjoyed seeing Dr. Gray lighten up a bit for once. "Now you're just being mean, teasing me like that." She stayed close to Kelly, still careful to keep her face hidden, then said abruptly, "What time is it? Do you want me to tell Cyke we're finished here, and we'll be on our way shortly to pick them up? Are they just going to meet us in the SeaWorld parking lot since Kelly is banned for life?"

Kelly rolled her eyes and elbowed the chimp woman, half-annoyed and half-embarrassed that Miko brought up *that* part again. But then she chuckled reluctantly. "Kelly Parker. Banned from SeaWorld. It's kind of funny, isn't it?"

"Kind of inconvenient is more like it," said Dr. Gray matter-of-factly. "But it won't be too hard to find shark DNA elsewhere, and with you being a child . . . well, you're much less suspicious-looking."

Miko patted Kelly's shoulder reassuringly. "It would have gone flawlessly if you hadn't hit the trainer ladder. That's what made you lose your concentration, wasn't it?"

"I suppose," muttered Kelly.

Dr. Gray gave a rude snort of laughter as they walked, as if he were remembering the scene. Reluctantly Kelly had to admit that the part where the aquarium workers hauled her out of the shark pool must have been quite a sight to witness.

The doctor soon became preoccupied and thoughtful again. "I imagine Dr. Sharma chose to use the cuttlefish for the Mark Four because of its amazing camouflage ability. You were clever to realize how to take full advantage of that power by replicating the animal's hypnotic pulsating ability. That kind of ingenuity is valuable to me. How did you know you could do it? Did Dr. Sharma tell you?"

Kelly beamed from the rare compliment. "I don't know what Dr. Sharma meant to do with the cuttlefish ability. She never said anything to me. When I originally read about it in the Project Chimera papers and tried it out the first time, I thought all I could do was camouflage. Even when I went to L.A. to be on *LIVE, TONIGHT*, I didn't know the ability could expand to hypnosis or I would have used it then to get that creepy host to let go of me." She frowned a moment, remembering, then shook her head slightly. "It wasn't until I was on the bus ride back to Arizona that I started studying more about cuttlefish. That's when I found out they can use that camouflage technique not only to hide, but also to mesmerize their prey. I figured I should at least give it a shot, so I practiced when the lady next to me fell asleep—I used the camera on my phone to see if I could get the pulsating-stripe thing going. Once the lady woke up, I tried it on her and it sort of worked. She was really confused at least. Enough for me to know there was something to it."

"I'll bet she was freaked out," said Miko with a chimpy laugh.

The walkway they were on rejoined the main road that would take them to the exit.

"Anyway," Kelly continued, "after I joined your team, I knew I had to do something to keep my parents from worrying about me, and everyone at school from looking for me. So I kept practicing while you guys were searching for a place to go next. I managed to hypnotize Mega in the backseat of the van." Kelly snorted. "But don't say anything; I never told her. I was really nervous to use it on my teachers, but when it worked on Mr. Anderson, who knows me better than practically anyone, I knew it could actually work on my parents, too. And it did. They . . ." Her expression flickered. "They pretty much forgot all about me."

CHAPTER 2

Deep Thoughts

After Kelly had visited the school the first time with her hypnotic plans, she'd realized that convincing Mr. Anderson she didn't exist would only cause a stir with the students—there was no way she could have hypnotized everyone in her school and life to think that. So she'd gone back and rehypnotized him and the rest of the faculty to believe she'd moved away instead. But her parents— she'd had to make them forget. There was no other way to do it.

It hadn't been hard to convince them to forget about her either, which bothered Kelly a little. She thought she'd have to work on them a few times . . . but no. She scowled and tried to rid her thoughts of home and her former life. Sure, it was a bummer that she missed being in the school musical—hopefully whoever had gotten the lead hadn't messed it up too badly. But she didn't miss the drama of her parents fighting. She didn't miss that whenever they weren't yelling at her they mostly ignored her. Skipping out on their messy divorce process was actually kind of convenient. It was a relief to leave that stress behind.

This life using her animal abilities was more the style Kelly craved—where she could take the spotlight. Be important and do things nobody else could do. And have people appreciate her, like Dr. Gray did. Obviously, Kelly knew he wasn't perfect—far from it. After all, he'd done some pretty bad things to Mac Barnes, but Dr. Gray had told her that was all because of a big misunderstanding with Charlie's bracelet. And sure, he'd kept Charlie's dad and the other scientists in his lab when they didn't want to be there. But Dr. Gray had explained that he'd really needed their help to proceed with his amazing work—which was top secret kind of stuff for the government, he'd told her. And those other scientists had been the ones trying to stop him, so didn't that make them the bad guys? Kelly didn't really know much about them, other than the fact that none of this weird stuff started happening until Charlie's family moved in. And Dr. Sharma and Ms. Sabbith had tried to take Kelly's device away. So they did seem suspicious.

Anyway, now that Dr. Gray had fixed the machine they'd all built together, he'd turned his full attention to his work and was back to being super focused on finding the right combination of animals to make the ultimate chimera.

Besides, this science experiment was exciting. Better and more important than the kinds of things Kelly had done in school. She liked being a part of it. And unlike the other scientists, Dr. Gray didn't want to take her bracelet—he wanted her to use it! His trust in her made her feel important and necessary in ways she'd never felt before. Hypnotizing zoo and aquarium workers so she could grab DNA from the animals? Okay, so that part felt a little bit wrong, but Kelly wasn't trying to harm anyone. And it was for a good cause. It seemed like such a small sacrifice for these people to make, especially since they wouldn't remember it anyway. Kelly was sure they'd be happy they'd helped to advance science if they ever found out what Dr. Gray was doing. And for Kelly personally, acting in this powerful role was like being the star of a new show every day. It was thrilling and a little dangerous. While the soldiers had been skeptical of her at first because she was just a kid, Kelly had been respectful, and they'd come to accept her. And Dr. Gray was on her side. She could control people and animals to her heart's content without anyone judging or looking down on her.

She frowned. Control *most* animals, anyway. That shark at Sea-World hadn't fallen under her spell, and the whole experience had been a nightmare. And if she was being honest, while Kelly loved having abilities in general, she didn't totally love her bracelet's specific abilities. If it had been up to her, she would have picked different ones. Even though the Mark Four had been designed using water animals, that didn't mean Kelly liked the water any more now than she had before. Not to mention sharks were just plain scary, no matter how fast Kelly could swim now.

As the three of them continued toward the zoo exit, Kelly thought about how things had gone down the previous day. The plan had been for her to sneak into the shark enclosure and lean over the edge of the pool to try to hypnotize a swimming shark so it would stay close by and give Kelly an opportunity to swipe its skin with a special tool. No big deal . . . if you forget about the teeth. And it had started off all right, but then everything had gone wrong. Some workers had seen her and rushed in, and Kelly couldn't hypnotize them fast enough—not while trying to get the sample, too. They'd lunged at her, and Kelly had panicked. She'd wanted that shark DNA and wasn't about to leave without it. So she'd yanked herself away from the workers and had fallen into the pool.

Her dolphin ability had kicked in, and so had her freak-out mode: was she about to get eaten? But Kelly wasn't going to go down without a fight. She'd decided that chasing the shark was a better idea than being chased by it, so she'd done just that. Following a shark around and trying to scrape its skin while not getting attacked or caught by the aquarium workers had been ridiculous. When the shark noticed her, it turned sharply and came after her. She'd tried to get away and bonked into the ladder, and in the end, she'd failed. But she hadn't gotten eaten, so there was that.

Dr. Gray wasn't mad at her, but Kelly had unfortunately made such a big scene in the shark pool that she'd been kicked out of the park. For life.

Ugh. She still hated the water. "You know," she blurted out as she, Dr. Gray, and Miko neared the Safari Park exit, "I'd easily trade the dolphin ability for something else someday." Doing *anything* underwater would probably never be something Kelly would outright enjoy. If she hung around Dr. Gray long enough, maybe he would give her some new powers. If he was going to give each of the soldiers new abilities, why not her?

"You might like it more once you get some practice," said Miko.

"Maybe," said Kelly with a sigh.

"Now that the lab's set up," said Miko, "and Dr. Gray has a couple samples to start working on, we could have some downtime. I'll take you swimming. You know? So you can practice using multiple abilities at once before you try going for the shark DNA again. We should have thought of that before. If Zed were still here, she would have."

Dr. Gray frowned. Talking about Zed, the panther hybrid, had been a tender subject with him. She'd been a fellow biologist from all the way back in his Talos Global days—an original member of Project Chimera. She'd made the Mark Two, and had been his most faithful ally and the very first test subject with his Mark One. And now she'd left without a word. It had shaken up the team a bit. Dr. Gray had even stayed hidden in the Phoenix area for a few extra days hoping she'd come back, or at least make contact through the communication system that was built into her suit. All the soldiers had tried talking to her since then, but not even Miko—who Kelly learned was the nicest of the pack—could get Zed to respond. Still, every now and then Miko made another attempt. "You never know," she would always say. "Zed might change her mind and come back. I'm not giving up on her."

They exited the zoo and entered the parking lot unhindered, and when she was sure they were out of earshot of anyone else, Kelly turned to Dr. Gray and tried again. "So now that we have the condor DNA for Miko, could we search for something to add to my device?"

Dr. Gray's expression clouded. He didn't answer at first. Then he muttered, "We'll see about something for you eventually." He hesitated, then added, "But even after I've had the chance to create Miko's formula, the others are still patiently waiting for their second abilities. And you already have four. Trust me, I have a method here that I'm trying to follow."

"You have Braun's porcupine DNA already."

"True," said Dr. Gray, wincing a little as he remembered how he'd gotten it. "But I've barely just finished fixing the *machine*. And there's a lot more DNA we still need to gather. I have a great deal of work ahead of me." He paused, then reminded them that Zed had thrown a wrench into his plans. "Twice as much work as I'd expected to have to do."

"Oh. Right." Kelly stared at the ground as they walked. She sighed deeply.

Dr. Gray glanced at her. "I really value the gifts you bring to the team," he said carefully. "So please don't be upset—you will definitely be rewarded . . . in the end. I'm just not quite there yet in the process. I—I want you to have . . . something special."

Miko's expression flickered.

Kelly frowned. Was he talking about the formula for his perfect chimera? How long would *that* take? After a minute she said, "I don't see why we can't try out one of these new animals on me while you're testing them on the others anyway. It wouldn't take much extra time to inject the formula into my bracelet, would it?"

"That's not how it works." Dr. Gray sighed loudly, as if annoyed. "And let's not forget you have plenty to work on with your current abilities first."

Kelly's face burned. She dropped the subject and got into the van, brooding about things. It was moments like these that made her unsure about her decision to join this team. But her uncertainty flickered and mostly went away. Kelly settled into the backseat and mused about how she'd gotten to this place where acting and looking like animals was normal. There was no turning back now.

Obviously, the whole chimera thing was awesome. And getting to work on a secret project that the government trusted Dr. Gray to do made Kelly feel pretty special. But sometimes . . . well, the experiment sounded a little *weird*. Especially when Kelly spent a lot of time thinking about it as she was now, stuck in the van in Southern California traffic with no cell phone to play with. And she still didn't quite understand everything. Like, *why* did the government want Gray to do this? Just to see what would happen? Just to say they'd done something no other country had? Is that what scientists lived for? Or did they expect to have to actually *use* this ultimate chimera to fight off some other enemy?

Kelly still wasn't quite sure how she felt each time she learned something new about Dr. Gray's progress—there were moments when it almost seemed like he was planning something bigger than what he was telling her and Miko and the other soldiers. But Miko seemed to be fine with everything. She, like the other soldiers, was obviously willing to be involved in this. And Kelly generally took her cues from her, the one she had grown to trust the most.

Not to mention Dr. Gray had said he had a method he was trying to follow. Kelly understood methods—she used them for acting. She'd used them in soccer, too. They worked. She respected methods and found it strangely comforting to know Dr. Gray had a way of doing things. That he wasn't haphazardly trying to create these chimeras. It made him seem disciplined. And less . . . insane.

Not that he was insane, Kelly thought hastily. She was sure he wasn't. Pretty sure, anyway. He just . . . *seemed* less so when he was talking sense. Talking about methods. Like . . . a teacher might.

Kelly shifted in the backseat and stared out the window, not really seeing anything out there, but wrapped up in her thoughts. She had a method here, too, she realized. Collect DNA to prove her value. Wait for the reward. Find fame and make it stick this time. After that she could kiss Dr. Gray good-bye if she wanted to. But she was still on step one. For now, the more DNA Kelly could gather for the team, the more valuable she'd be. And the closer Dr. Gray would get to creating the perfect chimera formula for the government. Hopefully Kelly would get her promised reward too, somewhere along the way. And then she could be one of the strongest, most powerful people in the world. She'd break the freaking internet with her awesomeness.

As Miko drove onto the interstate on-ramp heading back to Sea World and Dr. Gray studied some papers on his lap in the passenger seat, Kelly closed her eyes to meditate. She never noticed the SUV zipping past them, loaded with suitcases and three twelve-year-olds chattering noisily in the backseat, heading for a week-long vacation.

But someone in that vehicle did notice the familiar old white van.

CHAPTER 3

A Break from Reality

"Was that . . . ?" said Charlie Wilde softly, twisting around in the backseat of the Barnes family SUV. "No. It couldn't have been." She peered over the suitcases. Her two companions turned to look. Charlie pointed at a white van behind them moving slowly in the more congested right-lane traffic. It was soon hidden behind a couple of buses and a semitrailer truck as Mac's mom, Claudia, slipped into the commuter lane and zoomed ahead.

"I don't know," said Maria Torres, one of Charlie's best friends. "I didn't get a good look."

"That was it, all right," muttered Mac, who'd spent some time tied up in the back of it. "I'd recognize that van anywhere."

"So this is where they went?" asked Maria.

Charlie held a finger to her lips and glanced at Mac's parents in the front seat. Then she leaned in and whispered, "Ms. Sabbith tracked their license plate to the Arizona-California border, but then she lost the trail. She's still trying to find them. I'll text her that we spotted the van." She kept her voice low. "Do you think Dr. Gray saw us? Is he following us?" Charlie was confused. And while she was always on the lookout for soldiers in black bodysuits, the white van, and the awful Dr. Gray, she never expected to catch sight of them in such a random place as this.

The kids hadn't seen any sign of soldiers or danger since Gray had packed up his lab and left Navarro Junction, taking Kelly with them. But the arrogant biologist had foolishly spilled some details to Mrs. Wilde and the kids when he thought he'd had them beat. He and his hybrid soldiers were secretly trying to change everyone in the world into chimeras. And Charlie's dad and his fellow scientists were working just as hard and even more secretly to stop them.

"He's probably forgotten about us by now," said Maria, but she bit her lip anxiously anyway and glanced at her bare right wrist, where her Mark Two device used to be. She didn't have possession of it at the moment—Dr. Nubia Jakande, also known as Zed to Dr. Gray's team, was trying to fix it.

In the time since Nubia had left Dr. Gray and joined their side, she'd already managed to change Maria back to normal. It was a huge relief for Maria because she no longer had to worry about turning into a weremonkey at inopportune times anymore. The task, though time-consuming, had seemed simple enough. All Nubia needed was some of Maria's old, unaltered DNA—which they collected from a hairbrush—to concoct a formula that changed her back. But now Dr. Jakande had to reconfigure the Mark Two so that same problem didn't happen again the next time Maria put it on, which was a great deal harder. At the same time, the scientists were designing a few other improvements to the bracelets to help protect the kids in case they ended up needing to fight Dr. Gray's soldiers again.

Not having the bracelet left Maria vulnerable and unable to train, and she felt a little lost without it. She looked out the back window again. "That dude makes me nervous."

Mac saw Maria's worried expression. "I hear you," he said, noting the right lanes had slowed to a crawl. "But they're stuck way back there. And they'll never find us, if they even saw us in the first place. Besides, Charlie and I have your back." The silver Mark Three device shone on his arm—Dr. Goldstein had been planning to upgrade it too, but let Mac keep it while he did the prep work. And Charlie's old Mark Five was back on her wrist while she waited for her father to put the finishing touches on the Mark Six—which would have *her* DNA tied to it instead of his.

"I just don't like being anywhere near those soldiers without my bracelet," said Maria.

"Don't worry," said Charlie. "Remember, Dr. Sharma told us that the bad guys have everything they need now, so they don't have any reason to come after us. They've moved on and they're not even thinking about us. We should be safe until *we're* ready to go after *them*."

As Mrs. Barnes began crossing lanes again to get to their exit, Mr. Barnes half turned in the front passenger seat. "What are you kids playing?" he asked. "It sounds interesting."

Charlie froze. Maria looked sharply at Mac.

"Um," said Mac, clearly realizing that his dad had heard them talking and assumed they were playing some sort of game. "It's a new one." He lifted his iPad and waved it a little, making sure his dad didn't see the screen. "Oh, what's it called again, Charlie?"

Charlie laughed nervously. "It's, um . . ."

"It's a sci-fi adventure game," Maria said smoothly. "An evil scientist wants to take over the world and turn everybody into . . . uh . . ." She hesitated and gave Mac a look.

"Chimeras," Mac blurted out, then cringed but kept going. "And . . . we're trying to defeat him."

"That's a cool concept," said Mr. Barnes. "A chimera—that's one of those mythical creatures, right? Some kind of combination of—"

Mrs. Barnes put her hand on her husband's arm, interrupting him as she took the exit and slowed for a red light. "Help me with the directions here, will you? We want SeaWorld car parking."

Mr. Barnes turned to face the front and pointed out the huge sign indicating SeaWorld Drive ahead. "Pretty sure we'll find it eventually if we take this street," he said. "We've only been here five times before."

"Don't get cocky," Mac's mom warned, though there was laughter in her voice. "I've got too many other thoughts crowding my mind to keep directions to SeaWorld in there. You are free to drive if you don't want to navigate."

Mr. Barnes grinned. "Sorry, honey." He studied the GPS and pointed to a spot on the screen. "Yep, just keep going this way. Avoid the tour bus lane."

Crisis averted, the kids sat back and breathed again. Charlie sent a group text to the other two. "Great idea. Now we can use the game as an excuse if we get caught talking about this stuff again."

"Sorry I said chimera," Mac replied. "It just came out. Oops."

"It's fine," Maria wrote back. "It's not like anybody would ever expect this to be happening in real life."

"Good point," said Charlie. "May as well keep the story close to the truth—then we can talk about it without worrying about messing up. Should we come up with a name for this game in case Mac's dad asks again?"

"Yeah," said Mac. "If I know my dad, he'll definitely ask again."

They dropped their phones in their laps and thought about it, trying to come up with a good name as Mrs. Barnes pulled in to the correct SeaWorld lot and followed the flag-waving parking attendant's directions. Soon the kids were straining to catch a glimpse of the attractions out the window, forgetting about names. The top of a water ride was visible from the car.

"Look!" cried Charlie, who'd never been to California before, much less this park. "This is so freaking exciting! I can't believe we get to do something new every day this week."

Finally Mrs. Barnes parked the vehicle and everybody piled

out, anxious to get moving.

As the kids ran ahead of Mr. and Mrs. Barnes toward the entrance, Mac grabbed the other two. "Hey, Maria, Charlie, I've got it," he said excitedly. "A name for our fake game. We can call it *Clash of Beasts*. It sounds just like a game I'd play online."

Maria and Charlie quickly agreed to it.

By the time they reached the attractions, the white van had vanished from their minds. They never expected it to pull into the SeaWorld parking lot fifteen minutes behind them.

CHAPTER 4

Supernormal

Mac's parents let the kids go off on their own, which was an exciting development for them in a theme park. Mac took the lead. "Can we go to Ocean Explorer first, then Orca Encounter?" he asked. "They're both pretty new and I haven't done them yet."

"Mac goes to SeaWorld almost every year," Maria explained to Charlie. "He knows his way around this place like it's his neighborhood."

"I figured that out already," said Charlie. She and Maria almost had to jog to keep up with him.

The Ocean Explorer realm was right near the park entrance, so they hopped in line for the Submarine Quest ride. While they waited, they talked quietly about how Dr. Jakande was coming along with Maria's bracelet. They were hoping the biologist would be done fixing the problem by the time they got home from this trip.

"My dad said they're planning to add tracking and communication capabilities to our devices," said Charlie. "They're going to test everything out on Maria's device this week, and maybe the Mark Six if all goes well."

"When will they work on mine?" asked Mac.

"Soon I guess," said Charlie with a shrug. "Same with the Five." She flashed her wrist. "My parents wanted me to hold on to this for now, just in case I needed it for anything."

"Getting some extra safety features is cool," said Maria. The line moved, and she glanced around uneasily.

"What are you looking for?" asked Mac.

"I'm not sure," she said. "Nothing, I guess. I'm just feeling weird after seeing the van."

"I'm sure it's long gone by now." Mac shrugged and turned back to Charlie. "The scientists are still going to give us new abilities like you're getting with the Mark Six, right? Have they decided on the animals for them yet?"

"They've been talking about it a lot," said Charlie. "I've been dying to tell you, actually, but wanted to wait until we had some privacy away from your parents."

"Tell us what?" asked Mac.

Charlie leaned in. "Last night I hung out with the adults as they were discussing options. And my dad turned and asked me if *we* had any ideas for animal abilities! So I played it cool and said I'd ask you."

"Seriously?" asked Maria, gripping Charlie's arm.

Charlie nodded. "I don't know if they were just being nice or if they really meant it. And maybe they'll have decided by the time we get home. But it wouldn't hurt to do some research in case they ask again."

"That's so cool!" said Mac, whipping out his cell phone to start the search immediately.

The line continued to move surprisingly swiftly. As they chatted about animals, Maria and Charlie turned the research into a game, trying to guess which animals they each would add to their devices if they could. But they hadn't narrowed down the options at all before they were next in line.

Once they climbed into a mini submarine, the conversation became all about the sea life around them. The ride took them underwater through ocean habitats. They saw crabs, which reminded them of Morph—she was one of Dr. Gray's hybrid soldiers they'd fought who had a supersonic crab-claw punch. She had a second ability, a chameleon's, to camouflage herself as well.

A huge octopus came up to the glass, which made Charlie grateful that Gray hadn't tried to make a hybrid with that animal yet—she wasn't sure how dangerous octopuses were, but they looked . . . sneaky. And like they had really big brains. Not to mention all those arms.

Next they went through a segment of the ride that had tons of clear jellyfish with brightly colored insides. There were hundreds of them, in all sizes, some almost too small to notice.

Soon the ride was over. When they exited their submarine, thinking about standing in line for it again, a flash of black caught Charlie's eye. She turned in the crowded merchandise area and thought she saw someone in a black bodysuit moving through the far end, near the jellyfish tank. Charlie gasped and grabbed Maria's sleeve. "Look," she said in a low voice. "Is that Cyke?"

He was far away. Maria squinted. "I don't see him."

"I could have sworn it was him," said Charlie, though she doubted herself. "Then again, I think I see soldiers everywhere." She laughed uneasily. "Am I losing it?"

"Probably," said Mac with a grin. "I know we saw their van, but what would they be doing here? Maybe their new lab is around here somewhere." His grin faded. "Oh, wait. Between the zoo and SeaWorld, San Diego has all sorts of animals."

Charlie's eyes widened. "And my dad said that Dr. Gray probably doesn't have access to animal DNA from a lab like we do, so . . ."

"So it sorta makes sense that they'd have to . . . collect it," said Mac. "Themselves."

"Yes," said Maria thoughtfully, "I'll bet you're right. How else is Dr. Gray going to make his ultimate chimera?"

"Exactly," said Charlie, edging for the door. "Come on. Let's figure out where Cyke went." Charlie started jogging in the direction of where she'd seen the soldier, and the other two followed. As they moved through the crowds, Charlie spoke over her shoulder in a low voice. "The scientists said Dr. Gray is probably going to be doing more experiments on his soldiers, trying out different variations like he's already started doing with Morph and Fang. They think he'll be doing that until he figures out what the perfect combination is." She slid through the crowd, with Maria and Mac right behind.

They sneaked around the back side of the attraction and could see into an area enclosed by a chain-link fence. On the door was a sign that read Employees Only. Through the links they spotted a line of doors on the building with signs on them that apparently led to the control rooms for the various sea-life habitats within.

At first the friends didn't see anyone wandering around inside the fenced-in area except a landscaping crew laying fresh mulch along a sidewalk. But then Mac pointed at one of the doors on the building a few hundred feet away. It stood ajar.

Maria glanced at the fence door with the Employees Only sign on it and saw that it was unlocked, probably so that the landscapers could get in and out. "Come on," she said. She looked over her shoulder, then opened the door, and the three of them went inside.

Someone on the landscaping crew looked up and saw the kids. He started toward them, saying something in Spanish and trying to get them to leave the area. Maria had a conversation with him, though. After a minute, the man shrugged and went back to what he was doing.

Maria turned to Charlie and Mac. "Come on," she said, and beckoned them toward the ajar door. When they were out of earshot of the landscapers, she explained, "I asked if anyone else had come back here wearing black bodysuits. He said yes. He thinks they're divers or animal trainers. I told him we are at a kids' summer camp, and we're supposed to shadow them."

"That was quick thinking," Charlie said.

"Come on," said Maria. "They're back here in the jellyfish section."

They went up to the open door. Charlie shielded her eyes from the sun and peered into the crack. When her sight had adjusted well enough to see inside the room, she spotted a uniformed zoo employee lying on the floor, unconscious. She covered her mouth and held back a gasp, then spied a built-in ladder and looked up. Cyke and Prowl were standing on it, way at the top of the aquarium. Cyke was reaching into the water with a net. Charlie's bracelet grew warm on her wrist.

Quickly she stepped away and told Maria and Mac what she'd just seen. "Do you think we should go after them?"

"They're obviously doing something sneaky," said Maria, "and they already hurt one of the workers in there. But I don't have a bracelet right now, so I wouldn't be able to help you much."

"Yeah," said Mac, looking anxious. "Do we really want to get involved? They're not doing anything to *us*. I think we should get out of here and tell someone in charge at the park. And then hide. The soldiers don't need to know we're the narcs —they probably don't even suspect we're here. Who knows how many of them are around? Cyke and Prowl could call for backup with their little walkie-talkie buttons on their suits. And without Maria being able to change into a weremonkey, we'd have a tough time trying to take them all on."

Charlie stared at him, confused. It seemed so unlike Mac to want to run away.

Mac saw her look, then said with a cringe, "And just imagine explaining this to my parents."

"Oh no," said Maria, impassioned. "You're right. We *can't* let your parents find out. It'll ruin everything."

"Good point," said Charlie, a bit reluctantly. She didn't want Mr. and Mrs. Barnes to find out anything about what they were doing—it could wreck their plans to stop Dr. Gray. She took one more look as Cyke scooped awkwardly at some jellyfish, then turned away. "Okay. Let's go get them in trouble."

They went back the way they came, past the landscapers and out the gate. They rounded the building and exited the ride area, and went to the nearby park entrance. Two male and one female security officers were standing there chatting.

"Excuse me," said Maria. Charlie and Mac stood behind.

"What's up?" said one of the men.

"There are some strange men in black bodysuits trying to catch jellyfish. They went around the back of that building." Maria pointed to the Ocean Explorer ride. "Two of them. One is really big and the other one is smaller and . . . slinkier."

"Hmm. Bodysuits?" said the officer.

The female guard looked concerned. "Like yesterday with the

sharks?" she said to the first guy.

"What?" He seemed confused. "I was off yesterday."

"We had an incident in the shark habitat with some perps wearing bodysuits," she explained, annoyed. "Read your updates. Something weird is going on. Let's go check it out."

The man frowned. "Right. Thanks for reporting it, kids." He and the woman set off, leaving the second man still standing there.

Maria, Charlie, and Mac glanced at one another, the same question on their faces. Charlie looked at the remaining guard. "What happened yesterday with the sharks?" she asked.

"Hmm?" He scrutinized the kids, then shrugged. "Oh, some girl managed to get around the blockades to the edge of the shark pool. When the workers went up to her to get her out of the restricted area, she jumped into the tank. She started swimming around, chasing a shark. It was nuts."

"A girl?" asked Maria.

"Yeah. Some girl about your height wearing a bodysuit, probably trying to look like a trainer. We hauled her outta the pool. Kicked her butt to the curb. People are stupid." The guard turned away, keeping watch over the attraction entrance and now and then glancing in the direction of where his coworkers had gone.

Charlie, Mac, and Maria exchanged glances. They retreated, making a beeline toward a shaded area where they could hide and talk quietly behind some palm trees and a souvenir cart but still see the entrance to Ocean Explorer.

"Do you think that girl in the shark tank was Kelly?" Mac asked the other two once they had their stakeout under way.

"Could be," said Maria. "Or one of the soldiers."

"I'll bet it was Kelly," said Charlie. "She's the only one who has water abilities."

"As far as we know," Mac reminded her.

They waited. Charlie's device remained warm, and she checked it quickly, seeing the cheetah lit up. Now that she'd gotten the device out of defense mode, where it had been stuck for weeks, Charlie could click the buttons to manually turn on her abilities. She switched on strength and climbing, just in case something went down.

A few minutes later the three kids heard a shout from the area behind the building. They stood alert. The third security guard turned too, his radio crackling. He pulled it out and started talking into it. Seconds later Cyke and Prowl came tearing around the corner, dodging people and knocking snacks and souvenirs out of their hands. A cry rose up from the bumped individuals. Prowl and Cyke kept running. People dived out of their way.

The guard took off sprinting toward them, arms outstretched and palms out, demanding them to stop. Prowl lithely jumped into the air and used the guard's shoulder to spring over him. He landed on the ground and darted sideways, then sprang again over some kids who were screaming and running for safety. Cyke plowed through anyone in his way, knocking down some bystanders.

"Oh my," muttered Charlie. "This could be bad."

Maria gripped her arm. "Remember the parents—we have to keep a low profile."

Charlie nodded, her eyes glued to the action.

"Here come the guards!" whispered Mac.

The two security guards rounded the corner chasing after the soldiers. "Stop!" cried the male guard. The woman officer flung herself forward, diving at Prowl and catching him by the ankle. Prowl lost his balance and thudded face-first to the pavement. The woman jumped on top of him, trying to pin him with her knee in his back. Onlookers skittered away. Prowl twisted violently and knocked the woman off balance, then swiped his claws across her cheek, drawing a shriek and a long line of blood. But she flattened and managed to keep Prowl down while shouting for her fellow guard to help her.

Cyke galloped back around and yanked the guard off Prowl as the second guard stepped into the fray. And as Cyke tossed the woman aside, the male guard punched Prowl in the jaw.

"Should we do something?" Mac whispered. "I'm afraid if I activate my pangolin suit, people will freak even more. Plus, look at all the phone cameras coming out."

Charlie looked around wildly. A few civilians were screaming and others were filming the scene. Things were out of control. She wanted to help but didn't want people to get a look—or photo—of her face. "I'll go in really quickly to mess up the soldiers and give

the guards a chance to nab them. Then I'll take off running and disappear."

"We're coming too," said Mac.

Maria looked panicked. "I can't fight without my ability."

"I won't use my device either," said Mac. "We'll just be there to help if we can."

"Okay," said Maria. "Let's grab hats or something for a disguise. I saw some right there at the souvenir cart."

Charlie saw that it sold giant orca hats and octopus masks with dangly legs, among other items. The employee working there had already run for cover. Charlie snatched one of the masks and pulled it down over her face. Eight plush legs dangled over her chest and back. Maria and Mac grabbed orca hats and smashed them low on their foreheads. Half-blinded by the stretchy mesh, Charlie charged through the onlookers with octopus legs flapping. She checked her device to make sure her elephant ability was still activated, then sprinted toward Prowl and Cyke, dodging and weaving around trash receptacles, vendors, and people, trying to stay safe. Mac and Maria followed but fell quickly behind.

Charlie rammed into the horse hybrid, knocking him hard into Prowl and sending them sliding across the ground. Prowl's claws sprang out and he swiped the air, slicing Charlie's shirt but thankfully not her skin. Cyke flipped around and stumbled to his feet, looking bewildered—he hadn't seen Charlie coming, and he didn't recognize her now with the octopus mask covering her face.

Charlie darted around a tree while Mac and Maria sneaked closer and took cover behind the trash and recycling receptacles. Then Prowl leaped to his feet and pounced on Charlie. She fought him off, slamming her fist into his face and knocking him senseless. He slumped to the ground as Cyke ran at her. Feeling her fingers tingling, Charlie lunged up and stuck to the tree trunk, hoping nobody was noticing her but not having much of a choice. Cyke grabbed her by the leg to yank her down, but she hung on to the trunk and smashed her other foot into his chin, leaving him stumbling backward and howling.

Quickly Maria and Mac sprang out from behind the trash receptacles. Mac tripped the stumbling soldier and Maria shoved him. Cyke slammed into a light pole and landed hard on his stomach.

"Security!" Maria yelled as she and Mac grabbed Cyke by the wrists and stood on his forearms, pinning him to the ground. Mac shoved his orca hat over Cyke's face while Maria whipped off her sweatshirt and used the arms to tie one of Cyke's wrists to a light pole.

Mac saw the guards approaching and glanced at Charlie. "Go! Hurry!" he said in a harsh whisper as the security guards came running up. With Prowl knocked out and three guards coming for Cyke, Charlie jumped out of the tree. She slipped away into the crowd, keeping her mask on to avoid being caught by any cameras.

"Let's get out of here," Maria muttered. They hopped off

Cyke, leaving the three guards to handle him. But as they sneaked away, Cyke ripped the sweatshirt tether off his wrist and tore the hat from his face. He got to his feet, leaving the guards with a challenge they couldn't win. Prowl came to and together they knocked the guards flat and sprinted toward the park exit.

As Charlie ran past the cart she flung the mask at it, then continued at high speed so she could get far away from the attraction. She zigzagged through the park so no one could possibly follow her. When she got to a section where it seemed nobody had a clue that anything was going on, Charlie slowed down. She texted Mac and Maria to let them know where she'd ended up so they could find her.

Twenty minutes later, Maria and Mac came walking swiftly toward her. They were hatless but wearing wide grins.

"Nice job, Chuck," Maria said when they reached her.

"You too," said Charlie. She grinned back, relieved that they were all together again. "Did the soldiers recognize you?"

"I'm not sure," said Maria. "We tried to keep our faces hidden. Mac thinks they might wonder about us but bets they'd expect us to use our abilities if it really *was* us. So that'll help them believe it wasn't." She paused. "Does that make sense?"

"Sort of," Charlie said with a laugh.

"Nobody followed you?" Mac asked, looking around and breathing hard. He wheezed, then pulled out his inhaler and used it.

"Not at cheetah speed," said Charlie. "You?"

"We slipped out through the chaos," said Maria.

"What happened?" asked Charlie. "Did the guards arrest them?"

"Nope," said Mac. "They got away. At least we stopped them from really hurting those guards. Maria and I tailed them to the passenger pickup area, and we got there just in time to see the white van speeding off with them inside."

"Darn," said Charlie. "I hope they didn't get away with any new DNA samples."

"I doubt they did," said Mac. "After the van took off, we went back to the park entrance and hung out there for a couple minutes to eavesdrop. From what the guards said, it didn't sound like they got away with any animals."

"Yeah," said Maria, "and they won't be getting back into the park anytime soon. Those bodysuits are a dead giveaway. Plus, somebody got a good photo of them and turned it in."

"I hope they didn't get you guys in it," Charlie muttered.

"If they did," said Maria, "we won't be recognizable with those big manatees on our heads."

"Orcas," said Mac patiently. "They're not even similar."

"Whatever." Maria smoothed her hair.

Charlie glanced at Mac, waiting for him to scold them as usual about how animal facts matter, but he was distracted by his cell phone ringing. He pulled it out of his pocket and looked at the display, which read Malik Barnes. He quickly answered. "Hi, Dad," he said. "What's up?"

Mac listened and the girls could overhear concern in the muffled voice on the other end. After a moment Mac said, "Wow! Nope, we're nowhere near there. We're just getting in line for Orca Encounter. No crazy masked men out here that we can see." He flashed a grin at Maria and Charlie, and then they started walking toward the ride. "Everything is super normal."

CHAPTER 5

Being a Kid Again

Once they'd combed the park, ridden the rides, and chatted more about potential animal abilities, Mac suggested they go back to Ocean Explorer to try to figure out why Dr. Gray's soldiers had been after a jellyfish. Maybe that would give them a clue into what he was doing.

But when they got there, they realized there were lots of species of jellyfish in the tank, and nobody had seen which one Cyke was trying to catch—in fact, he'd been so clumsy with the net that he seemed to be going after anything that would miraculously fall into it.

Maria took photos of the description placards in the exhibition area so that they could look up the various names and try to figure out if there was anything great about a jellyfish besides its sting. Then they went to the shark attraction and tried to make friends with one of the workers over there, asking questions about what had happened the previous day.

But the worker seemed suspicious and told the kids to move along. Then she followed them when they went near the shark viewing area, like she thought they might also try to sneak in or something. Eventually the three left. As evening fell, they stopped at a stand for something to eat and to talk more about what had happened earlier.

"Do you think we should be trying to gather DNA too?" Maria asked. "I mean, since we're here anyway?"

Charlie tilted her head thoughtfully. "We don't know what animals the scientists will choose for us. And we have no idea how to actually collect a sample. Besides, Ms. Sabbith will take care of getting that stuff from the Talos lab in Chicago when we're ready."

"But . . . what if we see something cool that could offer a really great ability?" Maria replied.

Mac frowned. "I wouldn't want to stress out any animals just for the heck of it. I already feel bad for that poor shark and those jellyfish that Kelly and the soldiers traumatized."

"Good point," said Charlie. "If we see something that could work well for a new ability, we can just text Ms. Sabbith and ask if she has access to it. Then see if the scientists think it would be a good fit for one of us."

"Okay, I like that idea better than trying to collect it ourselves," Maria said. "We should stay away from anything that could mess up what we're trying to do. That includes touching the animals and fighting bad guys—that was a close call. Let's just, you know, not worry about it for once."

"You mean act like normal kids on vacation?" asked Mac,

dipping a dolphin-shaped fish nugget into some tartar sauce and shoving it into his mouth.

Maria wrinkled up her nose at him. "Is it horrible that they have fish nuggets on the menu at SeaWorld, or is it just me?"

The Barnes family and Maria and Charlie stayed at SeaWorld until closing with no further incidents. Then they dragged their tired bodies back to the SUV. By the time they got to their hotel, they were almost too exhausted to eat the warm chocolate chip cookies that the front desk offered them.

Claudia and Malik Barnes had booked them a suite with a kitchenette. Charlie zonked out quickly, and before she knew it, Mac's parents were rustling about making breakfast for everyone.

After a hearty meal, they set out again for another long, exciting day, this time to the zoo.

Unlike at SeaWorld, Mr. and Mrs. Barnes stayed with the kids this time, because the zoo was such a huge, sprawling place. There wasn't much of a chance for the kids to talk privately. Whenever they did, they tried to make it sound like they were talking about their new made-up game. It was fun for a while because it felt like they were talking in code. But eventually that got boring and they stopped.

Mostly they focused on the animals. And Charlie, Maria, and Mac were looking at animals in a different way, as research instead of purely entertainment. They took the time to read all the placards, and whenever one of them found an animal with an interesting feature, Maria took a photo of it and its plaque so they could look up more information and bring their findings back to the scientists.

When they got to the reptile area, Mac pushed his way through the crowd to see the various lizards. Charlie and Maria followed him, with Mac's parents trailing behind.

"Is there a pangolin in there or something?" Maria asked, curious as to why Mac was so interested in the reptiles. The metallic suit from Mac's bracelet had been designed to mimic a pangolin's features—scales that protected him and claws tough enough to dig through cement.

"A pangolin is a mammal," said Mac. "Not a reptile."

"Oh yeah, right on," said Maria. "I knew that. I was just testing you." She rolled her eyes at Charlie, who grinned. They looked over Mac's shoulders through the glass and saw a couple of lizards with thornlike skin.

"Whoa," said Charlie. She looked around for its description. "We don't have those in Navarro Junction, do we?"

"What are they?" asked Maria.

"They're called thorny dragons," said Mac. "And they're natives of Australia. We definitely don't have them where we live. Aren't they awesome?"

The lizards were small, but their skin looked like it was sprouting fin-shaped thorns like the ones that grew on rosebushes. "I wouldn't want to touch that thing," said Charlie.

Mac glanced over his shoulder to see where his parents were, and spied them a dozen feet away looking at something else. "It could be a great feature to go with my suit," he said. "Can you get a photo of it, Maria?"

"On it," said Maria, snapping a picture and making notes. "But you already have really great defensive scales."

"That's true." Mac looked at the lizard again. "It would be cool to collect different kinds of scales, though."

"I don't know," Maria said, noncommittal. "Seems too much the same. Wouldn't you want something different from the pangolin?" She moved to another section of the reptile house that had a pond in it, and beckoned the other two to come. "Look at that one with the weird feet," she said, pointing to a smooth green lizard about two feet long from nose to tail. Its back feet were large and the center toes were unusually long. She found the information about it. "Basilisk lizard," she said. "Get this—it runs on water!"

"Are you serious?" said Mac. "I've always wanted to see one in real life!" He slid up to Maria and peered into the habitat. "When I was little I had a book with one of these in it—it was my favorite! Their feet make upside-down cups. That's how they stay up." He studied one. "They can also run fast."

"You could use a little help in that department," said Charlie, then cringed—she hoped she didn't hurt Mac's feelings. But it was true. He wasn't much of a runner to begin with because of his asthma, but Charlie was talking about his pangolin suit, which slowed him down even more. It left him unable to keep up with the girls. "I mean . . . speed is always good, for all of us," she began to explain, but Mac didn't seem offended.

Maria studied the placard. "It can go five feet per second across the water. It has extra skin by its back legs that creates air pockets so it doesn't sink." She looked up. "That's pretty cool."

"You kids are really taking these animals seriously," said Mr. Barnes, who had appeared behind them without them noticing. "Are you having fun?"

Mac nodded and looked up at his parents. "I really can't think of anything better than animals," he said. "Remember the basilisk lizard from my zoo book when I was a little kid?" He pointed to it.

"I do," said his mom. "You loved any animal book, but especially that one. You knew all their features by heart and were always spouting off animal facts. I'm glad you've got friends who love them too."

Maria and Charlie grinned. They'd both liked animals for a long time, mostly in a pet kind of way. But the more they learned about them since they'd found the devices, the more they realized just how little they knew about the animal kingdom. "They're fascinating," said Maria. "They have so many cool abilities most people don't even know about."

Charlie nodded. "We could go on all day about them," she warned Mac's parents.

"Oh, trust me, Charlie," said Mrs. Barnes with a laugh and a shake of her head, "I know better than to get you all started."

CHAPTER 6

Shark Training

In the days that followed the trips to SeaWorld and the San Diego Zoo, Dr. Gray worked tirelessly in the makeshift lab in their rented house. On the table along the side of the room were containers that stored the formulas for all the various animals he'd worked on to this point: leopard, chimpanzee, horse, bull, rhinoceros, rattlesnake, wolf, chameleon, crab, panther. On the other table were the new DNA samples that would give wings to Miko and quills to Braun. It was painstaking work making the formulas. Victor's eyes weren't as good as they used to be. And things went much slower without Zed to help him. Why would she leave without so much as a note of explanation? And why now? Just when he was closing in on his endgame. Her timing was severely inconvenient.

Maybe she'd just gotten tired of being treated like another one of the soldiers. He should have continued to call her Dr. Jakande, perhaps, rather than the code name she'd adopted to fit in better with the others. He should have elevated her somehow to let her know she was more important to him than them. Her abilities and her intellect far exceeded those of anyone else he'd kept close to over the years.

Victor had been angry when she first left, and very hurt. Now he mostly felt regret. Maybe he should have shared with her his secret plan to change everyone in the world into chimeras. Surely, she would have stayed around to be part of that if only she'd known. She was a scientist after all. And he would have given her some credit, too, if that was what she needed.

"She probably knows by now, though," he muttered under his breath. "And she didn't come back." He'd made the arrogant mistake of revealing his plans to Dr. Wilde's daughter and her friends before he'd shut them into the bank vault. He'd assumed they'd never make it out of there, but somehow they had. Now Zed was probably with Charles and Jack and Quinn. And those little monsters most certainly would have told her what he'd said.

Sharp-eared Prowl, who was standing guard near the door without his mask, acted as if he hadn't heard the scientist. On the one hand, Dr. Gray had lightened up a bit since the time he'd held the other scientists captive—that had been a stressful period for everyone. Prowl and the others had become worried about being discovered or the police showing up. Or worse, the government agency that Dr. Gray worked for shutting them down. If that group ever found out they'd held hostages, they'd be furious. Prowl blinked. It reminded him that Gray hadn't seemed to be talking to anyone in the government lately. Not in a long time, in fact. That seemed strange.

But they hadn't been stopped. And they'd gotten out of that

jam, so the stress levels in the lab had decreased of late. Dr. Gray was calmer—some of the time, anyway. Earlier that day, Miko had told Prowl that the scientist was acting like his old self at the zoo, which was good news. The man seemed to find some level of energy trying to keep their newest team member, Kelly, happy. Maybe the old guy was worried about her platypus spikes, Prowl thought sardonically. He rubbed the spot on his thigh where Kelly had previously stabbed him and injected her poison.

On the other hand, Dr. Gray had become even more reclusive and focused when working in the lab. Having to fix his machine had set Dr. Gray back weeks. And without Zed to do half the work, the pressure to hurry seemed to intensify. Victor had been known to fly off the handle at the smallest provocations. Prowl, Braun, Mega, Cyke, and Miko had been around the man a lot of years, since he first recruited the young outcasts to be test subjects. And even though Gray didn't talk about Zed much, the leopard man knew he was stinging inside. Heck, Prowl was hurt, too—he and Zed and Miko had gotten pretty close after working together all this time. As much as Dr. Gray tried to appear stoic, he was more sensitive than many people, and Zed's leaving had been a huge blow to Victor's ego. Prowl missed her badly. No doubt Dr. Gray missed her even more.

Something moved outside the window. Prowl's green eyes turned sharply, but then he relaxed. It was just a bird. If he hadn't been on guard duty, he might have gone after it for fun. But he took his assignment at the door very seriously, especially after the last attack in Navarro Junction. He folded his arms and turned his furry leopard face back to the doctor, who was mumbling about phenotypes and genotypes. It sounded like a foreign language to Prowl. He and the other soldiers were limited in what they could do for the scientist.

The soldier dropped his gaze and his mind wandered again. He wondered what sort of second ability was in store for him. Dr. Gray hadn't disclosed anything, though Prowl knew he was planning something. He wished the doctor would consult with him first to see if he'd actually like the ability. It only seemed polite. But Gray didn't really see the soldiers as equals. He paid them generously and figured that was enough to maintain their loyalty. He was definitely not known for his politeness. Sometimes he was downright mean.

Prowl's expression flickered as he remembered how Gray had left him and Miko and Kelly stranded in Navarro Junction after the last fight. Thank goodness Cyke had come back for them. Prowl knew when he'd signed up for this job that even though the money would be great, life would change drastically. And Dr. Gray would be calling all the shots. But after all these years devoted to the man, was it asking too much of a favor for Prowl to at least be consulted before the scientist just sprang a new animal's DNA on him? Wishful thinking. Besides, it's not like he could leave, looking like this. Gray had them all in a corner, and he knew it.

At least Miko knew what her new animal would be now, and she seemed happy about it. And they all knew that if they ever managed to get shark DNA, it would be for Mega, the rhino-woman hybrid. But no one knew who the jellyfish was for. Prowl and Cyke hadn't even been sure they'd found the right kind the other day—it had been hard to tell since there were so many of them in that tank.

And unfortunately they'd failed to capture anything before they'd been caught and pounded senseless. Whoever came in and clocked them was lucky they had run off just as quickly. At first Prowl thought it might have been the Wilde child and her friends, but why wouldn't they have put up more of a fight like before? Too bad he didn't get a good look at them. All Prowl knew was that he hadn't expected to get knocked out over some stupid jellyfish.

Prowl wrinkled his nose, remembering. Much like a cat, he was not a fan of getting wet. He grimaced as he imagined falling into a tank full of jellyfish and getting his fur all soaked . . . blech. Not to mention getting stung, though being a leopard man had toughened his skin a bit. Still, no thanks.

Dr. Gray turned sharply toward him. "Is Miko back yet?"

"No," said Prowl, snapping out of his thoughts and looking up. "She and Kelly went to the beach to train. They told me they'll be gone all day."

"Right," said Dr. Gray, as if he was just remembering. "Good." He picked up a clipboard that held several pages of notes. "Get

Morph and Fang out to the backyard for their matchup and assessment. Let's see which ability outshines the others this time."

Not far away, at the beach, Miko sat down under a huge umbrella while Kelly put her hair up and fastened it.

"Go ahead," Miko instructed when Kelly was finished. "Do like we said. Just turn on your dolphin ability first and work on swimming and turning sharply. Then, once you've got the feel of it and you can really move with an instant's notice while concentrating on something else, switch on the cuttlefish and do your thing."

Kelly sniffed as she faced the crashing waves. It smelled nasty, like the seafood counter at the grocery store. "Do you think there are gross fish in there?"

"Nope," said Miko. "No fish in the ocean."

Kelly gave her a panicked look. "I'm serious, Miko. What if they . . . come *at* me?"

Miko sighed. "Come on, Kelly. You can do this. You did it before and saved three people—what's the difference now?"

"I know I *can* do it," said Kelly. "And in Cabo I didn't think about it first—I heard the shouting and ran to help. But now I just . . . ugh." She sighed. "Okay. Here I go." Without the adrenaline and the urgency that she'd felt when she'd saved those teenagers, it was hard to get up her excitement for this. But if she wanted the success and glory of procuring the shark DNA sample, she was going to have to rehearse this routine a few times, just like she had to do in theater class. Or like how she had to practice a lot to get better at soccer.

Stuff she probably wouldn't ever do again.

A dull pang swept through her at the thought, but she pushed through it. With a surge of determination, she jogged into the waves and waded out deeper than her waist. Once she was mostly hidden from other beachgoers, she lowered her goggles and clicked on her dolphin ability, then dived under.

The water was brisk on Kelly's face and she was glad her bodysuit had climate control to temper the highest heat of the Southwest as well as the shock of cold water. She surfaced for air and felt the breeze hit the fin that had pushed out of her back through the slit in her suit. Now she just had to be careful to stay away from the surfers so they didn't see it. Though, on second thought, maybe that would make them stay away from her.

She took a few deep breaths, then went back under and sped through the water, watching for fish ready to dart out at her, but realizing anything she could see was moving away from her. That relaxed her somewhat, and she began to meander around under the surface, looking at the shifting sand and shells and rocks below her. She liked how the sound of the world was muted down here. It made her feel like she was the only human left in the world and she imagined idly what that might be like. It would definitely solve a few of her problems, but Kelly wasn't sure it would ultimately be a great solution—who would be her future fans?

Eventually Kelly admitted to herself that swimming could potentially be fun if things remained calm like this. And being able to hold her breath for over five minutes like a dolphin was pretty excellent, too.

Once she was used to the water, Kelly got to work. She practiced sharp turns and making accurate moves at a high speed—things she hadn't had to worry about when saving those people. She took herself through a sort of obstacle course, using the ocean floor's natural rocks, sunken driftwood, and weed patches as things to dodge around. She was hoping to refine her skills enough that chasing a shark around a pool or aquarium would come more instinctively, without her having to concentrate on looking where she was going all the time. She closed her eyes, wondering if she also possessed the dolphin's sonar ability, but it seemed that feature hadn't been included in her device.

Maybe I'll just find a shark out here in the wild, she thought, and then her eyes flew open. What was she thinking? That would *not* be good. She looked all around just in case, then surfaced for air. She lifted her goggles and glanced at Miko, who was standing on the shore looking worried. Kelly waved to her, and Miko visibly relaxed and waved back—she must have been anxious about Kelly being underwater for so long. It was kind of nice having somebody worry about her for once.

Kelly floated for a moment, face to the sun, then went back down and diligently practiced her obstacle course again. After several times through it, she grew a lot more comfortable. Then, once she'd surfaced again for air, she clicked on the cuttlefish ability. As she went back down near the ocean floor, her body began to change color to match the spotty, shifting background. She kept intentionally turning and veering off course as she concentrated on bringing the camouflage to the more intense, pulsing level. At the same time, she focused on being totally aware of where she was moving at all times. She shot forward as if chasing after a shark, and concentrated on bringing on her hypnotizing ability, which would allow her to get close enough to scrape some scales without the creature tearing her arm off.

Finally, she could tell by the light pattern emanating from her that her facial colors had changed to pulsing, mesmerizing waves. She focused on keeping those going while traveling through her obstacle course.

It wasn't easy. She lost concentration the first two times and the pulses stopped. But Kelly wasn't the kind of person to give up. Even though she was growing tired after being out in the water for so long, she refused to quit until she did it right at least once. When she got her breath back, she dived down once more, determined. She stayed close to the ocean floor, weaving around like a bottom-feeder as her body blended in. Then she sped up, imagining pursuit, and concentrated on creating the hypnotic light pulses. Once she had that going, she dodged and weaved, knowing that when the real thing happened with the shark, she'd have to get its attention and keep it long enough to hypnotize it quickly and avoid attack. Was it even possible?

Maybe she could just try getting it from the safety of the pool deck again. But hypnotizing a shark that way, with it swimming all over the place, seemed almost more difficult to accomplish than being in the water, moving alongside it.

She turned sharply in the water and rose toward the surface, trying to imagine every obstacle she might encounter in a shark tank. As she dodged imaginary objects, a large shadow fell over her.

Kelly nearly gasped underwater. Her pulsing camo faded as she turned to look above her. A huge, solid *something* was passing above her. She began to panic. She flailed, trying to reverse direction, then attempted to get her speed up so she could flee whatever it was. But she lost her coordination and gulped down some seawater. Swiftly she righted herself and swept her arms to her sides to push herself forward, ignoring the sting in her throat and nose, and tried to get to the surface for a breath before whatever huge thing above her attacked. What could it be? A giant squid? A whale? A stingray?

Kelly's face pushed through the surface. She coughed and took a ragged breath, then down she went again, swimming with all her strength toward the shore. As she neared the beach, her kicking feet brushed the sandy bottom. She stumbled up and started running toward the beach, glancing over her shoulder, hoping there was no way a creature that size could follow her into such shallow water.

From the safety near land, Kelly spied the enemy: it was a treacherous wide-body sailboat. It had nearly eaten her alive.

Kelly doubled over in exhaustion and massive relief. Then she stumbled through the sand and fell on the beach blanket next to Miko, groaning at her own ridiculousness as she turned off her abilities. She'd have to practice hypnotizing sharks again tomorrow, because today? She. Was. Done.

CHAPTER 7

An Exciting Proposal

Charlie, Maria, and Mac spent the rest of their week in Southern California acting like regular twelve-year-olds. They rode roller coasters, ate junk food, and slept deeply at the various hotels in between. And when Mac's parents asked if they wanted to stop by Legoland, they decided that even though they were a little too old for it, they may as well go—being so close to it and all. Once they found out that it had a water park, and that the Sea Life Aquarium was right next door, it was a slam-dunk decision. It was like . . . like being a kid again. For a few days, they almost forgot about how Dr. Gray was planning to turn everyone in the world into chimeras. Almost.

By the time they returned to Navarro Junction, they were rejuvenated and exhausted in the best possible ways. But they were also eager to see if the scientists had made any progress while they were gone.

When Mac's parents dropped off Charlie at her house, Dr. Sharma's car was parked in the driveway as usual. Maria and Mac saw it and exchanged a glance. The three kids had agreed that they'd each go home to their families after the long drive and try to meet up again the next day, though it was tempting for Maria and Mac to run in with Charlie and ask what was new. But they refrained. Mr. Barnes hit a button to pop open the hatch, and went to get Charlie's suitcase.

Charlie flashed a secretive grin at her friends and got out of the car. It was sad to see the vacation end.

"Text me," Maria called to Charlie.

"I will."

"Me too," said Mac, though he didn't need to say it—they group-texted everything these days.

From the front seat, Mrs. Barnes looked amused. "I can't believe you three have spent the entire week together and you have to immediately start texting now that you're separating."

"We just can't stand to be apart," Maria said with a laugh.

"That's wonderful," said Mrs. Barnes. "Everybody needs friends like that."

Mr. Barnes set Charlie's luggage on the driveway and closed the hatch.

"Thank you for everything," Charlie said fervently, picking up her suitcase. "I had the best time."

"You're very welcome," said Mr. Barnes. "Do you need me to help you bring your bag inside?"

"No thanks. I'm good."

Mr. Barnes got back into the driver's seat. "Next stop, Torres Central," he announced to his passengers. Charlie moved toward the house, then set her things down on the step and stood in the oven-like heat to wave until her friends were out of sight. She'd had an amazing time and had grown even closer to Maria and Mac. Their bond was more solid than any friendships she'd ever had in her life. Sure, they'd had a few rough times at first, but those seemed to be over now.

The same could be said for Charlie's family. It had been hard moving here, and the stress of that had been compounded by her parents' crazy work schedules. Talk about rough relationships—back then Charlie had been pretty upset at her mother for working so much, and at her dad for taking a job right away when he really hadn't had to. At least, in Charlie's mind, he hadn't. But that stress had eased too. There was something about all the danger they'd been in that had brought them more understanding.

Now Charlie's mother was back working at the ER, but she'd cut back on her hours so she was home a lot more. Charlie's dad, who'd been teaching biology at a local college—before he was abducted, anyway—was off for the summer and working feverishly with the other scientists. Andy, Charlie's brother, was fully healed from Kelly's platypus sting thanks to the Mark Five's starfish ability, and he was busy doing his own thing with his friends, too.

After the Barneses' vehicle turned the corner and disappeared, Charlie picked up her things and went inside the house, eager to see her parents and brother and find out what happened while she was gone.

"I'm home!" Charlie called out as she walked in. She made her way into the kitchen and looked around. Everything seemed so much bigger after spending a week in hotel rooms, though the house had changed a bit now that they'd turned part of it into a science lab. "Mom?" Charlie put her bag on a dining room chair as Jessie, their dog, came bounding toward her and jumped up, her paws on Charlie's shoulders.

Charlie staggered backward, laughing, and hugged her. Jessie licked her face. "I'm so happy to see you, too," she said, and scolded, "I can't believe you didn't greet me at the door." Fat Princess, one of the cats, slid into the room but kept her distance, arching her back and acting coy, giving off an air of disdain. Their other cat, Big Kitty, stayed away, which was her style. The daily appearance of the extra scientists in their home had thrown off Big Kitty a bit. She liked to stay elusive and mysterious, spending most of her time on or under Andy's bed.

Diana Wilde came swiftly down the stairs. "Charlie!" she cried with a huge smile. "You're home early!"

"About a half hour," said Charlie. She pushed Jessie down and went to hug her mother.

"I think you grew taller while you were gone," said Mrs. Wilde. "Did you have fun?"

Charlie laughed. "It was the best." She released the hug and looked around. "Where is everybody? It's so quiet."

"Dad and the others are in the lab. The den, I mean. The lab den. Whatever we're calling it now. And Andy is going to be gone for a week—you just missed him."

"What?" Charlie cried. "Where is he?"

"A last-minute camping trip up north with Juan. They're going up to Flagstaff to get out of the heat and do some hiking."

"That's cool, I guess," said Charlie, but she was disappointed. She actually missed her annoying younger brother. It was a strange feeling. "I'm going to stash my junk and then I'll tell you all about our trip."

"Great. How does pasta for dinner sound?"

"Amazing," said Charlie. "I'm starving."

"I was about to make a huge pot of it anyway for the lab crew."

"Oh good—I wanted to talk to them too. If we all eat together I only have to tell the story once." Charlie grabbed her bag and raced up the stairs, with Jessie pounding up the steps alongside her. It was almost like the dog didn't want to let Charlie out of her sight again.

Charlie put her dirty clothes in the laundry bin and got cleaned up for dinner, her stomach growling. They'd stopped for lunch on the way home, but maybe Mom was right about Charlie growing— because she was hungry enough to eat her own fist right now. She paused on that thought. If she ate her fist, would her starfish ability make it grow back? She laughed and decided not to tell Mac she'd considered it, even jokingly, because he'd probably beg her to go through with it.

***

At dinner Charlie was the focus of the rapt attention of five doctors. She filled them in on the strange incident at SeaWorld with the soldiers in the jellyfish aquarium and what they'd heard about the girl in the shark tank, explaining that Gray and his team were probably trying to gather DNA.

"From what we overheard," Charlie told them, "I don't think either of the attempts were successful at SeaWorld. And I don't know if any of them will be able to go back inside that park now, especially if they're wearing the bodysuits, after what happened two days in a row. Security will stop them for sure."

Dr. Quinn Sharma tapped her forefinger against her lips. "Shark?" she mused. "And jellyfish? Interesting. Sharp teeth and more poison, like that rattlesnake-wolf soldier—what was his name again?"

"Fang," said Dr. Jakande.

"Right," said Dr. Sharma. "Do you think those kinds of abilities are what Gray is after?"

"Could be," said Dr. Goldstein. He sat slightly bent in his chair, for he was still not completely well after his traumatic ordeal, having been captured by Dr. Gray's soldiers and starved and mistreated for more than a month. "Should we be concerned that they are water animals?"

Charlie's dad lifted his gaze. "What do you mean, Jack?"

"I'm just not sure what those choices of animals indicate. The

69

machine he forced us to create wasn't meant for water distribution."

"Maybe it was totally destroyed in the fight and he had to change methods," said Mr. Wilde, though he appeared dubious. "But I don't think it necessarily means anything. I chose a starfish for its healing ability. The fact that the starfish is found in water didn't factor in. Dr. Gray might be at SeaWorld, but that doesn't mean he's investing in water-related abilities, per se."

"Kelly has all water animal abilities too," Charlie reminded them.

Dr. Sharma nodded. "But she can use two of the three on land."

"Right," said Mr. Wilde. "And like Quinn said, what comes to mind with a shark is its teeth, and a jellyfish, its poisonous sting."

"Even Morph's crab claw is something Victor chose because of its incredible punching ability," said Dr. Jakande. "Not because he wanted a water compatible hybrid."

"Excellent points, everyone," said Jack. "You're right. I'm overthinking things."

Mrs. Wilde tapped her lips. "It's interesting getting this peek into what they might have been up to all this time. I'll let Erica know that they seem to be stationed in San Diego. Maybe she can start fresh tracking them down." She pulled out her phone and started texting.

Dr. Sharma remained thoughtful but quiet. Then she turned to Nubia. "This discussion gives me an idea. You haven't decided on a second wereanimal for Maria yet, have you?"

Charlie sat up, wondering if Maria would have a chance to suggest animals for herself.

"Not yet," said Dr. Jakande. "I'll be diving into that soon. Fixing the Mark Two and trying to figure out my own personal DNA reversal situation has put me behind schedule, I'm afraid. But our other enhancements are built and should soon be ready to be installed in the devices—the GPS and emergency features. Erica's still finalizing things with that."

"Excellent progress. And you, Jack?" asked Dr. Sharma.

"I've got some ideas, but I'm still open to suggestions." Dr. Goldstein glanced at Charlie. "Have you spoken to Maria and Mac?"

Dr. Wilde looked at Charlie too. "Yes—have you and your friends come up with anything, Charlie? I meant what I said about wanting your input before I decide on your ability."

Charlie felt her face grow warm. "We spent some time talking at the zoos and aquariums," she hedged. It felt odd to be included in such important considerations, and she was suddenly shy to tell them about the specific animals they discussed—what if the scientists thought they were bad ideas?

"We'd love your thoughts," said Dr. Jakande, turning to Charlie. "All of you kids. It would be nice to have a bit of help there so I can focus on the other pressing matters. We still have a lot to do."

"Same here," said Dr. Goldstein. "I've been rebuilding the

graphics for the Mark Three since that never got finished the first time around. I'm ready to install it, but I haven't had much time to spend researching animals."

Charlie grew a bit more confident. "We'd love to help if you really think we can. We're meeting up tomorrow, and"—she grinned, slightly embarrassed—"okay, to be totally honest, we did *a lot* of research when we were out there."

"Good!" said Dr. Sharma. "After all, you'll be the ones using the abilities. They should be ones that speak to you. Ones you feel comfortable with."

"I agree," said Dr. Goldstein. "I want to hear from Mac before I make any decisions. You can tell him I said so."

Dr. Jakande and Dr. Wilde nodded.

"I will." Charlie's heart soared. She could hardly wait to tell the others.

While the scientists chatted about scientific formulas, Charlie finished eating, then texted Maria and Mac: "Be here tomorrow morning as early as you can. The scientists said we can definitely help pick our new abilities . . . They want *our* expert advice!"

CHAPTER 8

Decisions, Decisions

Maria and Mac showed up the next morning armed with phones and tablets. "My stepdad said I could borrow his iPad for the day," Maria announced, holding it up. "First time! I think he missed me while I was away because he was being super nice."

"Sweet," said Charlie. "And I have my laptop. We can do some more research this morning. The docs want to see us later this afternoon to update us on the bracelets and talk about the upgrades. Ms. Sabbith flew in late last night with some materials. Oh, and Dr. G. is ready to install some of the new safety and communication stuff in your device, Mac. He asked if you could bring it to him in the lab-den so he can get right to work."

"Cool," said Mac. He typed in the code and sprung the latch on his Mark Three, then disappeared down the hallway.

"Meet us in my room," Charlie called after him. She and Maria went upstairs to Charlie's bedroom. Charlie swiftly straightened the bedcovers. She grabbed her laptop from the side table and hopped on the bed. Maria climbed up too. A moment later Mac came in and pulled Charlie's desk chair over. He tossed his shoes off and used the bed as a footstool.

"Okay," said Charlie, excited to get started. "First question: Mac, do you think we even need to search for new options for you?"

"Why wouldn't we?" Mac seemed offended by the thought.

"Well, I just mean you've sort of already found a good one, right?"

Mac squinted. "You mean that basilisk lizard?"

"Exactly. It seems perfect for you. You love it. You know everything about it. And it can even freaking run on water, which is a very useful feature that nobody else has. What's not to love about that?"

"Okay, yeah," said Mac thoughtfully. "But what if Dr. Goldstein thinks it's . . . I don't know. Not tough enough. What if there's something better? We should at least spend a little more time looking. Just in case. We want the best thing, right?"

Charlie and Maria knew full well that Mac just loved researching animal facts. They also knew that the basilisk lizard was perfect for him and could be a great alternative armor for his device. But they looked at one another and shrugged. "Sure," Charlie said. "But let's start with Maria, since we don't have any ideas for her yet. Remember, we need to hurry. Now that we know Dr. Gray and the soldiers are out there gathering DNA samples as we speak, every day means he's closer to ruining the world."

"And the scientists are finishing up all the other modifications to the bracelets," Maria added, "so they'll be ready to get going on this pretty soon."

"All right," said Mac amicably. He thought for a minute and said sheepishly, "I really do love the basilisk."

"We know," said the girls together.

Charlie grinned at Mac. "Okay, let's try to come up with some options. Then the scientists can decide if any of them will work. We don't need final choices today."

The other two nodded and went through the notes they'd taken from their trip. Nothing stood out. Then Mac went to his default Google search: "cool animal abilities." He looked up and studied Maria. "So, I'm guessing since Maria's bracelet causes her to physically change, she can only do one animal at a time. Same with mine, I'll bet."

"What do you mean?" asked Maria.

"Well, you can't be two animals at once, can you? Or that could look . . . really weird, and the features might not work together."

Maria frowned, as though he were insulting her, but then she tapped her chin. "I guess you're right. So would I have to choose which animal based on what the situation is?"

"I don't know," said Charlie. "I hadn't thought of that but it makes sense."

Maria nodded. "We'll ask Dr. Jakande later. Meanwhile, what would be a good animal that would go well with my howler monkey?"

"How about . . . ," Mac began, thinking hard. Then he snorted. "A sea monkey?"

"You want me to turn into *fish food*?" Maria said. She threw a pillow at him, hitting him in the face. "Sure, and then I'd get eaten and you'd never see me again. Is that what you want?"

Mac pretended to consider it. "Could I still visit your family and eat their food and use the Wi-Fi?"

Maria threw a second pillow. This time Mac ducked.

Charlie stopped them. "Something that doesn't make loud howling noises would be great," she suggested. "No howler polar bears."

Mac turned to Charlie, eyes wide. "Is that a thing?" he asked softly.

Charlie lifted her eyebrows mysteriously. "Look it up."

He did. A second later he flashed Charlie a disgusted look. "It's not a thing."

Maria tapped her fingers on the frame of her tablet. "I know we talked about having a completely different creature from the pangolin for Mac's second animal. And we talked about that for me, too. But our devices don't really work the same way. I mean Mac's body doesn't physically change like mine does. So I'm wondering if maybe I'd want to have something closer to what I already have to make the transition easier. Like a different type of monkey. Would that make sense?"

"The changes to your body might be similar," Mac mused. "Is that something that matters to you?"

Maria typed into her tablet. "I don't really mind looking

77

different anymore, as long as it's not too weird, if that's what you mean."

"I meant it could be hard morphing from one animal to another if it changes your body a lot," said Mac. He went back to studying the page he'd pulled up.

"Oh. Yeah, I guess that's a factor. But maybe Dr. Jakande can, like, control that a little bit?" Maria typed "kinds of monkeys" into her iPad and clicked on a few entries, then stopped. "What is this . . . this water monkey?" She read further, her mouth agape. Then her face fell. "I don't think it's real. Definitely not the same as a sea monkey. A water monkey is some sort of Chinese mythological thing." She kept reading. "Dang, though," she muttered. "This thing totally gets who I am. All of these characteristics are, like, me."

"Maria," said Charlie with an edge to her voice.

"All right, all right," said Maria. "I'm focusing. But this would be really cool, is all I'm saying."

Charlie leaned over. "I'd stay away from any full-on water animal," she remarked. "Mythical or not."

Mac looked up. "Better check with Ms. Sabbith to see if mythical DNA is readily available," he added drily. Then he tilted his head thoughtfully. "Why would you want a sea creature anyway? You probably wouldn't be able to use it on land, you know."

Charlie rolled her eyes. "That's practically what I just said."

"I didn't hear you. I was checking out the polar bears." He

looked at Maria. "I'm just not feeling multiple monkey types for you, Maria."

"Not enough variety," Charlie agreed.

Maria frowned. "Yeah, I guess you're right. Maybe something a little more ferocious."

"Well," said Mac. "What features do you want? Poison? Spikes? Sharp teeth or anything like that?"

Maria shrugged. "I haven't really thought about that yet." She paused, then said apologetically, "I just really like being able to outsmart someone and use my monkey limbs and tail to smack them in the face if I have to. But I guess I should have some sort of alternate power move."

The three of them considered animals. After a moment Mac lifted his head. "What about that crab-claw woman—what was that all about? She could punch the stuffing out of somebody with that thing."

"And a crab can move fast if it needs to, right?" said Charlie. "They seem pretty smart and sneaky."

"I don't know." Maria looked unimpressed. "What kind of crab?"

"A ghost crab can move pretty fast," Mac said. He looked it up and read a few things about it out loud. Then he stopped. "Nope," he said. "It doesn't have a supercool claw. Besides, you can already move pretty fast."

"That's kind of a relief," said Maria. "I would worry about

those bug-out eyes happening to me. That might be a little too weird."

"True," said Charlie. Something on her laptop screen caught her eye. "Wait," she said, clicking on a link. "What about this arowana fish? It's a real thing. Unlike the water monkey."

"A fish?" said Maria, wrinkling up her nose. "I thought we agreed no full water animals."

"Yeah, but this one can jump out of the water and catch bugs."

"O-kaaay, gross. And boring."

"But it's really flexible. Check out the tail. I bet you could slap somebody with it."

Maria perked up a little, so Charlie played a short video that showed the fish jumping high out of the water and grabbing a spider from a tree branch. "You'd be able to swim. And jump. And slap people."

"Ooh," said Maria.

"Hey," Mac said sharply. "Remember what we just talked about five seconds ago? The limitative water principal?"

Charlie smirked. "Right. The ol' LWP."

"Be quiet," said Mac, trying not to laugh. "That's what I'm calling it."

Maria shrugged. "You're right," she said. "Enough of this." She cleared her search and started over. "Now forgetting the water stuff forever."

Mac glanced at Charlie. "Speaking of water animals, I just

realized *you* have an ability from a sea creature. Do you think your starfish mode allows you to breathe underwater, too?"

Charlie looked up and blinked. "I have no idea."

"Have you been swimming since you put the bracelet on?" Maria asked.

"Not really. Just the water park at Legoland with you two, but I didn't really spend much time underwater. I didn't notice anything weird." She thought for a moment. "My dad said it was the healing power of a starfish, so I don't think there would be anything else."

"But remember what Dr. Sharma told us after we saw Kelly talking to Mr. Anderson with that pulsing light?" said Mac.

Maria nodded. "She said it was probably hypnosis, which is an extension of the cuttlefish camouflage ability."

"And Dr. Sharma said she hadn't intended for that to be there," said Charlie. "So maybe my dad didn't plan for other abilities from these animals, but they could be there accidentally."

"We can test it out at my house sometime," said Mac, who had a swimming pool. "You never know."

"Yeah," said Maria, "but the hypnosis thing is not technically a different ability. It's another use of the camouflage, so it makes sense that it would be there. Charlie's starfish's healing ability doesn't have anything to do with breathing underwater."

"You're probably right." Mac went back to his tablet.

"We could still test it out sometime, though," said Charlie. "It's a hundred and ten degrees outside. I know we have a lot to do here, but a swim wouldn't be the worst thing in the world, you know?"

"Yep," said Maria. "Mac's pool is finally just about warm enough for me to swim in it. Any water temperature below eighty-eight is too cold for this girl."

Charlie shook her head and laughed. "You would *not* do well in Chicago. If Lake Michigan hits seventy we consider it warm."

"That sounds like torture," said Maria. She shivered.

"Maybe we should start thinking about warm-blooded animals for you, Maria," suggested Mac, typing again.

Charlie laughed.

"No, I'm serious," said Mac. "So Maria can handle cold situations better. A weremoose maybe? Were–arctic fox? Or . . . I know." He looked up, unable to disguise the mischievous expression on his face.

Maria eyed him warily. "I do not like that look."

Mac grinned, trying to look innocent. "What?"

"Just say it. Get it out there. What ridiculous animal do you have in mind for me now?"

Mac's face fell. "Werehamster," he mumbled. "It's funny."

Charlie laughed. "Or, like, a wererabbit. Like Bunnicula!"

"Dios mío," muttered Maria. "Bunnicula is a *vampire* rabbit." She sounded disgusted. "Vampires and werecreatures are not even in the same monster class. Good grief, Chuck. Sometimes I'm not sure I can hang out with you anymore."

Charlie laughed and sank back against her pillows. "I'm hope-less."

Maria raised a skeptical eyebrow. "Anyway, Mac. Hamster not funny."

Mac sighed. "Okay, sorry. What's next?"

"Oh!" said Charlie, something on her screen catching her eye. "Here we go. One of us should definitely have the attack ability of a sarcastic fringehead."

"I think we've got that covered," said Mac.

CHAPTER 9

Making Progress

Charlie, Maria, and Mac eventually stopped goofing around and got serious, writing down a few real options. That afternoon the scientists and kids, plus Ms. Sabbith and Charlie's mom gathered in the Wilde living room. Dr. Jakande, who still wore her soldier bodysuit minus the mask, opened the meeting. She stood with the slight unease of a visitor even though she'd been part of the group for weeks now. Maybe it was the fact that she hadn't been able to change herself back to normal yet that made her feel apart from the others somehow. It was a constant reminder that she'd been on the other side.

There was something about Nubia's distance that made Charlie wonder if she were entirely trustworthy. She'd felt it off and on ever since the woman had joined them. But thoughts like that were always on Charlie's mind these days. She didn't truly trust anybody except Maria and Mac and her family. Not after what she'd seen and experienced. Not after Kelly had turned her back on them. And it wasn't like Nubia had steered clear of Charlie in the battle—the two had physically fought. The memories of that clouded Charlie's view a bit too, she supposed.

Even though Dr. Jakande had apologized and had worked diligently to fix things for Maria, maybe Charlie hadn't quite accepted that the woman's motives were exactly what she said they were. She'd had Maria's device this whole time. Why was it taking her so long to fix it? And a week after Nubia had joined them, Charlie had overheard a voice that sounded like Miko coming through the communicator in Nubia's suit. Nubia hadn't answered Miko, but she'd looked around like she was worried someone had overheard. Charlie had kept an eye on her after that. She was still wearing the suit, after all.

In Dr. Jakande's hand was the Mark Two, nicely polished and fully assembled. She held it out to Maria. "All fixed," she said. The woman glanced at Charlie's dubious expression and added, "And the other doctors checked my work. The howler monkey is still there, but it won't permanently change your DNA ever again. You'll be able to turn it on and off." She paused. "Are you ready to give it a try?"

Maria jumped up and took it. "I want to but I'm a little scared," she admitted. She turned the device over and studied it. "Are you *sure* I won't be stuck like that this time?"

"I'm ninety-nine point nine percent sure," said Dr. Jakande with a small smile.

Charlie frowned. Was Nubia trying to do something sneaky? "What if you're wrong?" she challenged.

"Then we immediately inject Maria with the other formula like we did before to fix the problem. I kept extra just in case."

"Oh," said Charlie. That seemed okay.

"How will we know if it happens?" asked Maria.

"Once you put it on, we'll have you activate the device and change into your monkey form. Then you'll take the bracelet off. If you change back to your human self, we've done it right." She pointed to the device. "I've installed a key-in code so you can quickly take it off anytime."

"That all sounds pretty good." Maria shrugged—she was surrounded by four experts, so her fears were quickly fading. Nubia's explanation seemed great to her.

Maria took a deep breath, then cringed and slapped the device on her wrist. She did the clasp and looked at the screen, then tapped it. The graphics looked updated—Nubia had really done a lot of work to improve things. She held her finger above the howler monkey icon, then clicked on it.

Black fur sprouted from her arms and neck and a beard grew from her chin. The hair on her head became coarse and fur-like. A tail pushed out. Maria reached back and guided it over the waistband of her shorts and let it drop.

"You look like the same old monkey," said Charlie.

Maria hopped a few times, feeling the spring in her step after a few weeks without it. It felt good. Like jumping on a trampoline after a long time away.

"Okay, now take it off." Nubia gave Maria the code to unlock the bracelet. "If the physical traits disappear, then we're good to go. If they stay, well, then it's back to the drawing board, as they say."

Maria glanced nervously at her friends, then entered the code to unlock the device. The clasp clicked free and Maria slid the bracelet off her wrist.

Nothing happened at first. Then a second later all the monkey features disappeared and Maria was back to looking like her old self.

"Whew!" she said.

"It works!" said Charlie, relieved. She felt a pang of guilt for not trusting Dr. Jakande. She still wasn't sure the woman was totally on board with them, but everyone else seemed to think so.

Maria put the bracelet back on, and since it was already set to monkey mode, the features immediately returned. She clicked through the various screens, landing on the Turbo option and tapping it. Her limbs immediately started growing slowly, about four inches each, making her taller than Charlie and Mac and giving her the ability to reach farther and jump higher. She checked herself over and nodded. "This is just like it was before," she said. "I love it! Thank you so much, Dr. Jakande. I'm so glad to have it back again."

"You're welcome," said the woman. "But . . ."

Everyone looked at her. "But what?" said Maria, alarmed.

"Oh, it's nothing to be concerned about," Dr. Jakande said hastily. "It's just . . . well, two things, really. Let me explain." She smiled to reassure Maria, who looked mystified. "First, I found something while working on the device that gave me an idea about how to reverse my own predicament. You see, for me, going back to my human form is not as easy. Dr. Gray's Mark One permanently changed my DNA to a panther-human hybrid, but it was different from how I set up the Mark Two. Add to that the fact that I . . . well, I don't have any samples of DNA available from my former life. I left that world behind years ago, so there's no way for me to do what we did with yours."

While Dr. Jakande talked, Maria quickly powered down the bracelet's effects and returned to normal. She listened solemnly.

"But I saw something in the device that I want to study again, if you don't mind."

"Oh!" said Maria, crestfallen. "Well, sure, if you think it'll help you." She wanted Nubia to have the freedom to look human again, too. She unclasped the device. "What's the second thing?"

"Well, you already know we want to give you an additional wereanimal as we gear up for a potential major fight with Victor Gray and his soldiers. So I'll need the device back for that part anyway."

"Well, I figured that," said Maria, blushing. "And I can't wait."

Sure, she was disappointed that she couldn't mess around with the bracelet now that it was fixed, but this was more important— not to mention exciting. Maria held the device out to Nubia. "Here, go for it. Charlie, uh . . . ," she said, glancing sideways at her friend and then back at the scientist. "Charlie said you were maybe looking for . . . our suggestions?"

"Absolutely. After what happened in the last altercation, I was originally thinking of something venomous since that can be so debilitating."

"Oh," said Maria, realizing in that instant that having a poison ability didn't sound fun at all. "Okay. I mean, whatever you think is best." It was another letdown. But Maria knew that the bracelet wasn't technically hers. It was Dr. Jakande's—or the government's, she supposed.

"But," said Dr. Jakande, "I've since changed my mind. I just wasn't feeling a venomous vibe with you, Maria."

"You weren't?" Maria said, looking up.

"And after thinking about you and my own situation," Dr. Jakande continued, "I realized that the animal should be the kind that *you* would be most comfortable with. So, I'd love your input on what sort of creature feels right."

"Really?" Maria asked. She was relieved she wouldn't have to poison anyone. "That would be awesome. I'm . . . not really feeling anything in particular yet." She blushed. "But I've been thinking about it."

"That's okay. I've got this other work to finish," Dr. Jakande said, shaking the Mark Two. "Keep looking until the right thing clicks."

"I will."

"I'll need to collect your device as well, Mac," said Dr.

Goldstein as he walked over to the boy. "For the same reasons."

"Sure," said Mac, excited about what would happen next.

"Of course, I'd love to hear your ideas as well," said Dr. Goldstein.

Mac beamed and handed over the bracelet. "You got it."

Charlie looked at her father. "What about the Mark Five? You don't need this, do you?"

"Sorry, kiddo, but I do. Ms. Sabbith brought more materials for the communication and safety systems. And Dr. Sharma's going to see if we can add another animal ability to that one."

"Plus, I've got some other ideas for making the Five more . . . universal," Dr. Sharma chimed in.

"I'll keep working on the Mark Six for you, though," Charlie's dad continued.

"Oh. Okay." Charlie punched in her code, took off the Mark Five, and gave it to Dr. Sharma. She rubbed her bare wrist. It felt weird not having something there . . . not having her abilities after living with them for so long. They'd become a part of her. She had so many great ones, and she was really skilled at using them now. And they were perfect—they'd be perfect for anyone.

Suddenly Charlie looked up. "Hey, Dad," she said. "Since my device is so cool, have you ever thought about making copies for Mac and Maria? Then we'd all be the same! Or . . . is that too hard?"

Maria and Mac glanced at each other uneasily. "I'm not so sure I'd want that, to be honest," said Maria. "I mean, I already know how to use mine. I don't really want to change."

Mac nodded. "Besides, our devices have cool features that do things yours can't do, Charlie. Like swinging from trees and being able to cut through things like concrete."

"And protecting us from sharp-clawed attackers, and being able to jump far," said Maria.

"Right," said Mac. "We cover the gaps." He shrugged. "We're a team. We each have our strengths and weaknesses."

"And we like it that way," said Maria. "It's kind of like in soccer. We'll get rid of the pesky defenders while you take the ball to the goal."

Charlie smiled at the analogy. Her friends had a point. And Charlie couldn't imagine giving up her abilities either. Mac's and Maria's devices not only had a lot to offer, but it was true her friends were already familiar and well-trained with them. Starting from scratch with five new powers would take too much time to become skilled. Time they didn't have if they were going to stop Dr. Gray from wrecking the whole world.

"Sounds like we're settled on that," said Dr. Goldstein. "Continue your research and we'll send Ms. Sabbith back to Chicago in a few days to get the necessary samples. We'll be ready to start working on that soon. In the meantime, we've got other tasks to finish."

Charlie and Maria grinned and Mac lifted his chin, looking deadly serious as he clutched his iPad to his chest. "Time to get down to business," he said.

CHAPTER 10

Easier Than It Looks

While Dr. Gray worked long days to create and perfect the formula for Miko's condor wings and Braun's porcupine quills, Kelly and Miko repeatedly hit the beach.

"You're going to practice this until you can do it in your sleep," Miko declared.

"Easy for you to say," said Kelly, "sitting here in the sand."

"It's not like I'm getting a tan," said Miko. "You can imagine how boring this is for me, quite honestly. I can't do anything fun with all these other people around. I just have to sit here and not be noticed."

"You could swim too," suggested Kelly.

Miko blinked. "Hmm," she said. "I guess I could, couldn't I?" She thought about it for another moment, glanced around, then got up. "All right," she said. "I'll go in with you."

"You mean it?" said Kelly, a grin spreading over her face. "Cool, I'll use you as an obstacle. Let's go!"

Miko hesitated. "I . . . I'm not sure if I can actually swim. You know? I haven't . . . I mean, not since before."

"Before what?"

"Before I joined Dr. Gray."

Kelly looked at her. "How long has it been?"

"Six years. Almost seven, I guess, since I ended up like . . . this."

Kelly nodded sympathetically. "It's okay. Could you swim before?"

"Yes."

"Do . . . do chimps swim? Does it even matter since you're human too?" Kelly squinted at Miko in the bright sunshine. She wasn't sure how things worked for the soldiers. Miko's arms were slightly longer than an average person's and she could swing and jump like she was practically floating on air. But how much chimp was she, exactly? It was a subject Kelly had been curious about since she joined up with Dr. Gray, but she'd always hesitated to ask —it seemed like too personal a question.

Miko gave Kelly a long look, as if she were wondering the same things. "I honestly don't know. My instincts are to go for it, though. I don't feel afraid or anything."

Kelly smiled encouragingly. "Well, I'm probably the best person you could go into the ocean with," she said. "I'm kind of famous for rescuing struggling swimmers, you know." Then her grin faded. "I was, anyway." She started walking to the water and Miko fell in step with her.

"The hype has really died down, hasn't it?" asked Miko.

"I guess. I haven't been able to check since Dr. Gray took my phone."

"I . . . can't. My nose doesn't really protrude enough for me to plug it."

"Oh." Kelly thought a moment. "Breathe out when you go under, then."

Miko nodded. "That's what I used to do." She stayed upright as the waves lifted her off her feet, then lowered herself underwater.

Kelly went under too and watched her. The chimp woman floated for a minute, then she flailed and found her footing again. Her head surfaced and she coughed once. "Okay, that was a little different from what I remember. But not terrible."

"Why did you join Dr. Gray's team?" Kelly asked suddenly, thinking about everything that must have changed for Miko once she'd made that decision.

Miko was taken aback. "Well, to be honest, I needed the money. The experiment was a huge commitment, but it came with a big reward." She hesitated. "Dr. Gray was looking for outcasts. Loners. People who could leave everything behind."

"And . . . that was you?" asked Kelly gently.

Miko nodded. "That was me." She paused. "That was all of us."

They swam for a while and Kelly practiced her obstacle course again. Miko went into shallower water and moved about, trying to throw Kelly off by jumping and splashing and doing handsprings and flips when she neared. Moving and avoiding objects was becoming routine for Kelly, and eventually she could dodge Miko without having to think about it.

After a while Kelly turned on her cuttlefish ability and blended to match the mottled sandy background of the ocean floor. Then she concentrated even more until the mesmerizing pulsing began.

As a joke, she stayed just below the water and faced Miko, moving slowly toward her, completely visible to her friend. She assumed Miko would swiftly look away or turn around like she usually did when she knew Kelly was going to use her hypnosis ability. But Kelly hadn't warned her this time, and Miko focused an instant too long. She couldn't pull her gaze away in time.

Kelly didn't realize it until she stopped in front of the soldier. Still pulsing she stood up, wrung out her ponytail, and lifted her goggles, and saw that Miko had a glazed, faraway look in her eyes. Kelly stared. Then she grinned, tempted to make Miko do or say something embarrassing. Or to try to get her to tell her more secrets about her past.

She touched Miko's arm. "Miko?"

Miko blinked. "Yes?" she said softly. She was completely mesmerized.

Kelly frowned. She clicked off her cuttlefish ability and slowly the pulsing faded. Miko wasn't some stranger at a zoo that she'd never see again. She couldn't take advantage of her like that. It wasn't right.

When Miko snapped out of it, Kelly peered curiously at her. "Are you okay?"

Miko seemed startled to see Kelly standing right there. She shivered and hugged herself in the water to try to warm up. "Freezing," she said. "My suit isn't temperature-controlled like yours. I'm going in."

"Okay," said Kelly. She pressed her lips together, not sure if she should tell Miko what had happened. But she figured that since

Miko had only been hypnotized for a moment and Kelly hadn't actually done anything to her, she didn't have to explain. Why did she feel guilty, though?

Miko went back to the beach to try to unobtrusively dry out her fur, though it would certainly be a horrible matted mess to brush through once they got to the house.

Kelly continued practicing for a while until she tired of it. Then she joined Miko, her heart not quite in it today. "I think I'm ready," Kelly announced as she toweled off.

"Ready to go back to the lab?" said Miko.

"No," said Kelly. "Ready to go after the shark DNA again."

CHAPTER 11

Charlie Chooses a Sixth

Back in Charlie's bedroom, the kids tackled their job of picking their new animal abilities much more seriously than they had done before. Now that they knew the scientists were counting on them, they wanted to get it right.

Charlie's wheels were turning. "I wonder what would be the best thing for me," she mused. She'd eliminated everything they'd written down from the zoo and the aquariums they'd visited. Nothing seemed like a perfect fit. And she already had a really well-rounded set of abilities. But what was missing? What was her device's weakness? She began searching randomly. The room was quiet for a long time.

Over the next few hours Charlie found a number of animals she thought were cool. But none of them really seemed like they would add much to what she already had—or what her friends could help her with. She put down her laptop and started pacing the bedroom. Maybe she was going at this all wrong. She was thinking a lot about what was cool. But maybe she should be thinking about what would foil the bad guys. Was there anything that would give her an advantage over Dr. Gray and his soldiers? And Kelly now, too?

She looked up suddenly. "That's it," she said. "That's what matters."

"What matters?" said Maria. Mac looked up, curious.

"Kelly."

Mac raised an eyebrow. "Why?"

Charlie explained. "I got to thinking that it would be great if my new ability could be something that could combat the soldiers. But we don't know what new abilities Dr. Gray is going to give them. I mean, we can expect one of them to have some sort of jellyfish stinger or something. I'm not sure how worried we need to be about that."

"I'm safe from it, anyway," said Mac. "With my pangolin suit."

"Right. But we're not sure Dr. Gray will end up using it in the end. But we do know one thing."

"What Kelly's abilities are," said Maria, sitting up.

"Exactly. So maybe I should try to combat those in some way."

"As long as it's an animal you like and feel good about," said Mac, "I think that's a great idea."

"The thing I feel best about," said Charlie, her expression stern, "is being able to beat Kelly before she beats us. And there's only one ability she's got that can do us in."

"Which one?" asked Mac.

Charlie looked from Mac to Maria and back again. "The cuttle-fish."

Maria stared. "Seriously? That's the one you're worried about? Not the platypus?"

"Well, sure," said Charlie. "The platypus spikes would hurt, but I can heal pretty quickly and probably still stop her from doing anything if I saw her coming. But that's the important part—what if I don't see her? It's her invisibility I'm worried about. And worse, the hypnotism thing. That's really scary. What if she tries to convince us that we should help Dr. Gray?"

The others' eyes widened at the thought. It was horrifying but entirely possible. After what Kelly was able to do to convince all her teachers that she no longer went to school at Summit? Convincing her parents that she didn't *exist*? Charlie was right. That made them all vulnerable.

"The hypnotism is mostly effective on people who aren't expecting it," said Mac. "But we know about it. So we can always look away. Nine times out of ten I bet that'll work."

"Good point," said Charlie. "So it's the invisibility that is the biggest threat."

"What kind of ability can counter that?" asked Maria.

"I can't think of anything, unless there's some animal that spits paint or detects motion that the human eye can't see," said Mac. He frowned.

"I know," said Charlie. "This is a tough one."

They sat quietly again, then went back to their research to see if they could find any animals that could detect invisible predators. A while later, Charlie landed on a page made of gold. "Ahhh," she said.

"Did you find something?" asked Mac, leaning over to look at her page.

"I think so," said Charlie, skimming the information.

"What is it?" asked Maria. She scooted around to get a glimpse too. "A pit viper? What's that?"

"It's a type of venomous snake," said Charlie. She scrolled and kept reading.

"I don't get it," said Maria. "I thought you were going for something to detect Kelly when she's invisible. Did you change your mind? Are you going to try to match her poison with some of your own?"

"No," said Charlie. "Not the venom part. This." She turned her screen to face her friends and pointed. "Infrared heat vision."

Maria and Mac read the description. "Whoa," said Mac. "This is pretty cool. It's kind of like those night-vision goggles that hunters use. And spies and stuff in the movies."

"Yep," said Charlie, looking smug.

"But you already have night vision," said Maria. "From your bat. Won't that work?"

"No, my echolocation only works when it's dark. This would allow me to see someone invisible like Kelly anytime of the day or night by detecting the heat she gives off."

"That could really help us out," said Mac.

"And the best part about it," said Maria, "is that Kelly will never see it coming."

CHAPTER 12

More Decisions

The next day, after spending all morning researching with Mac and Maria, Charlie was even more convinced she'd chosen right. "I'm going to go talk to my dad," she announced right before lunchtime. "I've made my decision."

Mac and Maria stayed behind. Charlie found her father alone in the lab and told him her idea. "A pit viper," Charlie explained, "has heat sensors on its head. They're, like, actual pits near the snake's eyes —that's where the name comes from."

"Hmm," said Dr. Wilde. "Go on."

"Some scientists think the pit viper can use the sensors at the same time as their regular eyesight," Charlie continued. "They use the infrared to detect live prey in hiding. Day or night, they can tell if there's something alive nearby—they can see it because its body temperature gives it away. It shows up differently to the snake than a tree or a building, for example."

"And the tree or building—you can already see those things in the dark with your bat sonar."

"Right. I mean, with the night vision I'd see a silvery outline of a person, too, because people are solid. But it only works in the dark. And I wouldn't be able to tell the difference between, like, a living person and a statue. So with the viper's vision, whether it's day or night, I'd be able to detect body heat."

Her father frowned like he wasn't quite understanding Charlie's enthusiasm for this feature, but then his face cleared. "Ah," he said, beginning to nod. "So it would help you see Kelly when she uses her camouflage."

"Exactly," said Charlie.

"Yes," said Dr. Wilde, leaning forward. "That's very smart. Not only does Kelly have her cuttlefish ability, but that soldier, Morph, also has a chameleon camouflage feature. It's an extremely dangerous power if none of us can see them coming." He scratched his stubbly chin, then squeezed Charlie's shoulder. "Nice thinking. I'm game if you're settled on it. I reckon this will foil their plans pretty well, don't you?"

Charlie nodded as Dr. Jakande breezed into the lab with Maria's device. She glanced at Charlie and her father while flipping the high collar of her suit down, covering the built-in microphone. "How's the researching coming along?"

"Okay, I guess," said Charlie, eyeing the woman. "Maria is still looking for animals. She had a list started, but I think she just scrapped everything on it."

The earpiece in Dr. Jakande's mask crackled and Charlie could hear a muffled voice on the other end. She couldn't make out what the words were.

"Who's talking to you?" Charlie asked, trying to act casual.

Dr. Jakande's expression was worried—or guilty. Charlie wasn't sure which.

"It's, um . . . it's Miko. She tries every now and then to get me to talk to her. I've thought about answering it so I could maybe, you know, find out where they are. But I decided . . . not to."

Dr. Wilde smiled sympathetically. "It must be hard not to be in touch with your old friends," he said. "But it's for the best."

"It's just that I'd thought there might be a way to figure out where they're set up," Dr. Jakande explained. "That's all I wanted. I don't . . . I don't miss them."

"I doubt Miko would tell you where they are if she's still loyal to Gray," said Mr. Wilde. "And we don't want them to suspect we're looking for them. I believe Victor thinks we're no longer a threat because we're not organized enough—or ambitious enough—to go after him."

"Or foolish enough," agreed Dr. Jakande.

"So we don't want to give any hint at all that we're working to stop them."

"Of course not," Dr. Jakande said quietly.

Charlie looked at the floor, feeling awkward. And wondering again if they could trust Dr. Jakande.

Luckily the conversation was ended by Maria and Mac, who came running into the lab. "What did your dad say?" asked Mac.

"Thumbs-up," said Charlie, beaming. "We're doing it."

"Oh," said Dr. Jakande. "You chose your animal ability?"

"Yep," said Charlie. She hesitated. Should she tell her? What if Dr. Jakande wasn't really on their side and going straight back to Dr. Gray or Miko with the information?

"Well?" prompted Dr. Jakande with a grin. "Are you going to keep us in suspense?"

Charlie's face grew warm. She told the woman what she'd chosen, hoping she wouldn't regret it.

"That's a great idea," said Dr. Jakande. She turned to Mac and Maria. "And you two?"

"We're not quite at that point yet," said Maria.

Mac concurred, then listed off the variety of animals they'd researched for Maria. But none of those animals seemed quite right now.

"I just can't decide what I want," Maria lamented.

"Why don't we ask you some questions?" said Dr. Jakande. "That might help you figure out what you want."

"Okay," said Maria. "Go for it."

"First, what do you like and dislike about the monkey feature you already have?"

"I don't like the howling part," said Maria. "It's embarrassing."

"Ah, but if you ever get separated from the others, they'll be able to find you," the biologist pointed out.

"True," said Maria. "I hadn't really thought about that." She pursed her lips. "I love being able to swing up above people's heads, and do parkour moves like running up walls and jumping from building to building. And swinging around poles and slamming into the bad dudes."

"Those are great things," Dr. Jakande said. "Is there anything else you *don't* like about it, though? Or, to rephrase the question, what do you wish you could do?"

"Well," said Maria thoughtfully, "I'm not very strong or ferocious. You know what I mean? I'm not dangerous. I don't have sharp claws or horns or teeth or anything like that. And if I'm out in the open, there aren't many options for jumping and swinging. So that leaves me sort of useless."

"Okay," said Dr. Jakande, nodding approvingly. "You want something a little more ferocious. You want to be able to attack someone who is after you even if you don't have something to swing on."

"Right. So maybe an animal that would give me some serious power or sharp claws and teeth in case we end up fighting in a field, or a parking lot, or whatever—that might be good."

Dr. Jakande nodded solemnly. "You do have some vulnerabilities as a monkey. I agree something to balance out your current abilities is the direction we should lean toward. What about physical features? I heard you were quite upset at first about the look of the howler monkey changes."

"I was," Maria admitted. "Mostly because I wasn't expecting it. But the worst part was that I thought I'd be stuck like that forever. Now that you've fixed that part, it's not so bad. So I guess I'm not going to rule out an animal based only on its physical traits. But it's a factor."

"And we have a little leeway with that based on how I put the formula together," said Dr. Jakande, nodding thoughtfully. She turned to Charlie and Mac. "Okay, well, it looks like you have a lot to go on now, so come back to us with a new list when you're ready. If it helps, I brought in a set of encyclopedias and *National Geographic* magazines from the library that might give you ideas as well. I left them on the table."

"Oh cool," said Mac. "Thanks! I brought a book too."

"The one about the lizard?" whispered Maria.

Before Mac could answer, Dr. Goldstein and Dr. Sharma came in carrying sandwiches from the local deli. "How goes the research?" Dr. Goldstein asked.

The kids filled everyone in on their progress.

"Got your eye on anything, Mac?"

"Um, not really."

Maria elbowed him.

Mac gave her the stink-eye.

Charlie could tell he was nervous to make a suggestion to the biologist. And she totally got it. Dr. Goldstein was a genius and Mac was just a kid—even if he was pretty great with technology. What if the man thought his idea was dumb? Charlie gave him an encouraging look.

Dr. Goldstein peered quizzically from one kid to the next, not sure about the silent conversation going on between them. Then his face cleared. "You know, kids, a lot of what we do as professionals is come up with ideas and figure out if they're any good or not. Sometimes we have some pretty crazy ones, too, right?" He turned to his fellow biologists, and they nodded.

"And sometimes they don't work. But we don't make fun of an idea that isn't viable," said Dr. Wilde. "Sometimes that idea can spark a new one that leads us to a winner."

Mac pursed his lips thoughtfully. "Well," he admitted, "there's an animal I keep coming back to, but I'm worried that I only want it because it was my favorite animal when I was little."

"That's not a bad place to start," Dr. Goldstein said. "What is it?"

"It's called a basilisk lizard," said Mac.

"A lizard," Dr. Goldstein mused. "I'm listening. What does it do?"

"It can run on water."

The scientists exchanged intrigued glances.

"I can show you—I have my zoo book with me." He hesitated. "It's a little kid's book. I don't read it anymore or anything."

"I understand," said Dr. Goldstein. As Mac went to get it, the scientists pulled up the basilisk lizard on their phones. When Mac returned, he opened the book to the right page and Dr. Goldstein set his phone down and read it silently.

Mac's expression was strained, which made it clear to Charlie just how much Mac wanted this to be his second animal. No wonder he'd been so scared to suggest it—what if Dr. Goldstein thought it was a bad choice?

After a moment, Dr. Goldstein set the book down. "This looks promising for a number of reasons, Mac," he said. "I'm very interested in giving you an option to be nimbler when you need to be. Don't get me wrong—your pangolin protection mode and your claws for attack are working great. But I'm less satisfied with how your suit slows you down. Not to mention the noise it makes. It puts a target on you."

Mac nodded and looked more hopeful. "Yes," he said with a rush of air. "I was thinking the same thing. I want to be able to sneak up on people."

"And walking on water is an excellent feature. Nobody would see that coming. You could get places no one else could go. I'm going to read up on this lizard some more. The mechanics of it seems promising."

"Cool," said Mac lightly, but he looked like he was holding back a wide grin. Charlie held her hand up to high-five him. He slapped it and then bumped fists with Maria. The grin came out.

The scientists laughed. "That wasn't so hard, was it?" asked Dr. Sharma. "Nice presentation."

"Thanks," said Mac.

"Mind if I hang on to this book for a few days?" asked Dr. Goldstein.

"Not at all," said Mac.

The man tucked the book under his arm and picked up his lunch. "Let me know if anything else strikes your interest."

"I will."

The three kids returned to Charlie's room, this time determined to focus on Maria's new animal. Maria was starting to wonder if they'd ever find the right one for her.

CHAPTER 13

Maria Begins to Doubt

The scientists had entrusted the three friends to do this very important job. Mac and Charlie had chosen their animals well, and they wanted to continue to prove that they made good decisions by finding something right for Maria. They began jotting down notes as they paged through encyclopedias and other books and magazines full of animals. Every now and then they'd share an interesting finding with one another.

"The cone snail has enough venom to kill twenty people," Charlie remarked.

Maria wrinkled her nose. "A snail? Slimy. No thanks."

"The poison dart frog is pretty awesome," said Mac. "You could be bright blue—that would be cool. But if we touch you, we're basically dead."

"So much death, you two," Maria muttered. "Can't I be ferocious but in a non-killing way? Like scary and able to fight, but not to accidentally kill my best friends?"

"I'd prefer that too," Charlie said.

They went silent again, and then Maria muttered something about a grizzly bear. She seemed to rule that out too, for reasons unknown. "Hyena?" she said.

"I thought you didn't want anything with a strange howl," said Mac.

"Oh yeah."

"What about a spider—"

"NO."

"Okay, okay," Mac said. "I'm with you on that one—just thought I'd mention it."

Charlie flipped past a whole section of poisonous creatures in pursuit of something ferocious. "How about a hippopotamus?" Charlie suggested after a long silence. "They're the most dangerous animal in Africa. They can destroy a whole vehicle." She looked up. "You could take out the white van!" She showed Maria a picture.

"*Qué bárbaro*," muttered Maria. "Hippos are huge. I wonder what features I'd take on. The mouth is great, but it seems like it would be uncomfortable to open it that wide." She rubbed her jaw, imagining it, then looked at the other stats. "It can run fast, so that's a plus. But I'm not sure growing to thirteen feet long and three thousand pounds would be very convenient—that could really hurt. Plus, it's hard to hide a hippo, as they say."

"Who says that?" asked Mac.

"I guess I do." Maria hesitated. She looked doubtful. "I'm starting to wonder if we'll ever find the perfect one. Let's just put hippopotamus on the list with a question mark. It has some of the things I like, anyway."

Charlie patted Maria's shoulder sympathetically while Mac wrote it down. They searched on.

"Any interest in snakes?" Charlie asked. "Nonpoisonous, I mean," she hastened to add. "A python has teeth to catch prey, but then it squeezes it to death."

"No snakes," said Maria decisively. Then she added, "I think I'd like an animal that nobody else has."

"So that's a no on the African elephant, too, I take it?" said Mac.

"You are correct, my clunky friend." She looked up at him. "What's on the new list so far?"

"Uh," said Mac, looking at his notes, "hippopotamus."

"That's it?"

"Yep."

"Sheesh," Maria said. "I'm so picky."

"It's fine to be picky," said Charlie. "You didn't get to choose the monkey, and the shock of that one nearly put you out of commission."

"Yeah, well, I'm over that shock. The monkey, anyway. Now that I know my appearance will change, I'm pretty good with the idea of it, I guess. It's . . . it's kind of exciting, you know?"

Charlie tilted her head. Maria didn't sound very excited. She sounded more like she was trying to convince herself that she was.

"But still," Maria went on, "some animals seem like a better choice than others when you take the physical changes into consideration. There are definitely things I don't want."

"I would imagine any new animal is going to take some getting used to," Charlie replied. "Like Dr. Jakande said, you should choose something you really want. An animal that you like. Let's keep searching until we find the exact right thing."

Maria nodded at Charlie. "Thanks," she said.

Several minutes went by, and then Maria said, "Hmm."

Charlie looked over. "What? Did you find something?"

"All this time I was thinking I didn't want to be a reptile, so I've been skimming past those. But then I landed on this page about alligators."

Mac perked up. "Totally ferocious," he said. "But crocodiles are better."

Maria scoffed. "Better how? They're practically the same thing. I like alligators."

"Well," said Mac, moving to his iPad and typing swiftly. "I read once about the Nile crocodile—they can grow to be twenty feet long and they've killed more people than alligators have. Or something like that."

"Isn't that a book?" asked Charlie. "*Nile, Nile, Crocodile?*"

"That's *Lyle*," said Maria, rolling her eyes. She turned to Mac. "And that's exactly my point. I just want to scare people and be able to defend myself and you two. I think an ordinary, smallish alligator is more than tough enough." She studied the page. "Besides, I like the wider shape of the alligator snout better than the pointy shape that the crocodile has. I'm a little worried, I guess . . . ," she confessed. "Like what if my brain gets smooshed if my head changes too drastically?" Her brow furrowed as if she were picturing how her body might change. "Maybe I'm not so ready for a second animal after all," she muttered.

The other two were skimming the details and didn't hear her. "The alligator's teeth are hidden when its mouth is closed," Charlie noted. "The crocodile looks like it's grinning because some of the bottom teeth stick up over the top ones."

"See, Mac?" said Maria. "Alligators even have better orthodontics. No need for braces. And maybe not quite as hard to get used to as a croc mouth would be." She frowned.

Mac shrugged. "It's your animal. I'm just saying the crocodile is what I'd choose."

"Good thing it's my choice, then," said Maria, sitting up. "Put alligator on the list."

Mac obeyed and didn't argue further.

By the time dinner was ready, they were getting tired of all this research. And Maria, picturing herself as an actual hippo or an alligator, was starting to doubt both options and question her choices. Charlie was right—the howler monkey had taken a lot of getting used to. It had been so . . . so shocking to turn into an animal. Was she fooling herself, thinking that taking on features of a hippo or alligator was really going to be no big deal?

She'd have to get through it. What choice did she have? If

they were going up against the soldiers with new abilities, she was going to need another animal no matter what. Anything she picked would alter her body in some way. Could she really be as brave about it as she thought she'd be? With grim determination, Maria knew she had to suck it up and handle whatever came her way for the sake of humankind. This was not fret time—it was fight time. And boy, was she going to fight.

CHAPTER 14

Some Unexpected News

That night Maria called Charlie.

"What's up?" asked Charlie. "Did you finally make up your mind?"

"I'm sorry, but I have to go away," said Maria.

"What? Where? You can't leave! We need you."

Maria sounded torn. "I'm heading to Puerto Rico. Abu Yolanda called. She asked for help cleaning up her community— things have been a mess there from the hurricane but they finally have their electricity back. She wondered if I would come for a week to lend a hand."

"Oh," said Charlie, softening immediately. "Of course, you should definitely go." She hesitated. "When are you leaving?"

"Next Friday."

"Oh cool. That's soon." Charlie was relieved. Maria would probably return before anything important happened.

"Yeah," said Maria. "I hope it doesn't mess up the plans."

"It won't," said Charlie. "You'll be back before we know it." She felt glum, though. She didn't want to be away from her friend, not even for a week. "Does Mac know?"

"Yeah. He's bummed but he understands."

"I wish we could go with you," said Charlie.

"I wish you could come too. Abu could use more help."

"Aren't your parents going?"

"Nope. *Sin padres, chica.* They have the boys for the summer. Plus, Ken has to work."

"Dang. That's too bad." Charlie blinked and an idea began to form. She thought about the amount of work the scientists still had to finish before they could go after Dr. Gray. Then she thought about all the news reports she'd heard about the devastation in Puerto Rico: people without water or electricity, trees blocking roads, cars flipped over. Finally, she thought about her abilities. Strength would really come in handy there, she imagined. If the Mark Six was ready in time, her powers could be used to help those in need.

"Hey," she said softly, putting all her thoughts together. "Maybe we should go with you."

An hour later Charlie had talked to her parents and Mac had talked to his, and then they'd all talked to one another. They agreed it was a great opportunity for the kids to lend a hand where it was needed, and Charlie's parents were glad it would give the kids a chance to get away from the lab and do something good besides focusing on fighting a monster of a scientist.

When it was settled, Charlie got Maria back on the phone. "I can go!" she shouted.

"I know! Hooray!" Maria yelled.

"And Mac's coming too!" they both said together.

"Oh my gosh," Charlie said as the reality set in. The three best friends were going to Puerto Rico together. "I can't believe it. I'm really glad we can help Yolanda and her neighbors."

"And maybe if we work really hard, we'll get some of Abu's cooking," said Maria.

They discussed the trip for a while, and then Charlie moved the conversation to the work they were doing to stop Dr. Gray. "This means we need to focus hard to help the scientists before we leave," she said. "So they can be ready for action when we come back. We have to stay ahead of Dr. Gray no matter what. You know what this means, Maria."

"Yup," said Maria. "It means I need to make a decision."

"That's right. Have you?"

"As a matter of fact, I have."

Charlie's eyes widened. "What animal?"

"Can I talk to Dr. Jakande first? I want to get her opinion. Is she still there?"

Charlie made an impatient sound, then went to the lab where the scientists were just packing things up for the evening. "Dr. Jakande," Charlie announced, holding out the phone, "Maria wants to talk to you."

The panther woman looked startled, then set down her things and took the phone. "Is everything okay?" she asked. The doctor listened for a long moment, and then she smiled. "I agree, Maria," she said. "That is an excellent choice."

CHAPTER 15

Making Wings

Miko and Kelly entered the lab to see what Dr. Gray had in mind for them that day. Scattered on the table were the results of Fang's and Morph's recent evaluations. Kelly studied them curiously. On Morph's pages, "crab claw" was circled with a question mark next to it. "Chameleon" was crossed off. On Fang's, "rattlesnake" had a check mark next to it. Wolf was underlined twice with a few words in Dr. Gray's familiar scrawl: "Loyalty. Subspecies?"

Her eyes wandered to a clipboard near the landline phone. On it was a list of every zoo and aquarium in California. All of them had been scratched off and the word "banned" was written next to each one. At the bottom of the page were the letters "GDL" with three question marks.

Kelly wasn't sure what any of this meant.

The scientist beckoned to Miko. "Your formula is ready," he said gruffly. "And with any luck the machine should be working. I ran an H_2O test and all seemed well."

Prowl, from the doorway, looked up curiously. He still hadn't had a discussion with Dr. Gray about what his second animal would be. The wings would have been a good choice for him, he thought. He tried not to let his jealousy show—he wouldn't want Miko to feel badly about it. It wasn't her fault. It just seemed like Dr. Gray cared less and less about them, and their feelings and ideas, lately.

Gray used to consult with them all a lot more—he used to care about what they wanted, like with their initial animal. But not so much lately. He'd been in a terrible mood for the past two days, but no one knew why.

Miko bounded over to Dr. Gray, nimbly hopping over a lab table in her haste, while Kelly came and stood nearby to watch.

"Are you ready for this?" Dr. Gray barked at the chimp woman.

"Now?" she asked. "Like, right now?" She looked around nervously, confused by Dr. Gray's harsh demeanor. "Are you sure *it's* ready?"

Dr. Gray frowned at her. "Of course. I said it was."

Miko flushed. "I'm sorry. I'm just nervous."

The scientist grunted. He turned to the workstation in front of him and the genetic mist machine. It was the reconstructed masterpiece that he'd forced Charlie's dad and the other scientists to build for him during their captivity—the machine he hadn't been able to create on his own after all these years. And even though it had been broken in the fight, Gray had managed to gather the pieces before he fled.

It had taken him a while, but he'd finally got them put together properly again, and he was eager to test it out for real. With some slight alterations, this was the thing that would make his dreams come true. But its current form was perfect for the task at hand.

Dr. Gray poured a small amount of formula into the machine, which reminded Kelly of some kind of fancy espresso machine with an oxygen mask attached. He turned it on. It whirred, and Kelly could see a cloudy mist welling up inside through a glass window.

"Come on, then," the scientist said, glancing at Miko. "I haven't got time to waste. Take your suit off so it doesn't hinder the wings."

Miko had trouble controlling her nervousness. She pulled one hairy chimp arm out of her suit, followed by the other. Then she pushed the suit down to her waist, revealing tufts of fur poking out of the arm and neck openings of her tank top. Dr. Gray took a scissors and cut a slit down the back of her top.

"Have a seat." Dr. Gray pointed to a stool in front of the lab table. Then he explained what Miko would be doing.

"Rest your chin in this little holster," he said, "and when you're ready, put on the mask. Breathe normally until after the mist is gone and you feel something tingling. Then you can pull back."

Miko's eyes widened, but she did what she was told. She rested her chin on the curved bar and glanced anxiously at Kelly and Dr. Gray. Then she strapped the mask to her face and took a breath.

Dr. Gray muttered something to her that Kelly supposed was meant to sound reassuring. He turned to observe Miko's back, where the wings would emerge once the formula kicked in.

Miko kept inhaling and exhaling. Her fists clenched and unclenched on the table.

"You're doing great," Kelly called out.

"Remember to keep breathing even after the mist has disappeared," said Dr. Gray. "Wave your hand when you start to feel tingling on your back."

Eventually the mist cleared. After a moment, Miko waved her hand.

"All right. You can take it off," said Dr. Gray.

Miko took off the mask and pulled her face away from the mist chamber.

"What do you feel?" Dr. Gray asked Miko.

"The skin on my back is tight. It's trying to stretch."

"Good, good." Dr. Gray seemed to relax a bit, and laid a hand between her shoulder blades. A moment later Miko shifted uncomfortably and made an odd noise. "Oh! Something weird is happening!"

Dr. Gray pulled his hand away. Black and white feathers burst out of Miko's back. Kelly gasped. Dr. Gray stepped farther out of the way.

The chimp woman cried out again in surprise, but she didn't seem to be in pain. "Wow!" she said, turning to look over her

shoulder as the wings reached their full extensions. "Holy cow, they're big! And heavy."

Dr. Gray examined the wings all over. He stretched them out, then folded them, testing their joints, and seemed extremely pleased. "Can you move them?"

Miko strained, trying to figure out which muscles to use. The wings bounced a little.

"Great," said Dr. Gray. "Keep at it. Once you get used to controlling them, I imagine you'll be able to tuck them in closer."

"I hope so." Miko turned to Kelly, eyes worried. "What about my head? Is it still normal?"

"Hmm. Just a little pink," said Kelly, coming closer to see the wings.

"What?" cried Miko. Her hands flew to her face.

"I'm kidding," said Kelly. "It's normal. You don't have an ugly condor head."

"Whew," said Miko, visibly relieved. She checked the rest of her body, finding nothing else had changed, and returned her attention to her wings, straining to see the reflection in the window.

Nearby Prowl studied her new appendages and seemed impressed. "Nice. But they'll be difficult to hide in public."

"We'll come up with something to cover them," said Dr. Gray, giving Prowl an annoyed look. "That can be your job."

Prowl narrowed his eyes. "Is that supposed to be a punishment?"

"Whatever you want to call it," Dr. Gray said lightly.

Prowl stiffened and turned back to the window.

"Let's go to the mirror," Kelly suggested to Miko. "Then you can see better."

Miko looked to Dr. Gray for permission to leave, and he nodded slightly. "Hurry back, though," he said.

The two barely heard him as they went off to the bathroom to check out Miko's wings.

"What's his problem?" whispered Kelly.

"I don't know," said Miko. "Cyke and Morph were gone yesterday checking out zoos and came back empty-handed. Maybe Dr. Gray is running out of DNA to work on now that mine is done."

"Hmm." Kelly wondered if the clipboard zoo notes with "banned" written all over them had anything to do with Morph and Cyke's failure to get DNA. She hoped that didn't mean she and Morph would be stuck camo-ing their way through all the collecting from now on. Morph was dull and the only thing quick about her was her stupid punchy crab claw.

They stood in front of the broad mirror, Miko turning so that her back was to it and looking over her shoulder. The wings were thick at their base and hung at odd angles.

"I have a handheld mirror that I brought from home," Kelly said. "I'll be right back." She left and returned with it, then helped Miko hold it up so she could see her back better.

"Can you flap them?" said Kelly. "Have you figured out how to?"

Miko's look of concentration affirmed that she was trying. The wing joints moved a little. Then they moved a lot, haphazardly. "This might take a while," she murmured, still watching herself in the mirror. She kept at it for several minutes until the wings were moving together. With an enormous strain, she made them fold in like a feathery backpack.

"Okay," she said. "That was a workout. A bit of a learning curve, but I'm sure it'll come." Still, her face held a hint of concern. "Prowl made a good point. I can't really hide them," she said. "I mean, I'm not stupid—I knew that would be a problem. Dr. Gray said . . . Well, he insisted I'd be okay with it. It's just . . ." She glanced at Kelly in the mirror. "It's just that I was getting used to going outside without my mask. But now . . . yeah. Not so much going outside at all."

Kelly frowned. "We'll figure out a way to hide them if you want to. But you could just fly out in public, you know. Way up above people's heads so they can't tell what you are."

Miko recoiled at Kelly's insensitive choice of words. Her face hardened. "What am I?"

Kelly looked down. "Oh my gosh. Sorry. I meant . . . people wouldn't expect you to be human if you were flying above them."

"But I *am* human," said Miko.

"Right, of course, I know," Kelly hastened to say. "You just have . . . a unique look. More so now than before." When Miko's face didn't change, Kelly said more quietly, "I'm just going to stop

129

talking now. Other than to say I'm sorry again. And I think you look wonderful. Your feathers are really shiny."

"Thank you," said Miko, softening a bit. But the fearful look remained. Having wings would clearly take some getting used to, just like when she'd first become a hybrid. Abruptly she turned and headed out of the bathroom. "C'mon, Kel. Let's go see what these can do."

Kelly followed Miko out of the building. As they went past Prowl, he stopped them. "Did you hear the announcement? Gray didn't wait for you."

"What was it this time?" asked Miko.

Prowl looked annoyed. "We're leaving San Diego. Now that he knows the machine works, it's time to kick his plans into high gear and he needs more DNA. And apparently we're banned from parks across the whole state."

"What?" said Kelly, going pale. "Because of me?"

"Not just you," Prowl said, with a hint of kindness. "Cyke and me, too. Anyway, Gray thinks that the SeaWorld people alerted the other zoos and aquariums in the area about us. He's paranoid they've got the whole country's various attractions on the look-out."

"The whole United States?" said Miko. "No wonder he's been cranky today. What are we going to do? Where will we go?"

Prowl narrowed his eyes. "Dr. Gray said he has some associates in Guadalajara. We're going to Mexico."

CHAPTER 16

On the Road

While the soldiers spent the day before their departure prepping for the journey, Dr. Gray finished the formula for Braun and arranged for their arrival in Mexico. Once he had all the details secured, he called Kelly into the lab.

"You have your passport, right?" he asked her.

"Yes," said Kelly. "I took it from home when I hypnotized my parents, like you asked me to."

"Good. You probably won't need it, but bring it just in case."

Kelly frowned. "Why wouldn't I need it? You need one to get into Mexico—I was just there with my mother." She paused, thinking. "And I've been wondering: How are the soldiers going to get into another country? They'll have to take their masks off and they don't even look human." Kelly folded her arms and said knowingly, "They'll never make it through customs. I mean, Miko has *wings* now. Maybe you should've waited until later. . . ."

"It's under control," said Dr. Gray quietly. "Don't worry about it. I have an old friend—a Mexican official—who will meet our plane and take us in without asking any questions. That's all you need to know."

friends with the people you work for in our government?"

Dr. Gray's eyes flared. "No—I mean, yes. It's under control," he said again, clipping his words this time.

It sounded shady. And a little scary. "Why do I need my passport, then?"

The scientist's face turned red. "In case I decide to leave you in Mexico," he said indignantly, "for asking too many questions."

Kelly stared at the man. *What a horrible thing to say*, she thought. Tears burned her eyes and threatened to spill. She pushed her chair back and ran out of the office.

Dr. Gray called after her. "Kelly, come back."

But Kelly kept going. And the old questions returned. What was Dr. Gray's real goal? If he was working for the government, why did he have to be so sneaky? Why couldn't the government help him get the DNA he needed, rather than making him drag everybody to some faraway place in Mexico that wasn't even a resort town? What he was planning to do sounded illegal. Would the government want him to do that? They must have told him to do it this way. But it seemed weird.

Kelly didn't have any answers. As she burst out of the house into the yard to get some air, she saw Miko out there alone, trying to figure out how to fly. The chimp woman gave a lackluster wave.

Kelly wiped her eyes and went over to her. "How's it going?"

"Slow. The wings are heavy and floppy and I'm . . . I'm having trouble. . . ." Miko's eyes grew shiny. She couldn't speak for a moment.

Kelly forgot her own pain and reached out a hand. "Are you okay?"

"It's just hard," Miko whispered. "Frustrating." She turned her head away.

"You're like a baby bird," said Kelly. "It takes time to learn. But soon you'll be great at it. Just as great as you are at being a chimp."

Miko nodded. She took a deep breath and blew it out. "Thanks. I'm fine. I just need to work more at it." She looked up at a low-flying airplane that had taken off from the nearby airport and shook her fist at it. "I think it's mocking me."

"I'll help you if you want. Or at least hang out and watch. Like you did for me at the beach."

"That would be nice," said Miko. She laughed, a little embarrassed by her momentary breakdown. "I can't see what I'm doing, you know? Can you maybe just watch me and tell me what I'm doing wrong?"

"Sure, I'll try," said Kelly. "Go for it."

Miko ran through the backyard, wings flapping awkwardly, while Kelly shouted out suggestions and encouragement. She forgot about Dr. Gray's cruel words for the moment. But her uneasy feeling about his real motives was beginning to grow.

By the time darkness fell, Miko had managed multiple liftoffs after which she flew for a few seconds. But each successful takeoff ended with a crash to the ground, for she was still unable to maintain momentum.

Finally, exhausted and bruised, Miko called it a day. They went inside to pack for their trip. Then they checked in with Prowl, who was nearly finished sewing a canvas wing cover for Miko. He said it would look like she was wearing a large backpack. "I'll have it to you by morning," he promised. "See you bright and early."

Kelly and Miko turned in for a few hours of sleep.

Way too early the next morning, nobody seemed particularly excited to be awake.

Kelly stumbled into the kitchen to get breakfast and ran into Miko, who was carrying a floppy piece of canvas that had straps attached to it.

"How did you sleep?" Kelly asked, noticing Miko's red-rimmed eyes.

"Terrible," said Miko, pointing her thumb at the wings. "I can't lie on my back anymore. My muscles are so sore from practicing and falling. I'm covered in bruises." She groaned as she lifted the coffeepot and poured a cup.

"It'll probably be a while before flying becomes totally second nature," Kelly said, trying to sound encouraging. "But you came a long way yesterday."

"A long way *down*, maybe," said Miko, rubbing her lower back. "I can hardly walk."

"I can help you carry your stuff," said Kelly. She pointed to the canvas. "Is that your wing covering?"

"Yeah. Prowl left it outside our door. I'm not sure how to put it on."

"Let me see." Kelly examined it, then slipped what looked like the bottom part under Miko's wings. She helped Miko slide her aching arms through the straps and tightened them, which brought the upper part of the pack in place over the top of the wings.

Miko adjusted the straps to fit snugly. "Is this right?"

"Yeah." Kelly looked her over. "It's nice." It should sufficiently cover Miko's wings and hold them in so she would blend more easily in a crowd. And it looked like a backpack, as promised. It might be large and a bit bulky, but Kelly figured no one would suspect the woman had wings under it. "I think it'll work great. A few nice buttons or patches would make it downright cute."

"Thanks. Maybe you can help me decorate it in Mexico," said Miko, but she didn't seem enthused. When they finished eating, Kelly picked up Miko's luggage and carried it, along with her own, to the van in the dark. Miko sat by the window in the second row. Kelly got in after the chimp woman and sat down behind her. Kelly fidgeted with her Mark Four and checked the time. "I've never been to Guadalajara before," she said idly. "I wonder how long the flight is."

"It's a few hours," said Miko. "Dr. Gray rented a private plane, so that makes everything . . . easier. I guess." Miko sat awkwardly against the seat, her backpack full of wings keeping her from relaxing against the seatback. She looked uncomfortable. "Easier for people who look like me, anyway."

Kelly grimaced and changed the subject. "So, are we just leaving the van at the airport? Are we coming back here? Like, ever?" They had to. Right? Fear struck Kelly. What if they were never coming back to the United States?

"Cyke's dropping us off. He and Morph and Fang will be driving the van to Mexico later with the equipment. Prowl told me he thinks we'll come back here once we get all the right DNA."

That was a relief, though Kelly wasn't quite sure why. She had no one to come home to. She pushed the lonely thought aside. "What kinds of animals are we looking for in Mexico?"

"Jellyfish, for one. They've got a jellyfish display and a culture lab at the Guadalajara Zoo," said Miko. "I saw the website open on Dr. Gray's computer. Maybe they have the right kind there or something. The Mexican wolf is an animal Dr. Gray mentioned once, too, though he already has a different kind of wolf DNA left-over from Fang. And, of course, the elusive shark, if we can find one. I'm not sure what else."

Kelly frowned. "It seems like we should be able to find those all in the United States. Does Dr. Gray really think all the zoos and aquariums will be watching out for us? That's nuts. Besides, why can't Morph and I just sneak in using our camouflage? I mean, it's not my first choice spending that much time with her. But if it means we can stay here, why not?"

"Dr. Gray is paranoid," Miko said, sounding annoyed. "I don't understand him lately." She bit a hangnail on her monkey-like finger and spit it out. Then she examined it. Satisfied, she glanced out the window as Prowl came up. "But traveling by plane is kind of cool, I guess. We don't usually get to see much of the world except through the van windows these days."

"Who's the Mexican wolf for?" asked Kelly. "Me?" She hoped she wouldn't get the shark or the jellyfish. She had too many water abilities already.

"I doubt it," said Miko. "You heard what Dr. Gray said. Yours will mysteriously come later." She made a face.

Kelly sat back and studied Miko. It sounded like she didn't think Dr. Gray had meant what he said. Why were things so confusing with this group?

Prowl slung his bag into the back of the van with the rest of the luggage. "Mexican wolf?" he asked. "Hmm. Wonder if that's for me. A mix of canine and feline could be interesting. Though you'd think I'd be consulted." He sniffed.

"That combo could be a disaster," Miko declared. "You'd be constantly fighting with yourself."

Prowl scowled at her and sat next to Miko. "We'll see what happens, I guess." He looked back at the house impatiently   now that he was here, he was ready to get moving. Soon Dr. Gray came out of the building and held the door as Mega and Braun, the bull soldier, came outside. Braun was sporting new porcupine quills under an oversized coat. Apparently he'd gotten his moment with the mist machine last night. He walked gingerly, bickering with Mega as he often did. Neither seemed to be early morning people. They stopped talking abruptly when they got to the van.

Dr. Gray locked up the lab and followed. The three stashed their luggage and Dr. Gray slammed the rear door shut. The two soldiers eased their large bodies into the back with Kelly, and Dr. Gray went to the front passenger seat.

Braun snorted and shuffled to his seat. Kelly eyed his quills, which were showing through the opening in his jacket. She swiftly slid over to smash herself against the window, trying to stay clear. She didn't like the bull and rhino soldiers much. They usually ignored her, and that was just fine. They were cranky and loud, and they often argued about the fact that Mega was going to get the shark DNA. It sounded to Kelly like Braun wished he'd get that instead. It made Kelly feel uneasy. It seemed silly to argue when everyone was getting a new animal feature—they would all be excellent abilities, Kelly was confident of that. Dr. Gray was all about research and finding the best of everything, and porcupine quills were really dangerous, which was cool. So what was Braun's beef?

Soon they were on the road. With Morph and Fang staying

behind, only Zed was missing from their team. Nobody mentioned her.

Dr. Gray was quiet in the front seat, poring over his tablet, no doubt doing more research. Everybody else was quiet too, but it didn't feel pleasantly so. Prowl's sharp eyes followed the line of the roadside. Miko shifted uncomfortably. Braun farted and Mega slapped him, then cried out because a quill pierced her hand.

"Settle down," Dr. Gray muttered, not even bothering to look back. There was a strained tension in the air that had been developing ever since they'd left Navarro Junction. Everyone was anxious to move forward and get their new abilities. But then what? More testing? When would he determine what the ultimate chimera would be like? And who was getting it? Was *that* Kelly's special surprise—an updated Mark Four device with all the best features? Nobody seemed to know.

Kelly reached into her pocket for the cell phone that wasn't there, then laughed at herself—she hadn't done that in a long time. The action had once been so automatic every time she was stuck in a vehicle with one of her parents and didn't want to talk. She thought she'd broken the habit by now. Kelly looked around sheepishly to make sure no one had noticed, and caught her reflection in the van window. She was almost startled by it. Here she was in this van full of animal hybrid soldiers and a strange scientist, heading to Mexico to collect animal DNA from a zoo. It was super strange when she thought about it.

She glanced at the device on her wrist. Maybe she could play a trick on Braun by hypnotizing him. But the idea didn't sound nearly as fun as it had when Kelly was first learning about her new powers. Besides, Mega was sitting on the other side of him, and if she noticed, she'd just be cranky and make Kelly stop.

Kelly glanced at Miko, who was perched at the edge of her seat, strapped in by her seat belt but unable to sit back properly. She was looking out her window, her eyes shining again, and Kelly felt a wave of emotion for her. Wings were great . . . until they weren't. Miko's life had just changed dramatically, Kelly realized. Was her chimp-condor friend having an even harder time getting used to it than she'd let on? Kelly wanted to reach over the seat and take Miko's hand and assure her that she'd get used to the wings over time, but she felt weird about doing that. Miko was a grown woman, and Kelly was just a kid who was still pretty new here. It didn't seem like she could offer any real assurance. Besides, Kelly wasn't very good at close friendships. Sure, she was the most popular kid in her class—at least she used to be—but she'd never really gotten close with anyone. Maria was about as close as she'd ever gotten. But Maria had her best friends, Mac and then Charlie.

Not that Maria was even a distant friend anymore.

Kelly sighed and rested her head against the window, her breath fogging the pane, making the nearing airport lights seem like bright stars muted by a thin layer of clouds. Cyke stopped the van alongside a private hangar. Dr. Gray opened his door and all the interior lights turned on, making everyone blink. They piled out and collected their luggage, then trudged to a small plane. They'd be well on their way before sunrise with no annoying security lines to go through. *That's a plus*, thought Kelly.

As they boarded, the pilot poked his head out of the cabin to greet them. Kelly glanced over her shoulder and saw him give a curious look and a slight frown in Miko's direction, perhaps because of the bulkiness of her backpack. Kelly pushed up behind Miko to help hide it and tried to act normal. But then Braun came aboard. The pilot's expression changed for the worse, but Dr. Gray stepped up and greeted him. The pilot seemed to recognize him. They conversed for a moment, and then the pilot's face cleared and he nodded. Once everyone was settled he closed the cockpit door and went back to the controls. Dr. Gray sat down. Everything seemed to be going smoothly.

But getting into Mexico would prove to be harder than anyone ever expected.

CHAPTER 17

Detour Ahead

As the plane touched down, Miko leaned forward into the aisle and tapped Dr. Gray on the shoulder. "Are you sure we're not going to have a problem, Dr. Gray?" she whispered anxiously. "Won't the customs officials be suspicious of the way we look?"

"Not these officials," Dr. Gray said lightly.

Miko narrowed her eyes. "Do you know them or something? Are these your contacts?"

"I know a lot of people." Dr. Gray glanced out the window. "Like the pilot—you saw he didn't have any problem with you. So don't worry. I've got everything figured out."

Miko sat back, but her concerned expression remained. They taxied for a while, then came to a stop at a hangar far from the main terminal.

Kelly leaned toward the window and looked closer. Was this the kind of place where celebrities landed so they didn't have to walk through the crowded airport and get mobbed by fans? When Kelly became famous, she'd be able to say with a bored look that she'd already done the private jet thing. She smiled sleepily.

Dr. Gray sat up sharply, startling Kelly out of her daydream.

The doctor leaned over to his window and muttered under his breath, "Who on earth is that?"

Kelly looked. A small group of uniformed officials were walking toward the airplane. The pilot opened the plane door and lowered the steps so the officials could board.

Dr. Gray glanced wildly around, his face distraught. "This isn't . . . I don't . . ." He unbuckled his seat belt and stood up.

"What's going on?" hissed Miko.

Dr. Gray turned, looking panicked. "Everybody stay calm and cover up," he said, which only made Kelly feel like freaking out. Obviously, something unexpected had happened, but what?

"Aren't these your contacts?" Kelly whispered. "What's wrong?"

Dr. Gray shushed her, then grabbed her arm and tugged, but her seat belt was still on. "Get up!" he whispered harshly. "Everybody else stay seated."

As Kelly fumbled with her seat belt, Dr. Gray turned to Miko, who was the soldier closest to the front of the plane. "These officials shouldn't ask to see inside your backpack," he said, "but Kelly will help with that if there's a problem."

Kelly frowned and stood up. What kind of problem?

"Is something wrong?" asked Prowl under his breath. "Victor, for God's sake, tell us."

Dr. Gray ignored him and checked the window again. The officials had reached the bottom of the steps.

"Victor!" Prowl hissed.

Dr. Gray gestured angrily at him, then turned and spat out to the soldiers, "It's customs. I'd made arrangements but . . . something must have happened. Just act natural." Then he muttered to Kelly, "If they seem suspicious, hypnotize them."

"What? All of them?" said Kelly, startled. "Sheesh. Okay." Her palms began to sweat. She hadn't known she'd have to do something like that. Weren't these people like the police? It seemed a lot worse somehow to do that to a law enforcement officer than to a zoo worker. Especially in a different country. What if some weren't looking at her? What if it didn't work? Would she be arrested?

Kelly's heart raced as she watched through the window. The last of the agents climbed the stairs to the plane and the first ones were coming inside and greeting the pilot. One of the officers glanced at her. Kelly began to worry that if she didn't go into camo mode soon, she wouldn't be able to take it to the hypnosis level in time. But if she went camo now, they'd realize something was up. Even if she could stay hidden, at least one of them had seen her. And all her stuff was here. Plus, Dr. Gray wanted to block their view of the weird-looking soldiers. How was she supposed to do all of that? It was impossible. Kelly blew out a breath. She'd have to stay visible and hope everything went smoothly.

Miko shifted in her seat and Prowl growled under his breath.

The pilot returned to the cockpit and the first official came back into view. Dr. Gray stepped forward. "I'm Dr. Victor Gray," he said, handing them his passport. "Where . . . is Roberto Garcia Pérez? He said he was going to meet me. Us."

"Oh, really?" The official studied Dr. Gray through narrowed eyes, then looked at Kelly. "Officer Garcia Pérez was detained this morning."

Kelly wasn't sure what that meant, but it didn't sound good. Dr. Gray's hands tremored. The official took his passport and studied it, then handed it to one of the others, who scanned it. "What brings you to Guadalajara?" the man asked, leaning to see the rest of the passengers. His eyes widened.

"Medical procedures," Dr. Gray said. He tilted his head toward the soldiers and didn't elaborate. Kelly swallowed hard. She supposed collecting DNA could technically be considered a medical procedure, but she didn't think that was what Dr. Gray meant. He was pretending that the soldiers were patients who needed to be worked on. Kelly frowned. She wondered how they felt about that.

"Passports?" asked the official as he studied each of them with growing alarm. "We'll need you to take your masks off so we can compare your photos."

Miko froze. Prowl stiffened. In the back, Mega stood up. "I don't think so," she said.

"Mega." Dr. Gray held up a hand to stop her from doing something stupid. Then he turned back to the official. "Officer, when

I alerted Roberto of our visit and our special situation, I was told that removing the masks wouldn't be necessary because of the nature of their . . . conditions. They are at grave risk . . . for . . . acquiring diseases. They could die."

Kelly's heart pounded. Dr. Gray was scrambling. Everything felt awful.

"Roberto was lying," said the officer. He pushed past Kelly and Dr. Gray, reaching for the passports that a few of the soldiers held out. Not everyone was complying, either because of stubbornness or because they didn't have them.

"Remove the masks!" the officer said, his voice raised.

Dr. Gray elbowed Kelly and gave her a hard look.

Kelly startled into action. Abandoning reason, she tapped on her device, activating camouflage mode.

One of the other officials noticed her. "Eduardo!" she called out to the lead guy.

Kelly's heart flew to her throat. She concentrated, trying to hurry to get to the pulsating level.

Eduardo turned swiftly. He saw Kelly's strange pulsing and drew his weapon. "What's happening to her?" he demanded.

"That weapon is not necessary!" said Dr. Gray firmly, putting his hands up. "Please let me explain. I'll have them all take off their masks."

The official narrowed his eyes. "Do it, then," he said. "And explain *that*. What's happening to the blond girl? What's going on here?" He pointed the weapon at Kelly. "Where's your pass-port?"

Kelly started shaking. She couldn't concentrate with a gun in her face. Her pulsing stopped, leaving her camouflaged, but every-one had just seen her there a minute ago. She grabbed her passport from her bag and threw it at the woman, then tried again to get the hypnotic feature to kick in.

"Put your hands in the air!" Eduardo said to Kelly. "What is happening?"

"I—I don't know!" said Kelly. Her camouflage failed and she became fully visible again.

"Friends," prompted Dr. Gray, panic in his voice. "Do what the officials ask you to do."

The officials watched closely as the soldiers removed their masks. Kelly quickly returned to camo mode and strained to get back to the point where the pulsing began. Finally she could see from the corner of her eye that it was starting to work. With no time to spare, she darted into the aisle to draw the attention of all the officers. Then she swallowed hard, eyeing Eduardo's gun, and took a step toward him. "I think you've seen enough now," she said in a quiet voice. "Put the gun away."

The officer stared, then blinked hard and glanced at his fellow officers. His eyes weren't glazed over. "Excuse me," Kelly said. She jumped, desperate to make him look at her again.

He'd had enough. Whipping around with his gun, he yelled,

door to see what was happening. His eyes widened, and then he slammed it shut again.

"Stop this!" shouted Braun from the back of the plane, throwing his coat off and revealing his quills. He stomped up the aisle.

"Braun, no!" shouted Dr. Gray. "Kelly! Do your job!"

Frantic, Kelly stepped out of the aisle, camouflaged but unable to get to the pulsating level successfully. Braun lunged at Eduardo, knocking his gun loose and skittering under the seats, and leaving the lead officer crying out in pain, three quills stuck in his forearm. Braun kept going and Mega came behind him, roaring out.

A gun fired and hit the ceiling of the plane. Another bullet ricocheted and blew through a seat cushion. Kelly screamed and dropped to the floor. Still in camo mode, she changed to blend in with her new surroundings. Giving up on the hypnosis, she clicked on her platypus spikes and waited, hoping and praying to get out of there before she had to use them.

"Where'd the blond girl go?" cried one of the officers, arms outstretched, gun pointed. He swung the weapon wildly from side to side and started shooting over their heads.

Kelly screamed again, then slapped her hand over her mouth. She was a lot safer if they couldn't find her. She started sliding flat under the seat in front of her, trying to see a way to escape without getting stuck.

Dr. Gray's eyes went wild. Between fired shots, all his plans changed. "Get them, soldiers!" he ordered. "Knock them out. It's our only option!"

Braun slammed into another government officer in the aisle as Mega tried getting around him by jumping over the seats, swinging her big horned mug crazily to try to knock weapons loose and hoping to punch a few faces in the process.

Miko jumped on her plane seat and hopped back a few rows, opening the luggage bins as she went so she could swing on the shelves. She grabbed one, swung, and kicked forward, knocking a weapon from one officer's hand and slamming her feet into his face. Prowl caught the gun deftly, then pounced and sunk his claws into the officer, yanking him to the floor. "Kelly," Miko called out, "wherever you are, stay down!"

Kelly weaved slowly but stealthily under the seats, unnoticed, heading toward the exit at the front of the plane. Three officers were down and Mega piled them up in the aisle, unknowingly blocking Kelly's path. Eduardo, disarmed and with quills still stuck in him, was fistfighting Miko. One other officer remained upright, weapon in hand and shooting crazily. A stray bullet grazed Prowl's shoulder. He yelped in pain, then dived at the man. Miko swung from the overhead bins and punched her feet into Eduardo's stomach. He reeled backward and crashed into the seat where Kelly was hiding. He collapsed into her. Kelly felt a stabbing pain in her wrist, and somehow her bracelet became unlocked. The Mark Four slipped off and went bouncing into the aisle. Kelly's spikes disappeared and her camouflage ended abruptly.

"The blond girl!" Eduardo yelled, pointing. "Get her!"

CHAPTER 18

A Messy Getaway

Kelly scrambled into the aisle chasing after her device. Eduardo yelled out again, wedged awkwardly between rows. He struggled to get to his feet. Kelly grabbed the bracelet and tried to latch it around her wrist, but it wouldn't lock on. She held the device down on her wrist, connecting the band. With shaky fingers she reactivated the spikes.

Eduardo wriggled to his knees, then grabbed the armrest to pull himself up into the aisle. He reached for a loose gun. Kelly had no choice. Continuing to hold the device to her wrist, she swiveled and threw her leg into the air, slamming her platypus spike into Eduardo's stomach.

He let out a ghastly scream and dropped the gun. He turned to run, slipped, and fell backward, cracking his head hard on the armrest. Then he flopped to the floor, silent. Braun knocked out the last officer and stood there heaving.

Kelly gasped and stumbled toward the exit, putting her device in her pocket. Blind with tears, she dragged the other unconscious officers. Mega and Miko sprang to help her stack them in front of the cabin door to lock the pilot inside. Braun followed with the one he'd just taken down. Prowl tended to his wounded shoulder, then looked frantically around for their leader. "Victor?"

Dr. Gray opened the door of the lavatory and peeked out, unhurt but disheveled. "Is everybody okay?" His voice was shaking. He rushed forward and caught sight of Eduardo, who was lying still and silent now, bleeding profusely from his head and stomach. The man looked . . . dead. Dr. Gray turned away, shaken. "We need to move quickly. Gather your things. Walk off as if nothing happened and go straight to the limo—it's waiting for us a few hundred yards away."

"Let's hope the driver didn't hear the gunshots," muttered Prowl.

"Or the screams," said Miko.

The soldiers grabbed their luggage and disembarked the plane, walking in a line toward the awaiting vehicle. Dr. Gray swiftly gathered the strewn passports and his bag and brought up the rear.

On the tarmac, the doctor instructed the others to hold back a little. He jogged to the front of the line. When he reached the limo, he signaled to the chauffeur, who opened his door and hopped out of the driver's seat. The man wore earbuds and was talking on his cell phone. He rapidly hung up and pulled the earphones out. *"Lo siento,"* said the chauffeur, looking guilty for not having noticed the party approaching. "I'm sorry. Hello, are you Dr. Gray? How was your flight? Just set your bags by the trunk. I'll take it from there." He went over to Dr. Gray and they shook hands, the disheveled scientist turning so the driver wouldn't have a good look at the soldiers. He made small talk while the others skirted around them to drop their luggage and climb in the back section of the vehicle, hearts pounding.

Kelly got in. Miko spotted a control panel and found a button that raised the tinted glass, separating them from the front seat. Now they needed to move fast, because eventually somebody would discover that something bad had happened when the customs team didn't return. Kelly spied a box of tissues and handed it to Prowl—it wasn't much, but it might help stop him from bleeding all over. Prowl took it with a shaky hand and examined the wound. "It's not too bad," he muttered, and pressed a wad against it. Mega took some too and began wiping her suit clean.

The chauffeur loaded the bags in the trunk, suspecting nothing. Dr. Gray got in and closed the door. Everyone breathed a little easier, but knew they weren't out of trouble yet.

"How are we going to get out of this?" whispered Miko. She dropped her face into her hands.

"Shh," said Kelly. Now that the immediate danger was over, Kelly started shivering. She wanted answers too, but she knew better than to say anything. The driver got in the car and started it.

"Everyone stay quiet," whispered Dr. Gray under the roar of the engine. "Let me worry about the mess. Focus on the task we're here for. We have important work to do."

Kelly stared at him. They'd just gone through a traumatic fight with government officials of a foreign country. They'd just *assaulted* them. One of them could be *dead*. Was it Kelly's fault? Kelly's sight wavered, and she clutched the armrest. A wave of nausea went through her. They'd committed a terrible crime. And Dr. Gray was worried about his stupid DNA?

"This was a mistake," whispered Miko.

Prowl elbowed her. "Miko. Stop." He clipped his words, and his face was gray between the patches of fur.

Miko turned sharply toward him, face frightened. "How are we ever going to get back? They'll report us! And we're so easy to identify. We're freaks." She cringed and swallowed hard.

Dr. Gray shushed them again, so Kelly didn't answer. Not that she knew what to say. Were they stuck in Mexico forever? Would they wind up in jail or something? It made her stomach hurt.

"When we get to the zoo," muttered Dr. Gray to Kelly, "make the driver forget he drove us." He paused. "And don't screw it up this time."

Kelly flinched at the harsh words and resisted the urge to lash out. She'd been under so much pressure. Instead, she nodded numbly. She pulled the Mark Four from her pocket, studying it to see if she could fix it.

Miko noticed. After a moment she took the device and handed it to Prowl, who used a claw like a screwdriver. Soon the band was repaired and the device secure on Kelly's wrist, good as new.

"Thanks," Kelly said. She switched on her camo ability and faded into the seat. She wanted to have enough time to reach the hypnosis state this time. Miko threw her a sympathetic look before she disappeared.

After what seemed like an endless ride, the limo pulled into the Guadalajara Zoo and came to a stop at the drop-off curb. The chauffeur popped the trunk, but before he could get out and open the door, the soldiers were piling out of the passenger side and getting their luggage. They began walking swiftly away from the vehicle. Dr. Gray let camouflaged Kelly out the other side, then got out after her and they approached the driver. With his finger poking into her back, he averted his eyes and held out money for a tip. Kelly fidgeted and stepped forward, changing colors as she did so. She began pulsing, then approached the man, smiling disarmingly. He stared at her. "*¿Qué   ?*" he began.

"You're going to forget about us," said Kelly.

"I . . ."

"Forget all about us. Forget this ride. You never saw us. Got it?"

"Say *olvidar*," whispered Dr. Gray to Kelly.

"*Olvidar*," repeated Kelly, not breaking her gaze. "Okay?"

The chauffeur seemed taken aback, but he nodded. "*Está bien*," he whispered.

"Good. Now get back into the car." She flicked her finger impatiently at the limo door.

The man obeyed.

When Kelly was certain he would forget them, she turned to Dr. Gray. "All clear," she said, trying not to sound upset. "Let's get our bags and go."

CHAPTER 19

On the Run

After cleaning up and finding food, Kelly, Dr. Gray, and the soldiers regrouped under a tree on the outskirts of the Guadalajara Zoo. It was beastly hot, but the tree offered a small amount of relief from the sun.

"The way I see it," said Dr. Gray, "we have two choices. Speed up or slow down." Sweat beaded on the man's forehead.

"What do you mean?" asked Prowl, who looked a little more like his usual self now that his wound was bandaged properly. Miko had sewn up the tear in his suit, too.

"Either we go into the zoo now and get everything we need," said Dr. Gray, "or we go into hiding for a while. If we go after the DNA now we risk getting caught, but we can try to get out of Mexico tonight before the news breaks. If we slow down, we'll set up a new lab outside of the city, go into hiding, and hope there's no manhunt."

"The officers on the plane saw our faces," said Miko, distressed. "And they weren't hypnotized to forget. The pilot can identify us too. Sketches will be plastered all over TV."

"I'm sorry, guys," said Kelly, feeling miserable. She could

have prevented that if she'd only gone into camo mode earlier. But she'd had no idea they'd be in trouble—not until the officers were boarding. Why hadn't Dr. Gray told her ahead of time that this could be possible? He hadn't seemed to think anything could go wrong. She was furious at him for not preparing her better. And for being so selfish.

"It's done," said Braun gruffly. Sweat dripped off his porcupine quills. "No changing the past. I say we get in, do what we came here for, and get out as soon as possible. The longer we wait, the more recognizable we'll be."

The other soldiers seemed to agree, and looked to Dr. Gray for the verdict.

"All right," he said. "I'll go along with the consensus." He fished around in his bag for some papers and pulled one out: a color photo with a description on it. He handed it to Mega and Braun. "This is the species of jellyfish you're looking for. It's very small. Don't make a scene, all right?" He gave Prowl the side-eye. Prowl looked abashed and turned away like he was tired of being belittled.

Kelly didn't blame him. "Shouldn't we just try to get back to the United States right now?" she ventured. "Can't we get all these animals from there? I don't get why you put us through this . . . disaster. Can't your government people, like, help us out?"

Dr. Gray turned sharply, his face instantly red. "Obviously I made a mistake with our arrival. I didn't anticipate the difficulty at the airport. I—I'd checked into it. Thoroughly. Everything pointed to . . . to a perfect . . . outcome." His eyes narrowed and he slashed his hands through the air impatiently. "And I counted on you to do your job!"

"Wow," said Kelly. She took a step back at the injurious words.

"It wasn't her fault," Miko muttered. "You know it's hard for her to work in that kind of stress; it's overwhelming."

Prowl agreed. "You should have told us up front what the situation was so we could've been better prepared."

Dr. Gray softened and looked wearily at the soldiers. "You're right. But it doesn't matter now. We're stuck here for at least a few hours until I can find a way home. So you might as well do something while I solve our problem." He shook his head, looking old and disoriented, and Kelly wondered if the heat was getting to him. He began muttering. "With this new wrench in plans, I have to speed up our process. Finalize the perfect combination. I worry . . . the world's in danger. And if we don't succeed . . ." He got lost in the thought and didn't continue.

The soldiers looked uneasily at one another. The world? What was he talking about? Kelly frowned at the grass, tears pooling in her eyes. If they hadn't so stupidly left California, they wouldn't be in this kind of trouble right now. Was Dr. Gray starting to lose his mind? She wasn't sure she could trust his decisions after this mistake. And he could try to blame it on her all he wanted—she wasn't going to take responsibility for it. It was his fault, not hers.

Miko put a reassuring hand on the girl's shoulder, but the chimp woman's expression remained uneasy.

Suddenly Dr. Gray's troubled eyes cleared. "Kelly, you and Miko and Prowl can go after the Mexican wolf. If that goes quickly and without disruption, find the sharks and just get whatever one looks easiest. I'll stay here with the luggage, call Cyke to update him, and make arrangements for our transportation home."

CHAPTER 20

Close Calls

The zoo wasn't busy in the afternoon heat, and the animals were quiet. With the adrenaline of urgency fueling them, it didn't take long for Kelly, Miko, and Prowl to get to the wolves' habitat. They checked out the exterior of the vast enclosure, then went around to the deserted back part of it. Kelly spotted a young scrawny wolf below a rocky overhang, sheltered from the heat of the day.

"Is that it?" asked Kelly. "That scrawny thing?"

"It's probably just a young one," said Miko.

Prowl climbed the fence and made a hole in the netting. He dropped inside. Miko helped Kelly climb through, and Prowl broke her fall. The wolf stood up, alert. Kelly started pulsing. With Prowl by Kelly's side, ready to swoop in and protect her, Kelly carefully crept forward, hypnotizing the wolf. When it was complacent, she yanked out some of its fur.

Suddenly the wolf snapped out of its trance and charged at them, fangs glistening. Prowl pounced and held it down. Miko, hanging from the netting, grabbed Kelly by the hand and swung her up and out of there. She did the same for Prowl after he subdued the beast. The two climbed down the fence, while Miko unfurled her backpack and used her wings to help her descend. She was a bit unsteady, but made it to the ground successfully.

They moved swiftly out of the area and slipped back to the designated walking paths. Prowl helped Miko put the canvas cover over her wings again and showed her how to put it on by herself next time. Kelly removed a special bag from her waist pack and tucked the wolf fur inside, sealing it shut before putting it back.

"Whew," said Kelly. "Now let's go find a shark." She let out a shaky breath.

Miko glanced at Kelly. "You can do this," the woman said.

Kelly's face clouded. She tried not to let Dr. Gray's hateful words from earlier take up space in her brain or make her feel incapable, but the sting was still there. "I know." She pushed the insecurities away and glanced at the soldiers. "Thanks for sticking up for me earlier," she said, feeling awkward.

Prowl grunted. Miko nodded. "What happened on the plane wasn't your fault," she said.

"Dr. Gray . . . ," Prowl muttered, then shook his head angrily and didn't finish the thought. Kelly had never seen Prowl say a bad word about the scientist before, but he seemed like he wanted to now.

There was something else still clawing at Kelly's mind from the airport. She hadn't said anything before—it had almost felt like if she didn't say it, it couldn't be true. She closed her eyes. "Do you think that Eduardo guy is dead? Did I . . . do it?" She glanced at the soldiers, trying to read their faces.

"He turned and slipped and hit his head." Miko's expression was stern. "He's probably just unconscious."

"No one has ever died from a platypus sting," Prowl said, like he was reciting a fact that he'd recently looked up. Maybe because he had wondered the same thing.

Kelly swallowed hard. "Is that true?" she whispered.

Prowl nodded and Miko gripped Kelly's shoulder. "Today it is."

They continued in silence, taking long strides. Had the news surfaced yet? Had their descriptions been released? The three avoided crowds and focused on keeping Prowl's masked face and Miko's bulky backpack shielded so they wouldn't be recognized— especially now that they'd be wanted by police.

Kelly's stomach wouldn't stop hurting. What was this life? She could hardly believe that ripping fur from a wolf was only the second-most dangerous thing she'd done today so far. And the day wasn't over. Sometimes it seemed like she was in a giant theatrical production. She could use an intermission right about now.

Inside the humid aquarium attraction, visitors were sparse. Kelly and the soldiers could relax a little in the cover of darkness. Quickly they moved through the passageways, briefly looking at the smaller tanks of fish. They didn't see any jellyfish, though they knew Mega and Braun were taking care of that task. Probably not very well, thought Kelly, because the beefy duo weren't the brightest brutes in the group. But at least Kelly wasn't responsible for everything. She wrinkled up her nose at the briny smell.

They came to the large tank and scanned the placards to see what sort of sharks it held. "Shortfin mako," murmured Kelly, reading one of them. It was known as the fastest shark in the world. She frowned. "That seems like it might be too difficult to get."

"Here's another," said Miko. "Bull shark."

Kelly studied the description. "Osmoregulation," she said haltingly, sounding out the unfamiliar word. "It can live in salt water or freshwater."

"It's also one of the most likely to attack humans," Prowl read. "Right up Dr. Gray's alley."

"Yikes." Kelly looked at the picture, then peered through the glass to see if she could spot it. There were two that she could see. They were pretty big, but not enormous. "Bigger than Cyke," said Kelly, "but not too much." After all her practice with Miko, she thought she could handle that.

Miko touched Kelly's arm and pointed to an unmarked door in the shadows. "That's probably the access door."

Prowl nodded and protracted his claws. "I'll spring the lock. Miko and I will cover you so you can go to work." He hesitated, looking at Kelly, and said gruffly, "You know, sometimes I forget you're a kid. Are you sure you're ready for this?"

Kelly nodded and turned on her camouflage, ignoring the butterflies in her stomach. "I'm sure."

"If you get into trouble, escape at all costs. And use those platypus spikes on anything you need to. Got it?"

"Yeah. Thanks." Kelly appreciated Prowl's warmth, for it didn't come out often.

"Whenever you're ready." He stealthily moved over to the door and made himself small in the shadows, working the lock. Miko and Kelly moved that way too, distancing themselves from the other zoo visitors. No one paid attention to Miko, and no one could see Kelly.

A moment later Prowl had the door open and the three of them slipped inside. They went down a narrow hallway with the aquarium on one side and a cold cement wall on the other, looking for a way into the water. Soon they came to a larger open area with a built-in ladder. Near it was a closet with some buckets and towels and other supplies. The fish smell was even strong back here, and Kelly wished she didn't need to breathe at all.

"All clear," whispered Miko, looking around trying to address the invisible Kelly. "Where are you?"

"On the ladder." Kelly climbed to the top and opened the hatch to the aquarium. She took a scraping tool out of her pack, then clicked on her dolphin feature. "I'm going into hypnosis mode, so look away," she warned Prowl and Miko. "I want to try to do this without going into the water."

"Everything's quiet out here," said Prowl.

"Great." Kelly began focusing her concentration on

hypnotizing the sharks—and any other creature in the pool. Her heart thudded as she scanned the surface, looking for one of the bull sharks.

Pulsing now, Kelly prayed for a bull shark to swim close and become hypnotized, but the stubborn creatures swam right past and didn't notice her.

"Someone's coming!" hissed Prowl. "I'll take them out."

Kelly started sweating profusely. She had to do this. She didn't want to face an angered Dr. Gray and have to go through this all over again.

"Don't stress, Kelly!" whispered Miko.

That only made Kelly more anxious. "Come on, you stupid sharks," she muttered. But the creatures stayed far away from her.

Kelly and Miko heard a scuffle nearby. Then Prowl's voice in a raised pitch. Kelly lurched, trying to stay focused—she was so worried she'd lose her concentration again, like before at SeaWorld and on the plane. The scuffle grew louder.

Exasperated and out of time, Kelly glanced at Miko, who was dutifully staring at the floor, not looking at her. "I'm going in."

Miko nodded. "Spikes," she reminded the girl.

"Right." Kelly engaged her platypus spikes. Then, with only a slight hesitation, she dived into the water. She had to get this done.

Her dolphin swimming ability kicked in automatically to support her. With it she didn't feel the urge to breathe, so that calmed her down a little. Still pulsing, Kelly remembered what she'd practiced so many times in San Diego. She set off slowly toward the sharks, hiding behind rock formations and enormous, slimy vegetation. Her pulses were smooth and steady. She carried the sharp scraper in one outstretched hand and another plastic pouch in the other, ready to scrape off some of the shark's skin.

"Stay calm, stay calm," she told herself, like a mantra. She could see her mesmerizing lights reflected against the side of the tank, which gave her even more reassurance as she approached the area the sharks were in.

Suddenly one of them swooped around in a glorious arc, seemingly without effort, swimming close to the glass and past Kelly's shoulder. "Eek!" Kelly shouted in the water, and she nearly lost her concentration. But she clamped her mouth shut and kept moving forward. The other shark had begun swimming slowly, its creepy eyes on Kelly. Did she have it?

Oh my God, Kelly thought. She almost snorted down a gallon of water. Instead, she crept forward, staying in the bull shark's line of sight. It began to circle around her. Kelly changed course to swim alongside and in front of it so it wouldn't lose sight of her.

When she felt confident that the shark was fully hypnotized, Kelly slowed a little to let the toothy half of the creature move ahead. Then, cautiously, she reached out toward its tail. With shaking fingers, she scraped the shark's skin hard with the tool and slid the whole thing into the bag, sealing it immediately. The shark continued forward. Kelly turned sharply back toward the ladder, her heartbeat thudding in her ears. Risking a glance at the bag, she could see the slice of skin floating inside. Triumphant, but beginning to feel like she needed to breathe, she continued toward the edge of the tank. She didn't see the shortfin mako shark heading straight toward her at a ridiculous speed, jaws agape, until it was almost too late.

Kelly almost dropped the DNA sample. Instead, she looked around frantically and spotted the aquarium opening. Realizing her pulsating lights had faded, she glanced at herself to see if she was at least still camouflaged. She was, but that didn't seem to matter— the shark could sense her easily. She swam with a renewed burst of energy. The shark veered sharply to follow her.

Frantic and running out of breath, Kelly tapped her device, forgetting she'd already enabled her platypus spikes. If she could stay in front of the shark she had a better chance of hitting it with one of them and hopefully disabling it for long enough to allow her to escape. She swam as fast as she could toward the ladder.

The mako was faster. It bumped its nose against her toes. Kelly nearly screamed. She spun and yanked away, then tried to land a spiky kick and missed. Out of breath, she could feel her head growing hot, her blood pulsing. Demanding oxygen. Finally the ladder loomed. She reached out for it as the shark bumped her leg, harder this time. It opened its mouth around it.

Kelly screamed and swallowed water. She began to choke. She kicked out with both feet wildly, blindly, trying to connect

with the beast without getting her leg chomped off. Flailing with her free hand, she tried to reach the ladder without dropping the all-important DNA sample. Her vision dimmed. She needed air. Her limbs were weakening, giving out. Just before the world went completely black, two hands grabbed her by the wrists and yanked her up and out of the water. The shark's jaws snapped the air.

CHAPTER 21

Cause for Alarm

Prowl and Miko hauled Kelly's sodden, dripping body over the lip of the aquarium. Miko grabbed her around the waist and dragged her down to the floor while Prowl scrambled down after them. Kelly sucked in air, coughed violently, and breathed again.

Eventually the world grew brighter. For a moment Kelly panicked. Then she looked at her hand, still clutching the bag. "I got it," she gasped, holding it out.

Prowl took the bag. "That was impressive," he said with respect. "Let's get out of here. The workers I fought will be waking up any second. Can you walk?" He examined her leg where the shark had left its mark.

"I think so," said Kelly, though she had no idea if she could. She pushed herself to a sitting position. "Did anybody see me in there?"

"Nobody who matters," said Miko, helping Kelly to her feet. She grabbed a towel from the supply closet and quickly dried off the girl the best she could. "Prowl found a different way out of here. Let's go."

The three escaped and moved quickly through the back area

of the zoo. Prowl's sharp eyes kept a lookout for more workers. As Kelly clicked off her animal abilities, he guided the other two away from the more populated areas. After a quarter of an hour they were back to the tree, under which Dr. Gray sat, talking on the phone to someone. Braun and Mega were there too.

Kelly, occasionally coughing up some water and looking bedraggled, limped over to the group.

"Are you okay?" asked Braun.

"Did you get the DNA?" asked Dr. Gray.

Prowl looked at the man with disdain. He took the shark sample out of his pocket, and grabbed the wolf one from Kelly, then handed them both to Dr. Gray, who took them greedily. "Good, good," he murmured. "Now we're onto something. Too bad these two bozos bungled the jellyfish."

"We caught one," said Braun. "A really small one, like you said."

"It's not the right kind," said Dr. Gray impatiently.

"They all look alike," muttered Mega.

Kelly and Miko exchanged an uneasy glance. It was clear that Dr. Gray didn't care about whether Kelly was okay or not.

"Kelly's a champ," Miko said. "She's fine now," she added to Braun, answering his question from earlier. "She got a good chunk from that shark."

"What kind of shark?" asked Mega. "Great white?" She tried

and failed to look nonchalant.

"Uh, *no*," said Kelly. "A great white? Are you kidding me? I got you a bull shark."

"What?" said Mega. "What's that? I've never heard of it."

"It can survive in fresh- or salt water," growled Prowl menacingly. "And it's got lots of sharp teeth." He pointed to the blood trickling down Kelly's ankle. "Good enough?"

Mega snorted, her rhino nostrils flaring visibly through her tight face mask. "You don't scare me," she warned.

"Soldiers, that's enough," said Dr. Gray, packing the DNA lovingly into his suitcase. "We need to hurry. We have a bus to catch."

Everyone turned in surprise to look at him. "A bus?" said Miko. "What are you talking about?"

"You mean a bus back to the US?" asked Kelly. "Isn't that really far from here?"

Dr. Gray pressed his lips together. "Not exactly," he said, picking up his luggage and gesturing for the others to do the same. "We've . . . had a change of plans. We're staying in Mexico. For the foreseeable future. We'll just have to save the world from here." He paused, then added, "That's the great thing about the world, though. You can save it from anywhere."

The scientist began marching through the grass to the parking lot while the others stared at the back of him. Save the world? He was definitely off his rocker.

"What happened?" said Prowl, catching up to him. "Why do we have to stay?"

Kelly stared, her stomach churning. *We have to stay here.* The others followed Dr. Gray at a brisk pace, heading toward some unknown bus stop. Kelly stumbled after them.

Dr. Gray cleared his throat. "My, *erm*, my contacts in Guadalajara were, unfortunately, arrested this morning for, *erm*, committing some crimes. Which is why we had that little mix-up at the airport."

"Mix-up!" cried Miko, but Prowl elbowed her into silence.

Dr. Gray went on as if he hadn't heard her. "And now according to breaking news reports, we're highly, ah, *wanted*. Airport security, local police, and border patrol is on the lookout for us. So . . . we're not going home. We're staying here."

"Is—is that guy going to be okay?" Kelly asked, feeling nauseous.

Dr. Gray didn't look at her. "He is in a coma," he said quietly.

There was a moment of stunned silence. Kelly's face turned gray.

"It can't possibly be safe to stay here," said Prowl. "Soon there will be pictures—they know our names from the passports!"

"Well, we won't stay *here* here. We're going into hiding. Outside of Guadalajara. Before word spreads about us."

Despite her weakness, Kelly grew alarmed. "So now we're

fugitives?" She whispered the last word, as if saying it aloud would cause the police to swoop in and arrest them right there.

"I wouldn't say that," said Dr. Gray mildly, a strange look in his eyes. "They might not realize it yet, but we're actually gracing Mexico with our presence and giving them a huge gift. They'll be the first people we save with our scientific breakthrough."

"Dr. Gray," said Miko, "you keep saying things like that. What are you talking about? Since the beginning, you've told us that this was a secret government program. That they wanted to see if they could enhance human soldiers with animal abilities and features—see if it made us stronger than regular humans. You said that maybe someday we could return to the armed forces. But that's . . . that's not what this sounds like anymore."

"Yeah," said Braun. "You're making it seem like you have something different in mind."

"Victor," said Prowl, eyes narrowed, "what's going on?"

Kelly clutched her stomach. Maybe it felt queasy from the water she'd swallowed, but more likely from this conversation. They were stuck here, unable to go back home. They'd hurt innocent people. And Dr. Gray was acting strange. All the soldiers seemed to think so—not just Kelly. It made her want to call it quits on this whole thing—go back to her parents and try to un-hypnotize them, and return to school and be normal again. Who cared about fame now, when everything had been turned upside down? Kelly would gladly give the stupid bracelet back if she had to. If it meant she could get out of this nightmare.

Dr. Gray gazed thoughtfully at his soldiers and Kelly. "That was the plan at first, Miko. But I've changed my mind. The government . . . well, it gave up on us," he admitted. "A while ago. But it was clear to me that this experiment was invaluable, so I kept going. And just look at you all! You're superhuman!"

The soldiers stared.

Dr. Gray continued walking. "It's wrong to keep these amazing developments to ourselves. Mankind is hurtling toward extinction with pollution, climate change, and natural disasters. This is a way to save all of humanity by granting this amazing gift to all people. Don't you see? Once I've finished my formula, we're going to change everyone in the world into chimeras. And you are all a part of it."

"What the—?" sputtered Prowl. "What are you talking about?" Miko echoed him. Mega looked confusedly at Braun, and Kelly felt her stomach roiling again. As she stumbled along, half listening, half trying not to vomit, she could hardly believe what Dr. Gray was saying. It was like she was in a bad dream and she couldn't wake up.

A moment later, when they reached the bus stop, Kelly grabbed the corner of a bench. She bent over and threw up all over the grass. Before she could spit out the last of the bile, a bus pulled up to the stop. Miko, still stunned, managed to come to Kelly's aid and helped her onto the vehicle. Soon the team was on their way to some remote location that nobody knew anything about, with a scientist who had certainly gone mad.

Wanted as criminals, they couldn't do anything to stop it.

CHAPTER 22

Inching Closer

Now that all three of the new animals had been decided by Charlie and her friends, the scientists had their work cut out for them. Her dad was already finishing up the high-tech graphics in the Mark Six while he waited for Ms. Sabbith to return from Chicago. She'd be bringing the viper DNA so he could add the heat sensor ability to it, and alligator DNA for Maria's device. Dr. Goldstein, who used technology rather than biology to replicate animal features in the Mark Two, was already hard at work designing Mac's basilisk lizard feature. Which was a good thing, because his would probably take the longest to complete.

Dr. Sharma, who'd been working on the Mark Five, wasn't having quite as much luck. While she'd managed to smooth out the glitches that had plagued Charlie in the past, she wasn't able to add an additional ability to that device without destabilizing the other features. It would have to be sufficient as it was.

"That's not a problem," Dr. Wilde told Dr. Sharma before the scientists left for the day. Charlie hung out in the lab helping to tidy up. "Those five abilities are already incredible enough, as we've seen. And the last thing we want to do is overwhelm the person wearing it—the technology is ten years old, after all. And I don't think we have time to start from scratch."

"Agreed," said Dr. Sharma. "Besides, I have other things I'd like to fix in that device. And, of course, this frees up some of my time to work with Jack and Nubia on the Mark Two and Three, if they need help."

"Hey, why not build a device with, like, twenty abilities?" asked Charlie. "If you had the time, would you do it?"

Mr. Wilde pursed his lips. "I don't know. You'd have all those different kinds of DNA coursing through your body. It would be tricky to find the right balance and if too many activated at once."

"Yeah, it'd probably also get confusing," said Charlie. "It would be hard to remember what all the options are. Spend an extra half second deciding which one to activate and you could be a goner."

"Wise words," said Dr. Sharma with a laugh.

Andy was back home again, and the four Wildes were all together for dinner with no guests for once. It seemed so quiet. The kids filled in their mom on what she had missed that day.

"Ms. Sabbith flies in tomorrow with our DNA," Charlie told her. "She's got the goods—a viper for me and an American alligator for Maria."

"Dr. Goldstein doesn't need any actual DNA," Andy added.

"He told me all about it. He uses a metallic alloy to replicate the basilisk abilities."

"Impressive," Mrs. Wilde said. "That's a mouthful."

"That's right," said Mr. Wilde. "Jack has a head start but Nubia and I will be working on our formulas as soon as Erica gets here. With any luck," he said, glancing at Charlie, "we'll have them all ready before you kids go to Puerto Rico. If not, then soon after," he promised.

"Really?" said Charlie. "Sweet!" She could always take the Mark Five instead if she had to. But it would be great to have the new device to train with while they were gone.

"And then you'll make a device for me?" asked Andy with a hopeful grin.

"No way," said Mrs. Wilde. "Not a chance. You're sitting this one out."

"Rats," said Andy. But he wasn't too disappointed. After his run-in with the platypus spikes, Andy wasn't interested in being involved with that sort of fighting again.

Charlie, Mac, and Maria spent the remaining days before their trip trying to help the scientists as much as possible. The doctors also invited them to hang out in the lab and watch what they were doing. They gave them various science lessons as they worked, and let them do some of the more basic measuring and mixing techniques and applications. Dr. Goldstein let Mac work with tiny tools right inside of the device. He helped reprogram the existing code and moved gauges and electronics into place using mechanical instruments and a microscope to help him see everything better.

"This is way better than the insect cameras," Mac said.

"Hey, now," warned Ms. Sabbith with a sly smile. "Just remember who was the first to let you handle the goods." She unpacked a box and shook it, then set it mysteriously on the table.

"Oh, I couldn't forget that." Mac looked over at what she was doing. "So, uh, what do you have there?" he asked, turning away from his device.

Dr. Goldstein harrumphed, and Mac quickly refocused on his job. "Scientists mustn't get distracted," the man said gruffly.

"Sorry," said Mac, but he glanced once more at Ms. Sabbith, clearly torn.

Charlie and Maria grinned at each other. Dr. Goldstein often teased the kids now that they all had gotten to know one another better. He was like a grandpa with his goofy jokes. And the kids could tell he and Ms. Sabbith were pretending to compete for Mac's attention.

"Hey," said Maria. "What are we? Chopped liver?"

Charlie stared at her. "Chopped liver? What?"

Maria rolled her eyes. "It's a saying."

Charlie shrugged. "Anyway, let's go see what Ms. Sabbith is doing."

"Yes," said Ms. Sabbith. Come on over, you two. I've got some fun new technology to show you."

The girls gathered around Ms. Sabbith as she unpacked, explaining things as she took them out of their protective wrappings. "You know we've installed a communication system into your devices. Well, this is the control panel." She took out a piece of equipment around the size of a large computer keyboard, with buttons and toggles and lights on it. "Once I tie your devices to this, the system will be kind of like what Dr. Gray's soldiers use— you know how they press a button in their suits to talk to home base? Well, now you kids can do that too, only the button will be on your devices. And you'll be able to hear me through the earpieces that go with it."

"That's way better than using cell phones," said Charlie. "We all remember how well that worked out." She recalled with chagrin the moment Dr. Gray had captured them outside the vault because he'd taken over her mother's phone and texted her.

"Definitely more efficient," agreed Ms. Sabbith, "especially if your phone is stuck inside your suit. Ahem." She glanced sidelong at Mac.

Mac tittered from his lab table. He often had things stuck in his pockets that he couldn't access when his pangolin suit was activated. Like his inhaler, for one.

"What else do you have?" asked Charlie.

"All of our old drone friends," she said, holding up the ladybug.

"Except for the one Prowl ate," Mac called out.

Dr. Goldstein rapped on the table in front of Mac to get his attention. "I can send you over there if that's what you really want, but then you must never come back," he said in a mysterious voice.

"What?" said Mac, staring at him. "Why not?"

Dr. Goldstein shrugged. "Scientists are sensitive beings," he said. "Our feelings get hurt."

"Whatever," said Mac, laughing. "Okay, I'm staying with you. Happy now?"

Dr. Goldstein nodded, a small smile on his lips. "That's better. I demand loyalty."

"You sound like Dr. Gray!" said Maria over her shoulder.

"Oy," said Dr. Goldstein. "That's terrible. I take it back. Go wherever you want."

While Mac and Dr. Goldstein bantered, Ms. Sabbith pointed to a digital map on the control panel. "This is the GPS system so I'll always know where you are," she said. "You'll show up as dots."

"How will you know which one of us is which?"

"You'll be color-coded," said the woman. Then she pointed out a red alarm light on the board. "This will light up if you use the new emergency button on your devices. If I don't have my earpiece in for some reason, I'll be alerted that you need help." She glanced at the girls. "And if I do have my earpiece in, the emergency whistle is annoyingly, piercingly loud. So only use it if you really need it."

Charlie and Maria exchanged a mischievous glance. "What happens if we press the button by accident?" asked Maria.

"Then . . . I'll punish you by forcing you to work with Dr. Goldstein," said Ms. Sabbith with a grin.

CHAPTER 23

Loud and Clear

The scientists worked long into the evening leading up to the kids' trip. Finished packing, Charlie stayed up with them, worrying over their lab stations but doing her best to stay out of the way. They were trying to finish the bracelets—at least to the point where the kids could practice a little with the new abilities during their week away.

Dr. Jakande looked harried. "I'm determined to finish this."

"It would be ideal if the kids could give them a bit of a workout," said Dr. Wilde. "But don't stress it, Nubia. They don't have to be perfect yet." He peered into a microscope and adjusted something. "They'll figure out if there are any glitches and let us know what improvements are needed. Plus, that would give them time to get used to the updated graphics. That way we don't lose this week of training."

Ms. Sabbith's voice crackled through an earpiece on the lab table. Dr. Goldstein quickly placed the unit in his ear and spoke into Mac's Mark Two. "Come again? I read you." He was quiet for a few seconds. Then he smiled and looked up at the others. "It's working. At least on this unit. She tried the others already—you didn't hear anything? Quinn? Nubia?"

"Nothing," said Dr. Sharma. Dr. Jakande shook her head and didn't look up.

"Nope," said Dr. Wilde. "Charlie, put the Mark Six earpiece in and let me know if you hear Ms. Sabbith."

Charlie obeyed. "Nothing happening," she said. "Where is she, anyway?"

"Back in Chicago," said Dr. Goldstein.

Charlie's eyes widened. "I figured she was just in the living room or something."

A few minutes later, Jack pointed to his earpiece and paused in his work to listen.

Charlie watched his expression change. Finally he said into the device, "That's promising. Keep us posted."

Dr. Jakande looked up. "What's promising?"

"Sabbith is hot on the trail of our old government contact. Remember Captain Zimmerman? Erica thinks she's got a hot lead. She might be heading to Washington if she can get a meeting with her."

Dr. Jakande nodded. "I remember her," she said. "That was such a long time ago." She paused in her work to wipe her tired eyes, then put her safety glasses on and turned back to it.

Charlie narrowed her eyes. The panther woman wasn't acting like herself. She seemed stressed out trying to finish Maria's bracelet. It almost sounded like she didn't think she'd get done. Maria hadn't had her Mark Four in weeks. How were they supposed to train if they never had the devices? Or . . . was that part of Dr. Jakande's plan? Maybe she didn't want Maria to train because she wanted Dr. Gray to beat them.

Charlie frowned at herself. Now the stress was getting to *her*. She was being ridiculous.

The night wore on. Charlie rested her head on the lab table for what felt like a minute and woke an hour later to her father nudging her awake. "Did you finish?" Charlie asked sleepily.

"Not quite. I'm going to keep working. But you should go to bed. You've got a long flight ahead."

Charlie reluctantly agreed. She said good night to the scientists and slid off her chair.

As she headed for the door, Dr. Jakande's communication device crackled. Everyone turned.

"Is it Ms. Sabbith?" asked Charlie. "Did you get Maria's device to work?"

Nubia shook her head and pointed to her suit collar. "It's my built-in," she said grimly. "I thought I was done hearing from Miko. Let's listen."

Charlie's eyes widened. A familiar voice came through.

"Zed," Miko said in a harsh whisper. "I don't know if you're there, but if you are . . . well . . . something really bad happened.

187

Maybe you've heard by now. Oh—!" There was a sudden loud crackle and a voice in the background. Then silence.

"That was Kelly!" said Charlie. "Did she just shut Miko down?"

Dr. Jakande looked fearfully at the others. "Should I try to respond?"

Dr. Wilde looked at Dr. Sharma and Dr. Goldstein. Slowly Quinn shook her head. "We can't risk it—not if Kelly's there with her. She might tell Dr. Gray that Miko's trying to contact you, and we don't know what he could do to her. Besides, we don't want to give them any idea that we're the slightest bit interested in what they're doing." She paused, thinking. "We need to stay consistent and ignore."

Charlie watched Dr. Jakande carefully. Did the woman look the slightest bit guilty? Had she been telling the truth about not being in contact with Miko? Or . . . maybe that was worry on her face. It was sometimes hard to tell with the fur and whiskers.

The scientists debated a little more, but ultimately stuck with the decision. When nothing more happened, Charlie dragged her body to bed, wondering what the bad thing was that had happened.

By morning, all questions about Dr. Jakande and Miko were forgotten, for on the kitchen table by the cereal boxes lay three bracelets, a sealed envelope, and a note.

Devices are ready for action! Communication feature not working quite yet—will fix that and any other glitches when you return. Enjoy your trip.

Love, Dad

P.S. There's money in the envelope in case you need anything. If you have any left over, maybe you can do good with it. I know you'll think of something.

CHAPTER 24

Doing Good in the Neighborhood

Maria, Mac, and Charlie got off the plane in San Juan and saw Maria's *abuela* Yolanda waiting for them. She greeted them with warm hugs, then showed them the way to the car.

The long drive to her house was a big eye-opener. Near the ocean, sailboats were capsized on land and beaches washed away. Inland, buildings were toppled onto cars. Roofs blown off. Debris was everywhere, piled along the road, waiting for someone to haul it away.

"Puerto Rico will never be the same," Yolanda told them. As they finally neared her house, she pointed out a small grocery store that stood open and appeared to have had little damage. But next to it a row of houses had been flattened, as if a bulldozer had plowed them over.

Yolanda slowed the car in front of a narrow side road that led steeply uphill. "Look up there," she said. The street was covered in debris—large trees, overturned cars. Pieces of roofs and entire walls. The area around it was razed. "Nobody can get through."

"Does anyone live up there?" asked Maria.

"Lots of people," said Yolanda. "They're stranded on the other side of this mess until the machines can get here to dig them out. We don't know if they are okay or not."

The kids stared at the destruction. It was worse than they'd seen on TV. Way worse.

Yolanda continued with the sobering tour. "There are a lot of places that we can't get to. Streets unpassable. Businesses, houses . . . all of it is gone." She seemed like she was about to cry, and Charlie didn't blame her. This was Yolanda's island. Her home. And it was destroyed.

Maria reached for her grandmother's hand. "I'm glad you're okay, Abu."

The next day, Maria, Charlie, and Mac met the neighbors and together, with Yolanda, worked harder than they'd ever worked before in their lives. They cleared branches and pieces of wood and siding from houses that had been destroyed. They helped move a big fence out of the road. They ran down to the little grocery store to buy goods for an elderly man whose car had been destroyed.

They were constantly working alongside other people in the community, so it was hard to find opportunities to use their devices without being noticed, though occasionally Charlie's strength automatically kicked in when she was helping to lift something heavy.

That night after dinner, once Abu Yolanda had nodded off to sleep in her chair, the three looked at one another. They weren't done yet.

"Let's go to that one road," said Maria, rummaging in the garage for a battery-powered floodlight.

"The one with all the overturned cars," said Mac, knowing exactly which one she meant.

"Where the people are stranded on the other side," said Charlie. "If we can clear that road, maybe we can use our extra trip money to buy food and bring it up there."

"But can we at least try out our new devices first? They might be able to help us," asked Mac.

"Of course," said Charlie.

The three set off through the dark using their phone flashlights. Some temporary street lighting had been set up in spots, but not nearly enough.

They'd had time on the plane to check out their updated devices and scroll through the new designs. Mac had even tried out his basilisk suit in the airplane lavatory, but there was a line behind him so he hadn't had time to admire it for long. Besides, the tail had almost flopped right into the toilet, so the situation wasn't ideal. Still, he'd tried to get Maria to test her werealligator in there too, but she didn't dare after what had happened last time. If there were any sort of glitches it would be hard to explain that to a flight attendant.

The impassable road was deserted. When they neared the worst of the destruction, they stopped and set their phones down, facing them so they could see one another. Maria clicked on the floodlight and stood in its glow.

"I'm going to test the howler monkey mode first," said Maria. "Just to make sure that still works like it did before. I'm a little nervous to try the alligator." She tapped her bracelet and slipped into monkey mode. It worked as before. Then she smoothly went back to normal at the touch of a button. Returning to a howler, she retested what would happen if she took the bracelet off, and immediately turned back to her human self. "That all seems to be working great," she said. "One of you go next while I work up the guts to try my new animal."

Charlie's Mark Six had all five of her same abilities plus the new viper vision. The device's screen was larger and the interface was updated, so she got familiar with that before she poised her finger over the new viper heat-vision ability. "Okay," she said. "Here goes."

She clicked on the snake and waited, looking around. Mac and Maria took on a red tinge. "I see some red where your bodies are. So, I guess that means it works."

"What about out there?" said Mac, pointing to the piles of debris. "I'll bet you can see all sorts of animals. And people, too, obviously. You'll be able to tell if anybody's coming while we're working."

"That's cool," said Charlie. She turned and looked where Mac was pointing. After a minute, she noticed a few small red blobs moving around. "There! Oh my goodness! I see something!"

"What is it?" asked Mac.

"I think . . . it's rats! Or really big mice." She stared in horror. "I kind of don't want to see them, but now I can't look away."

"Gross," said Maria.

"Hey, as long as they're not bugs, I'm good," said Mac.

Charlie messed around a bit more with her device.

Mac was itching to move on. "Are you ready to see my basilisk lizard suit?"

"Yes," said Charlie, turning back to the others.

"Sure," said Maria. "I'll go after you."

First Mac double-checked his silvery pangolin suit to make sure nothing got screwed up in the process of adding the new ability. Everything checked out. Then he clicked on his new basilisk lizard ability. Instantly his silvery suit thinned considerably and clung to his body. It took on a greenish metallic tinge and the spikes melted into a smooth, streamlined skin. A long thin tail shot out from the back. The part covering his feet grew larger and cupped, and several metallic toes took shape and spread out.

"Wow, it's beautiful," said Maria.

"Thanks," Mac said, looking at himself all over. "I feel a lot lighter in this than with the pangolin suit. But these feet . . . seem . . . weird."

"Try running," Maria suggested.

"Maybe I'd better start with walking." Mac took a few steps, trying to figure out how to negotiate his new body dimensions. He took a few more. Then he stopped and hopped lightly over a tree branch. "I can definitely move better," he said.

"You've lost your clunk," noted Maria.

Mac hopped around a few more times. "I've never been a very good runner," he said apologetically, "so don't be disappointed if I don't go as fast or as smoothly as you expect."

Charlie smiled. "Don't worry. Go ahead. Give it a try."

Mac took a breath and let it out. "I forgot. My inhaler's in my pocket," he said, looking sheepish. While Charlie and Maria waited patiently, Mac powered down the suit, used his inhaler, took a few slow breaths, and then clicked on the basilisk lizard. This time green liquid poured from his device and formed the suit. His feet grew cupped and wide as before.

"Okay, cool." Mac took a few steps, then started jogging.

"You can do this," Maria encouraged. "Don't worry about it. It's the pangolin suit that's slow—not you, Mac."

Mac shrugged, knowing that was only partly true. He jogged across the dirt, getting used to his new strange feet and the stream-lined effect of the suit. He felt almost buoyant.

He looked that way, too.

"Go faster, Mac!" Charlie called out. "You're doing great."

Mac sped up. Surprisingly, he found his legs were incredibly strong—they weren't getting tired like they always used to when he tried to keep up with Charlie and Maria. He went faster, feeling like he was stepping on springs.

"That's it," Charlie encouraged. "You're moving really fast!"

"I am?" Mac shouted back as he turned to circle around.

"You're cruising," said Maria. Instinctively she clicked into monkey mode and ran for the trees so she could move along with Mac and encourage him. "Is your breathing okay?"

"This is hardly winding me at all," said Mac. "It's just so . . . easy! I've never . . . been able . . . to run like this before."

Charlie grinned. Whether he'd meant to or not, Dr. Goldstein had given Mac something that nobody had realized Mac wanted. He'd always lagged behind the girls when they ran, and he didn't have their soccer-playing stamina. He had to be careful because of his asthma. But the girls hardly ever thought about it. They never realized Mac might feel like he was missing out because of it. He'd never said so. But now he was moving like a track star.

Maria swung on the tree branches just behind Mac as he came back to where Charlie stood. Normal Mac would have stopped and probably collapsed, but lizard Mac didn't even slow down. He flew past Charlie and started up the road, hopping over debris, picking things up and chucking them along the side of the road.

Charlie knew this was important. They'd had to wait for Mac in the past, and that could put them all at risk. Now he could keep up a better than normal pace. If only they could find some water nearby to see how his ability worked. There were some flooded ditches and big puddles around that might do. But that might be dangerous if Mac fell in. Yolanda had warned them that the standing water left over from the hurricane could be filled with bad bacteria or have sharp objects hidden under the surface, so they should stay away from it.

The girls stayed within their lighted area. Charlie clicked on her elephant strength mode and began picking up large tree branches while they waited for Mac to come back. He was breathing harder now, for sure, but wasn't nearly as winded as he would have been. His grin was wide when he switched back to normal. "This," he said, wheezing a little, "is awesome."

"We'll have to find some clean water for you to try to run on," said Charlie.

"I could try Yolanda's bathtub," said Mac with a laugh.

"There's always the beach, though I'm not sure what's left of it," said Maria. "We'll have to see how much work we get done here first."

The other two agreed that the work was more important, at least for now. Then Mac and Charlie turned to Maria, who was still in monkey mode.

"Well?" said Charlie. "Are you ready to become an alligator? Maybe once you're strong you can help me roll some of these cars over."

CHAPTER 25

Like Old Times

Maria, still in monkey mode, gave Charlie a nervous look. "I'm scared."

"Still?" said Charlie. "I don't get it. You're not going to get stuck as an alligator. That part got fixed, right?"

"I know," said Maria. She sighed. "It's not that."

"Then what is it?" asked Mac.

"I guess I'm scared of the ferocious part," she said. "I mean, what if I start attacking people like Kelly did with Andy?"

"Oh, Maria," Charlie said, "you'll still be the same on the inside. Just like you are as a howler monkey. The animal doesn't change who you are. It just gives you abilities."

"Kelly made her own choices," Mac said. "The platypus spikes didn't make her hurt innocent people. She decided to use them, knowing exactly what they would do."

"Trust yourself," said Charlie. "We trust you."

"I know," said Maria. "Thanks for the reminder, though. I do trust myself." She pressed her lips together, then nodded confidently. She examined her device, took a breath, and clicked the alligator mode. She cringed and waited.

A split second later, Maria's body morphed wildly. "Whoa!" she cried.

Charlie and Mac jumped back and shone their flashlights on her. Maria flopped onto the ground, her arms and legs growing short and squat and her torso extending crazily. Her face flattened and her mouth protruded, her teeth grew more plentiful and bigger and sharper, her forehead sank and her eyeballs bulged. When she stopped moving, Charlie gasped. "Are you okay?"

"I'm fine, I think. Just . . . wow. I think we've got our first glitch."

Then Mac got closer to her and started laughing.

"Dios mío," Maria muttered, trying to look at herself. "Why are you laughing, Mac?"

"You're still covered in monkey fur, Maria," said Charlie, trying not to laugh like Mac was doing. "And you still . . . well . . ."

"You still have a monkey tail right above your alligator tail!" exclaimed Mac. "Oh wow. This is amazing." He started cough-laughing and held his stomach.

Maria curved her alligator shaped body sideways so she could see herself, and her bulging eyes widened even more in horror. "I look ridiculous! And I'm so . . . so . . ."

"So alligatory?" said Charlie.

"Yes! This . . . this isn't going to work."

"Can you go back to monkey mode?" asked Mac, who had stopped laughing by then.

"Yeah," said Charlie. "Try that. I'll bet you have both animal features because you went from weremonkey mode to werealligator mode. Click out of both and start from your normal human self. Can you even reach your device?"

"Ay caramba." Maria was still trying to see her full self and looking worried. "Sooo much alligator." She moved one clawed front foot to the other, where the device was tightly wrapped around her . . . well, her wrist-like area. She tipped her head sideways and peered at it with one bulgy eyeball, then tapped her claw on the device a couple times. Soon the alligator features disappeared and she morphed back into a more normal size. Then she turned off the monkey.

"Well," she said, happy to be on two human feet again, "that was quite an adventure." She looked at herself all over, checking for tails and fur and claws, and determined she was completely human again. "At least I can turn them off."

Charlie was relieved that Maria was handling the issues so well. "And like you said, it's a glitch. A pretty big one, but this is just a trial run. A chance to figure out the problems. I'm sure Dr. Jakande can fix all of this."

"Yeah," said Maria, "I know. I'm not worried this time."

"Now try the alligator directly," suggested Mac.

Maria took a deep breath and steeled herself for the strange morphing once again. She clicked the alligator, and this time, along with taking on a mostly reptilian shape, she showed no signs of being a monkey.

"That was it," said Mac. "Charlie, you were right. Hopefully that part won't be too hard to fix either. Do you want to try moving around?"

"Um . . . sure." Maria worked on walking first. It was harder than she expected with four limbs on the ground. Soon she got the hang of moving her right front with her back left, but she didn't like being so close to the ground. It seemed too difficult. She pushed herself up to try to stand on her back legs, then tried walking upright like a human. She staggered on her short limbs, trying to balance the weight of her long torso using her tail to lean back on. "I'm gonna need to look a lot less like an alligator," she said. "It's too hard to move normally and how am I going to be able to help fight the soldiers? I want my regular arms and legs back, at least."

"For sure," said Charlie. "And maybe not quite such a big alligator head and face?"

Maria put her head down and felt her cheeks. "It's so . . . warty."

"Well," said Mac, as if to remind her that she chose it, "it *is* an alligator."

"I know, I know. It's just so . . . dramatically different. I expected I'd be able to stay upright with maybe a tail, claws, and some teeth. Not this."

"Well, Dr. Jakande can take a look at that when we get back.

For now, let's see what you can do in this mode," said Charlie, anxious to keep working on their plan to clear the roadway. She walked over to a car that was blocking the street. Its windows and tires were blown out and the interior was destroyed by the elements. She caught sight of the rats again and hastily clicked off her viper ability—better to forget they were there. Then, putting all her strength into it, she picked up one side of the car and rolled it. And rolled it. And rolled it.

Maria joined her in alligator mode for one last heave onto the side of the road. Mac, wearing his pangolin suit, used his claws to break a huge tree trunk into more manageable pieces.

They worked until they were exhausted, but it hardly looked like they'd done anything—that's how bad it was. But they were determined to do everything they could to open up that road so that the people living up in the mountains could get through once more.

"This kind of feels like how things were when we first discovered Charlie had abilities," said Maria, wiping the sweat off her warty alligator brow. "Like when she saved those people from the burning house."

Mac smiled, remembering. "That was really cool," he said. "And this is even better."

"Like old times," said Charlie. "Helping people in the neighborhood. It's so much more fun than having to fight bad guys."

CHAPTER 26

A Change of Plans

By the end of the second night, Maria, Mac, and Charlie had cleared enough to be noticed by people driving by. It put them in a tough spot, because during the third day while they cleaned up Yolanda's neighborhood, people were talking about it. They speculated about why there were no big machines sitting there to haul off the stuff, and wondered if it was the work of someone other than the government contractors who were in various other parts of the island. The kids weren't quite sure what to do when people talked about checking things out at night.

"Charlie can see them coming, at least," Mac muttered to the girls.

"Maybe we should try to start from the top end of the road instead," said Maria. "And work our way down, saving the stuff nearest the intersection for our last night so we don't get caught in the act."

"Easy for a monkey and a gecko to climb over all the stuff," said Mac. He paused, thinking. "I wonder if my basilisk lizard might be useful for that too."

"With feet like that, how can you go wrong?" said Charlie.

"I think we should try it. We don't want to be discovered because then we can't work."

As it turned out, things took a turn for the worse in an unexpected way. That night they headed out to clear more stuff away. They climbed over fallen trees, cars, and debris, only to discover a big open area up ahead. At first, they were glad to see it—less wreckage to clean up. But when they moved closer and shined their lights on it, they realized it wasn't just an open space. The road had been totally washed away. There was a huge chasm, wide at the top and narrowing as it went down, with a river at the bottom. There was no way to get to the other side.

"Now what?" asked Charlie, her heart sinking. Had everything they'd done so far been for nothing? Or was there a way to get across?

The three friends thought about all of their various abilities and how they could use them in this situation. "I could climb down the rock face using my gecko ability," said Charlie, peering down the chasm. "But I don't think Maria's monkey would be able to—there aren't any handholds. And I'm not sure I can cross that river. We don't know how deep it is."

"If you were able to carry us down," said Maria, "Mac and I can both cross the river now."

"Yeah, but then how would we climb up the other side?" asked Mac. "We'd need Charlie for that, too."

"That's too dangerous for her," said Maria, "especially in the dark. We can't risk it."

"Maybe if we work together," Mac mused, "Maria and I could get you across. You could step on Maria's alligator back with one foot and I could help you as I run across the water with my basilisk lizard suit. . . ."

"That sounds disastrous," said Maria. "I mean, neither one of us has had the chance to try out our water abilities yet. We're not sure how they work exactly."

Charlie was not enthusiastic about the prospect. "There are too many things that could go wrong. Besides, what are we going to do once we get over there? If we're going to try to bring food and supplies, we have to think of how to carry all of that stuff, too. I mean, I'm strong enough, but . . ." She imagined trying to balance dozens of bags of groceries while trying to get across the gorge.

"The people up there need help," said Maria, tears springing to her eyes. "Nobody is coming! And now we can't get there either."

"Maybe I can throw things across," suggested Charlie. "Or use a tree like a giant pole to put things on the other side?"

"How does that help if nobody can get to it from the other side?" Maria pointed out.

"Can Abu Yolanda call them?" asked Mac.

"No electricity up there. No phones," Maria reminded him.

Mac sagged.

"We have to get to them," said Charlie, determined. "Some-how. We have the powers. We just have to figure out how to use them for this."

"Hey, Charlie," said Mac after a moment. "You mentioned using a tree like a pole. But what if you just put a tree across to make a bridge?"

Charlie stared at him. "Duh," she said. "Why didn't I think of that? Let's try it." She went for the longest uprooted tree she could find and brought it over, then held on to one end and tried laying it across. But the chasm was too wide and the tree wouldn't reach the other side.

"How close are we?" asked Charlie.

Mac trained his flashlight on the other side as Charlie held the tree.

"Not far," said Mac. "So close it's frustrating."

"The chasm narrows," said Maria. Her face lit up as an idea formed. "Try setting the tree in and see if it catches. Maybe we can wedge it in there a few feet down."

Charlie bent down, back straining as she tried to keep the tree as horizontal as possible. But it still didn't catch.

"You're so close!" said Maria. "Drop it!"

Charlie dropped the tree and it caught several feet below them, making a slightly uneven bridge to the other side. They peered over the cliff at it.

Maria held the light up. "Well," she said, "I wouldn't walk on it. But that's something."

"Yep," said Charlie. "Still too dangerous." Charlie's night vision made the log shimmer a silvery color. "We don't know if it'll hold."

They sat there unsure what to do.

"What if I put more trees next to the first one?" said Charlie. "Once we have a base of tree trunks, we can pile more trees and even other stuff on top. That'll help it wedge in there even more solidly. And we'll build a bridge."

"Yes!" Mac exclaimed. "A bridge! Then we can walk over, clear the road on that side, and then bring some supplies."

"And let the people up there know they can get through," said Maria. "That's it! Everybody move—we don't have any time to waste."

Even though she was completely exhausted, Charlie looked forward to morning, when she and her friends could work with Yolanda's neighbors again. She loved being part of a community. Everyone helping one another. Friends, strangers, all trusting one another.

Nobody suspected anyone of being there for the wrong reason. Nobody tried to take advantage of another person's weakness. Not one of them was there to compete. They were all there to help. To show love and solidarity and goodness during a time of disaster.

It made Charlie think a lot about how much suspicion she had in her life at home. How she often had to weigh people's motives, or expect the worst from them instead of the best, like here. It made her very thoughtful. She liked it better this way.

She also liked their secret plan to help. The bridge took them two nights to build. Charlie jammed uprooted trees into the chasm in a line while Maria, in alligator mode, moved more debris to the edge for Charlie to layer on top of the tree base. Mac used his pangolin claws to break an enormous concrete roof from a destroyed building into eight equal squares. Eventually Charlie could lay the pieces end to end to be the finishing layer of the makeshift bridge.

When it neared completion and there was nothing left for Mac to do, he pooled all the money the three had brought to Puerto Rico with them. Including the extra money from Dr. Wilde, they had $475, so they'd need to make a lot of trips to the grocery store—and he wanted to get started.

The moon was full and bright, casting an eerie glow on the devastation. Using basilisk mode, Mac ran down the road to the grocer to buy as much nonperishable food as he could carry, like peanut butter and soup and bottled water. After he paid, he stopped in the shadows outside the store to enable his basilisk mode again. He could hear the ocean nearby.

When he returned to the work site, he saw that Charlie and Maria were nearly finished. Charlie was carrying the last piece of the concrete roof over to the bridge. She laid it carefully on top, making a relatively even, smooth path across.

"There," she said, dusting off her hands. "That's it." It was well after midnight. She flipped on her gecko ability as a precaution and ventured out onto the bridge. She jumped up and down a few times. It was solid. She glanced at the others. "We did it!"

Mac nodded approvingly. "Now just three nights left to get the rest of this cleaned up."

Maria eyed the supplies that Mac had brought. "I hope the wild animals don't get into these."

Charlie and Mac looked at each other. "I didn't think of that," said Mac.

"Maybe we can hang the groceries from a tree or something," said Maria. "I saw people do that once on TV." She looked across the bridge and saw a light pole still standing, though it was bent. "Charlie, can you run back to Abu's? There's a rope in the garage and some canvas shopping bags with handles in the pantry. Mac and I will tie everything up while you're gone and get some of this little stuff out of the road."

"Back in a flash." Charlie sped to Yolanda's in cheetah mode and returned in a few minutes with the items. Mac packed the food and water into the canvas bags and strung the rope through the handles. Maria, in weremonkey mode, climbed the pole holding the ends of the rope and hung from the top by her tail. Charlie hoisted the stuff up and Maria tied the rope so the bags of groceries hung just above their heads.

Things were moving along once more. But the kids were beat.

By the sixth night, they'd cleared out most of the big stuff from the stretch across the bridge. While Charlie and Maria had continued moving the remaining debris off the road, Mac had made daily trips to the grocery store. Their food and water supply had grown large and they were eager to deliver it. They were running out of time.

Even if they didn't finish, Charlie thought, at least what remained on the road was something ordinary people could handle. With the last of a huge leafy tree moved aside, Charlie could make out the shapes of a few houses. That was a good sign. There weren't any lights coming from them, which worried Charlie, but then she remembered there was still no electricity up there.

Pausing to rest, Charlie tapped her device and turned on her new viper vision. She scanned the area, wondering if she'd be able to detect heat through the walls of the houses—was this ability that strong? She figured it wouldn't hurt to test it. Venturing closer, she heard a dog bark and quickly spotted it on the porch of a house. She focused on that home and thought she detected a couple splotches of red. Could it be? She was hopeful that it wasn't just her imagination.

Maria and Mac returned with one last load of supplies. Their money was gone. Maria untied the goods from the pole and Charlie hoisted them, like Santa Claus might, over her shoulder. The three of them trudged up the hill toward the houses.

Despite being the middle of the night, they left the goods on the doorsteps, knocked, then ran—they didn't want to have to explain how they'd gotten there, but they knew the people would figure out that the passage must be open again.

Their last task was to finish removing the debris from the bottom part of the road that they'd left so people wouldn't come in search of the midnight cleanup crew. It took them almost until morning, but they finished just hours before Yolanda would be taking them to the airport. It would be a big surprise for people driving past, but the kids wouldn't be there to see it. That part didn't matter. As they turned to go to Yolanda's house to catch a couple hours of sleep, Mac stopped the girls.

"Hey," he said. "We're not going to get much sleep anyway. Want to just stay up?"

"And do what?" asked Maria.

Mac pointed down the hill, past the store, where he'd heard the ocean waves. "Finally try out our new abilities on water."

Charlie's and Maria's faces lit up. "Sure, who needs sleep?" said Charlie. "Let's go!"

Maria led them down a path to what was left of a small beach. Mac clicked on his basilisk lizard mode. The light green metallic liquid flowed over his body.

Maria clicked on her werealligator. She was getting used to morphing into the creature now, though she still didn't like it. "Really gonna need to fix this back in Arizona," she muttered. But she was excited to try out her swimming in this mode.

Charlie found a spot in the sand to settle in, and smiled as she watched her friends: Mac running on top of the waves, Maria gliding partially underwater.

After a few minutes, Charlie remembered wanting to test her starfish ability, so she went in too. She dunked her head under to see if it gave her any extra water features, but it didn't appear to. Charlie wasn't surprised. She surfaced and bobbed, loving the coolness on her skin and the night sky above. And for a brief moment, all seemed well in the world.

CHAPTER 27
Back to Reality

They slept the whole way home. When they got off the plane in Phoenix, Charlie's mom, Mac's dad, and Maria's mom were there to pick them up at the gate. As Charlie ran to hug her mother, a TV monitor tuned to a news channel caught her eye. On the screen was a grainy photo from an airport security camera, showing two soldiers wearing bodysuits and face masks, getting into a limo. In the corner of the photo was part of a third person whose back was to the camera. All they could see was a swath of blond hair. The chyron at the bottom of the screen read, "Manhunt Continues in Guadalajara. American Suspects Armed and Dangerous."

Charlie's eyes widened. She pulled back from the hug and pointed to the screen. "Did you see this?"

Dr. Wilde nodded and gave Charlie a "boy do I have a story for you" look. "I'll fill you in later," she said as the group moved to the exit. Maria had seen it too, and she gave Charlie a wide-eyed questioning look. Charlie shrugged helplessly. They'd have to talk when Maria's and Mac's parents weren't around. But now they were all excited to see their kids and hear about their work in Puerto Rico. The mystery would have to wait.

The families parted ways at the parking garage elevator, and finally Charlie was alone with her mom. They walked arm in arm, Charlie pulling her carry-on behind her. "What was that all about on the TV? Was that Kelly and the soldiers? It looked like Mega and Prowl."

"That was them all right," said Dr. Wilde grimly. "I'm not sure what they're doing in Mexico, but they injured some customs officials at the airport and one of them is in a coma. They're in big trouble. Nobody knows where they are, though." She pointed out their car and they got in. "Your dad says Guadalajara has one of the best zoos in Latin America, which could be why they went there."

"Wow." It was a lot for Charlie to take in. After a week away from this mess, it was a harsh awakening. "What are we going to do?"

Mrs. Wilde backed out of her parking space and drove toward the garage exit. "Ms. Sabbith is trying to track them down. Once the news confirmed that they flew in from San Diego, she went down there and started looking for the van. She also finally got in touch with Captain Brenda Zimmerman—she was the one who originally hired Talos Global to work on Project Chimera."

"Wow, Ms. Sabbith has been busy," said Charlie.

"It's amazing how hard it was for her to find them, but when the government goes top secret, they aren't fooling around. Anyway, now Captain Zimmerman knows what Gray is up to. Whether she believes it to be as serious of a threat as we do remains to be seen."

"Why wouldn't she want to help?" asked Charlie. It seemed crazy not to.

"Maybe she'll decide to." Dr. Wilde didn't sound hopeful. "But this whole situation turning people into hybrids and chimeras is one you have to see to believe, you know? We need to convince her that this project evolved into something crazy after she shuttered it all those years ago."

Charlie let out a breath. "Wow," she said. "So now what? When do you think Dr. Gray will come back with his soldiers?"

Dr. Wilde glanced at Charlie as she headed for the highway. "Honey, I don't think they'll be able to get back into the United States. They're wanted . . . for a serious crime."

"Even Kelly?" asked Charlie, looking fearful.

Dr. Wilde nodded. "Especially Kelly. The officer who is in a coma had a head wound . . . and a poisonous puncture wound to the stomach," she said quietly. "It's pretty obvious Kelly hasn't stopped using her destructive powers to hurt people." She let the words sink in, then added, "I'm afraid she's gone too far to ever turn back."

CHAPTER 28

New Abilities

The next day Mac and Maria showed up at Charlie's house, eager to see what progress had been made in their absence. They'd seen the news. Now that they were here, Charlie told them everything her mom had said about Kelly and Dr. Gray and the soldiers.

"Whoa," said Mac. "Kelly put a customs official in a coma."

"We don't know for sure if Kelly did it," said Charlie. "He had a head injury too, which was probably from one of the soldiers."

"Are they still in Guadalajara?" asked Maria.

"My mom thinks they are. She said they'll be stuck in Mexico because of what they've done."

"Yeah—they'll have to go into hiding, I'll bet," said Maria. "Those suits they wear are pretty noticeable."

"The fur and other animal features underneath probably won't help," said Charlie.

"At least we know where they are," said Mac.

"But Mexico is huge," said Maria. "They could go a lot of places."

"Not if they're trying to hide," said Mac.

Charlie nodded solemnly.

Just then the scientists and Ms. Sabbith arrived for the day. They filed into the house and greeted the kids. Mr. and Mrs. Wilde came into the dining room as well.

"Since we're all here, let's gather around," suggested Mr. Wilde. "We can update everyone on a few things."

They sat at the dining table, Maria and Mac sharing a chair and Charlie leaning over the back of it behind them. The adults took the remaining seats.

"It's great to have our young team back again," said Mr. Wilde. "Welcome, and I hope you all had as much fun as Charlie did helping out over there. We're excited to hear how your new abilities are working."

"We tried them out, all right," said Mac. Maria grimaced, and then they both laughed.

"Before we go into that, though," said Charlie's dad, "Erica has an update on Dr. Gray." He nodded at Ms. Sabbith.

"Yes, I do," she said. "Here's what we know: Dr. Gray was with Kelly and four of his soldiers—Braun, Mega, Prowl, and Miko. They flew on a private plane from San Diego to Guadalajara, where they caused serious problems at the airport."

She paused, then added, "To be honest, I was really puzzled for a while about why Victor would try to leave the country with them—he had to know that even private planes would have to go through customs, and that his soldiers would still be scrutinized. But then Nubia told me he has some sort of nefarious connections

218

in Guadalajara. Apparently, he'd made several trips there while we were working on the devices initially. So maybe he thought he could get through without incident. Anyway, according to news reports, Gray and the team were questioned on board their plane. They ended up attacking the agents and fleeing in a black limo. Their driver doesn't remember them or where he dropped them off."

"Kelly," said the three kids in unison.

"I found the white van in California and monitored the house where it was parked. There appeared to be activity inside so I stayed to watch. Once darkness fell, Cyke, Fang, and Morph started loading up the van. When they finished I had an opportunity to attach a GPS inside the back bumper and a tiny camera to the windshield wipers."

"You're so cool," said Mac, shaking his head. "So freaking cool."

Dr. Goldstein playfully rolled his eyes.

Ms. Sabbith smiled. "Yes, I am," she said, giving Dr. Goldstein the side-eye. "I flew back this morning and I'm pleased to report that as of fifteen minutes ago, the van is on the move. Heading south toward Mexico."

"Oh," said Dr. Sharma, sitting up. "That's interesting. Are all three soldiers inside?"

Ms. Sabbith nodded. "Cyke is driving. The other two are with him. And if they make it across the border without getting stopped, they'll lead us directly to Dr. Gray."

A few of the adults frowned. "So . . . we actually want them to get through border control," mused Jack. "How do we make that happen?"

"I've got our old government contact in the loop now," said Ms. Sabbith. "She's agreed to help us with this part because of the wanted status of Dr. Gray. But it's been tough getting her to understand how advanced these devices and hybrids have become since she shut down the project ten years ago. She thinks I'm exaggerating. I tried to pull footage from the insect cams of the last fight we had, but Prowl and Miko destroyed that computer when they tied us up. Not to mention she really doesn't want to come back to this whole mess that she thought she'd buried ages ago."

"Getting Cyke across the border is a step in the right direction at least," said Charlie's dad. "You're doing great. We've got you running everywhere and you're killing it, Erica. Thank you."

Ms. Sabbith nodded. "This is serious business. I worry Gray is going to ramp things up and do something rash now that he's cornered."

Dr. Jakande, who'd been quiet until now, nodded. "The soldiers have been given more abilities. Did you notice the security camera footage of Miko? She's got something strange on her back."

"I thought it was just a backpack," said Dr. Goldstein.

"Look more closely." Dr. Jakande clicked on her tablet and brought up the photos. She showed one around the table. "It's huge. She'd never wear something like that—she'd carry a bag so she could drop it quickly if she needed to spring into action. The backpack would only serve to hinder her chimp performance." She sat back. "I think she's hiding something under that canvas . . . wings. Back when I was working with Dr. Gray that was the feature he most talked about wanting to give to a soldier."

"Wings?" said Charlie and Mac together. That was unexpected.

"Whoa, that's awesome. Why didn't we think of that?" added Mac, more to himself than anyone else.

The doctors murmured with one another. Charlie's dad gave Dr. Jakande a respectful nod. "Excellent deduction, Nubia."

"Thank you."

Charlie glanced at Dr. Jakande. The woman had just given them some important information. It certainly seemed like the kind of information she'd hide if she were secretly working with Dr. Gray.

Charlie thought back to how she'd felt in Puerto Rico. About trusting people. Maybe she had been imagining Dr. Jakande's sneakiness all along. It was true that Charlie had been overly suspicious of everyone ever since Dr. Gray's first attack and then Kelly's betrayal. But there was something that had changed inside her, at least a little. She wanted to trust people more.

"That's all I have for now," said Ms. Sabbith. "I'll keep you updated. It's a long drive—it'll take them a couple days if they want to stay off the radar and stop to sleep."

"Well," said Mr. Wilde, pushing his chair back. "I guess that's it, then."

"Dad!" said Charlie. "Not funny. What about the bracelets? We have to talk about them."

"Oh right," Dr. Wilde said in a teasing voice. "Well, we're dying to see how we did. Want to show us?"

Dr. Sharma chimed in. "Yes, we'd love to have a look. Then we can figure out how to fix them before we make the trip south, because it doesn't appear that our friends are coming back here."

"So we're all going there?" asked Charlie.

"From what Ms. Sabbith said, we're going to have to," said Mr. Wilde. "It's the only way to stop them."

Charlie looked at her friends in alarm. "Do you think your parents will let you come with us?"

"I don't see why not," said Maria. "It's only fair. You went along on our trips, after all."

"Yep," said Mac. "I'm sure my parents will be cool with it."

Mrs. Wilde spoke up. "Okay, so why don't you float the idea to them that we're thinking of taking a trip to Mexico before summer ends, and we'd love you two to come along. Then, in case we have to move fast, it won't come as a total surprise. Do you both have passports?"

"I do, Mrs. Dr. Wilde," said Maria.

Mac nodded. "Yup, me too."

"Sooo . . . ," said Charlie, lifting her wrist. "Back to the devices." She clicked on her viper sensor and looked around the room. "There is no one hiding in this dining room," she announced. "All clear. It works great—though sometimes I'd rather not see things like rats."

"Ha-ha. Well, that's excellent," said Dr. Wilde. He turned to Mac. "How about your basilisk lizard? Can you show us?"

Mac stepped back and clicked on the feature. The scientists oohed when the streamlined suit wrapped around his body and a tail shot out. "It's quiet, and I can run really well with it on land. And we had a chance to try it out on the ocean. I can zoom over the water, just like the real animal. It's super slick and I love it!"

"So, you think I'm cool too?" asked Dr. Goldstein with a sniff.

Mac grinned. "Totally cool."

Ms. Sabbith frowned. Maria and Charlie feigned bored looks.

"And, Maria," said Nubia, leaning forward, "how about yours?"

"Well . . . ," said Maria, "maybe it's better if I show you."

"Uh-oh," said Dr. Jakande. "That sounds like a problem."

"You could say that," said Maria. "Make some room." The people slid their chairs back and Maria hit the alligator button. Her body stretched and contorted into the animal's shape.

"Oh dear!" said Dr. Jakande, clutching her face in horror.

Charlie watched her. If she'd planned this error to sabotage their progress, she was surely hiding it well. Charlie cringed. She needed to stop looking for ways to suspect Dr. Jakande of working for Dr. Gray. It was obvious by now that she'd had a true change of heart. Still, Charlie couldn't let it all go. She'd been burned too many times.

"I'm so sorry, Maria," said Dr. Jakande. "It's clear I've erred in my calculations. You must have been terribly shocked."

"To be honest," said Maria, "It wasn't bad once I got used to it. And I knew you could fix it so I can feel a little more . . . human. Like with the monkey. And at least I didn't get stuck in alligator mode like what happened before. I'm really glad to be ferocious, but also glad not to have any killer instincts. So that's cool too."

Charlie smiled at her friend. Maria had come a long way when it came to her device and the physical changes it gave her. She seemed to actually like it.

"Also," added Mac, "when she went from monkey to alligator, she ended up with both animals' features."

"Whoops," said Dr. Jakande, looking embarrassed. "That shouldn't have happened either. I was rushing there at the end, and it shows. I'll get to work on it right away."

"We'll all do what we can to help you, Nubia," said Mr. Wilde.

Dr. Jakande smiled. "You've all done so much already." She turned to the kids. "I forgot to tell you the good news. While you were away, the scientists and I finally finished working on a new reversal bracelet, which I hope will be able to turn me back to my normal human self. I'm going to give it a try later today. Then I can jump right into the fixes for Maria, while the others continue building a new, less permanent version of a panther hybrid device for me."

"You're going to go back to being a panther?" asked Charlie.

"A werepanther," said Dr. Jakande. She turned back to Maria. "Just like you. I don't think your device will take long to fix."

Maria brought herself back to human form and handed the bracelet over to Dr. Jakande. "Thanks," Maria said. "I hope I'm not being too particular about it. It's just hard getting used to being so different."

"Trust me, I know that pretty well," said Dr. Jakande. "Looking different is hard. I'm glad we're both heading in the right direction with these."

The two exchanged warm looks. As Maria went to take her seat once more, Ms. Sabbith started typing furiously on her tablet. A second later she stopped and stared at the screen. "News flash," she said, looking up. "The white van has officially made it across the border."

CHAPTER 29

Unrest in the Ranks

They'd been somewhere in central Mexico for days, but Kelly still didn't have a good feel for *where* they were exactly. All she knew was that the bus had taken them several hours outside of Guadalajara. They were in the mountains. There was a lake a few blocks down the hill from the house Dr. Gray had rented. The lake had an island in the middle of it—Dr. Gray seemed unusually giddy to find that out.

Nobody else cared about it, though, or understood why it was so great. They were all edgy and on the verge of completely freaking out—at least Kelly was. And Miko and Prowl didn't seem very comfortable either. Knowing they were stuck here in Mexico and forced to hide felt so . . . so restricting. So stressful. On top of that, Dr. Gray's confession that he'd gone rogue from the government and started his own crusade to save the world, and had purposely withheld that information from even his most trusted soldiers . . . well, that just seemed preposterous. Cyke, Fang, and Morph probably didn't even know that part yet unless Miko had told them through their little walkie-talkie devices in their suits. Kelly had walked in on Miko talking sneakily to someone a couple days after they'd gotten here. But when she'd asked, Miko had refused to explain.

Most of the time Kelly wasn't overly worried that Dr. Gray could change everyone in the world into chimeras. How would he be able to manage something like that? It took him so long just to make the formula for one new animal ability. Though, admittedly, it was going much faster now that he'd fixed the mist machine and was collecting DNA regularly. But still, they could only do it one person at a time with that dinky machine. It just seemed impossible. Too impossible to worry about.

It was the fact that Dr. Gray *thought* he could do it that made Kelly feel increasingly uncomfortable.

While Braun and Mega remained supportive of the scientist even after the shocking revelations, Miko and Prowl at least seemed a lot more concerned about what he'd revealed. They were angry, too, and bitter that Dr. Gray had kept that little tidbit a secret from them until after they'd come here. Now it was too late for them to do anything about it. And they couldn't leave, or else they'd risk getting caught. So here they all were, trapped and huddled up in an old house, trying to rebuild Dr. Gray's lab without drawing attention to themselves so he could continue his work. If they refused to help, he could kick them out. And then where would they be with their faces plastered all over the news?

With the anxiety levels high everywhere, Kelly began sneaking around the house in camouflage, trying to catch others talking.

What did they say when Dr. Gray wasn't around? Were Braun and Mega really falling in line with this new development or were they pretending? And what did Prowl and Miko mutter to each other sometimes when they were alone? Kelly had seen them on numerous occasions, but they usually stopped talking when she walked up. That stung. Didn't they trust her? Not even Miko?

One day in camo mode Kelly slipped into the open doors of the living room, which had become Dr. Gray's new lab. The scientist was there, setting up a new piece of equipment that had been delivered that afternoon. She heard him talking, and at first thought he was speaking to himself. But soon she realized he was using the communication device in the collar of his lab coat—the same kind that was built into the soldiers' suits. She crept closer and listened to his half of the conversation.

"No, no. The shark is for Mega. The formula is finished, I'm just waiting for the machine. I've got other plans for—" He paused to listen. "Komodo dragon? Hmm. I was thinking a poison dart frog for you, but that's not a bad idea. I can find that one locally, I think. There's a zoo an hour from here. Or I suppose I could sneak back to Guadalajara with Kelly—her face isn't in any of the surveillance videos and she looks . . ." He paused again to listen, longer this time.

"I hate to take that much time away from my work to get DNA, but I don't want the soldiers leaving the house—we can't afford to be spotted just yet. Not until everything is ready."

Kelly frowned. Ready? Who was he talking to?

"Okay, so, electric eel, Komodo dragon. But very specifically, I need that *Linckia diplax*. You brought the wolf samples that were left over from Fang, right? Because he's been very loyal and . . . and I'm not as keen on this Mexican wolf as I thought. Excellent. What's that?"

Kelly shifted and her arm brushed the wall, making a small sound, but luckily Dr. Gray didn't hear it.

"Cyke, no. No, that's for . . . me." Dr. Gray straightened suddenly and glanced around the room, his eyes shifty like he didn't want to be overheard.

He was talking to Cyke! But *what* was for Dr. Gray? Was he still talking about the wolf? Or the *Linky diplax* thing, whatever that was? Or something else? If Dr. Gray was planning to change everyone in the world, did that include him taking on animal properties too? And what was that part about Fang being loyal? That was weird. Though she didn't blame him for not liking that scrawny wolf.

Kelly moved toward the door so she could escape and write down the weird words she'd just heard—maybe there was a way to look them up. If only she could get to Dr. Gray's tablet, but he took it everywhere he went. He probably even slept with it.

"All right," Dr. Gray continued. "Glad you made it across. Stay out of trouble and we'll see you soon." He read off the address of their house so Cyke could enter it into his GPS.

Kelly sneaked away, past Miko and Prowl who were whispering in the kitchen again, and went to the bedroom she shared with Miko. She found a scrap of paper and a pen in her luggage and wrote down the animals and strange words Dr. Gray had said. Then she pulled out some of Dr. Gray's books and searched the glossary for them.

When Miko came into the room, Kelly looked up. "Oh, hi," she said coolly. "You're not wearing your suit."

"Why bother?" said Miko. "Besides, even with a cutout I just hate how it feels. So . . ."

Kelly shrugged. "Cyke is coming. You probably already knew that." She was a little miffed that Miko had been talking to Prowl without her again.

Miko nodded. "Yes, he's coming with the equipment and all the samples from the old lab. Morph and Fang are with him."

"Oh. Thanks for letting me know." Kelly couldn't stop the sarcasm in her voice. She was feeling alone and the situation seemed awful, and Miko had distanced herself from Kelly since Dr. Gray had revealed his true purpose.

Miko stopped, then went back to the door and closed it. "Look, Kelly," she said softly, "I don't mean to be standoffish with you. But Prowl and I go back a long way. And even though he thinks you're great soldier material, he's still a little wary of you. Especially with this new development—Prowl and I aren't safe. And he doesn't trust anybody anymore."

"I suppose he has a right to be nervous about me," mumbled Kelly. After all, she'd put him through a lot of agony with her platypus spike attack. She looked at the floor. "I'm scared," she said. "I don't know what to do. I want to get out of here."

Miko sighed heavily and went over to Kelly. "Oh, honey, I'm sorry. We're trying to figure out what to do. It's all pretty confusing. And I don't trust anybody but Prowl and you right now. I don't think you should tell anybody else about how you're feeling—especially not Braun or Mega. They are definitely on board and excited about what Dr. Gray wants to do. Cyke is questionable—we'll have to see about him once he gets here—and the other two as well. They're newer recruits to the experiment . . . or *whatever* this really is . . . and we're not close with them."

Kelly felt better now that Miko was talking to her. "So what are we going to do? You don't really think Dr. Gray can change everybody in the whole world into chimeras, do you?"

Miko gave Kelly a wary look. "Never underestimate what that man can do," she said. "I hope you're right, that it's impossible. But he could do a lot of damage trying."

"Is there anybody we can go to for help? What about Zed?" And now that Miko was opening up, she ventured, "Is Zed who you were talking to on your comm device when we first got here?"

Miko hesitated, then flopped her arms. "Yeah. But she never answers. Either she's not wearing her suit anymore, or she's chosen not to respond to me. I think she's written us off. Or me, at least."

Kelly was quiet for a moment. Then she looked up. "What if we have to hide forever?"

"Then we hide," said Miko. "But you won't have to. Dr. Gray has your passport—I saw him pick them up. And the police don't have any good surveillance photos of your face. You look like a regular person. You'll be able to get back to the US if you want to. It's . . . the rest of us who can't. Not like this." She pointed at her features, the fur growing under her chin and close around her ears, and the wings that were now a part of her body forever. "When I was a kid, I always thought wings would be so cool," Miko said with a bitter laugh. "Now I'm just an extra-weird freak."

"No you're not," insisted Kelly. "You're like a superhero."

Miko shook her head sadly. "I used to think that. But the superheroes are the good guys. Now that I know what Dr. Gray is planning, I'm starting to realize we've been the villains this whole time."

The statement left Kelly cold. She knew that she'd done some bad things. But did that make her a villain? If it did, was there anyway she could undo it? Didn't heroes make mistakes sometimes? She looked up, scared and confused. "But Dr. Gray thinks we're the good guys—he wants to save the world. He told me so. Maybe . . . maybe this isn't so bad."

Miko frowned.

Kelly continued anyway. "What if we're just not seeing all the good that could come from changing everyone into chimeras? I mean, sure, it sounds really extreme. But if everyone had animal abilities on top of our human minds, just think how strong that would make us. And—maybe you wouldn't stand out quite so much with those wings on your back if you weren't the only one with them."

Miko eyed Kelly carefully. "Maybe you're right," she said in a stiff voice. She didn't sound convinced. She sounded like she was giving in. Like she didn't want to talk about it anymore. Like maybe she didn't trust Kelly now either after what she'd just said. Miko stood up and started toward the door.

"Wait," Kelly said, suddenly realizing that what she'd said had sounded a lot like she was defending Dr. Gray's plan. She ran to the door after Miko. "I'm just . . . I'm trying to make sense of things. I don't want to be a . . ."

The chimp-vulture turned and afforded a small smile. "I know, kiddo. It's all good. We're all trying to do the same thing. It's okay to talk things out. I just . . . I have to go help Dr. Gray now." She opened the door.

Kelly grasped Miko's arm. "If you learn anything else, will you tell me?" whispered Kelly. "Please?"

"Of course," said Miko, gently pulling away. "Don't worry about that."

Miko left the room with Kelly staring after her, the girl's heart sinking. Had she just alienated her only ally?

A tear slipped down Kelly's cheek and she turned back into the room. She sat on her bed, then buried her face in her hands. Everything was such a mess. And she had just made it worse. She didn't know what to do or where to turn.

After a few minutes, she heard a tap at the door. Kelly whisked her tears away and dried her eyes on her sleeve. "Come in," she said.

Dr. Gray opened the door a few inches and peered in. "It's time to visit a new zoo," he said. "Be ready in ten minutes." He closed the door, leaving Kelly standing there. Her shoulders slumped. She went to the closet to change into her camo suit. Hanging there were Miko's bodysuits. Kelly flipped past them, then stopped. She went back to one and peered at the communication device that was implanted in it. An earpiece was attached to the collar. She examined it, trying to figure out how it worked. She saw a small dial with names going around it—Dr. Gray, Cyke, Prowl, Zed, Team.

Kelly's heartbeat sped up. She touched the dial, then turned it to Zed. Before she could think about what a mistake she could be making, she pressed it. "Zed, can you hear me? This is Kelly Parker. We need your help."

Kelly let go of the button and pressed Miko's earpiece to her ear, half praying that Zed would respond, half hoping she hadn't heard her. After several moments, and with the clock ticking, Kelly blew out a breath and dropped the earpiece, letting it dangle from the suit. She quickly changed into her own suit and then, on a whim, listened again. But there was no one there.

After Kelly left the room, there was a crackle inside the closet, followed by a whisper. "Kelly? Are you there?"

CHAPTER 30

Changing Gears

Dr. Jakande had been in the Wildes' bathroom changing back into her human form with the reversal bracelet when she'd heard the call from Kelly. As soon as the last of her panther features had dissipated and she'd had a second to see herself the way she used to be, she slipped on her street clothes and reached for her suit. She squeezed her eyes shut, unsure what to do, then listened at the door for a moment. Torn, she went with her heart and answered. Kelly was just a kid.

But Kelly hadn't replied.

Dr. Sharma knocked on the door. "Is everything okay? Did it work?"

Dr. Jakande dropped the suit. "Fine!" she shouted. "I'm just . . . looking at myself. Trying to remember the old me."

"Great news! Come out when you're ready."

Dr. Jakande gathered her wits and folded up her suit, squashing the comm device inside the folds of it to muffle any noise that might penetrate if Kelly responded. She took another look in the mirror and opened the door.

"Wow," she said. "This feels strange." She emerged from the

Wildes' bathroom wearing a T-shirt and jeans and the slim reversal device around her wrist. Her panther fur was completely gone. In its place: brown skin and black hair. Normal fingernails instead of claws. She ran her hand down the skin on her arm, then looked up with a shrug and a self-conscious grin. "What do you think?"

The doctors and children crowded around her, congratulating her. She took the reversal device off and handed it to Dr. Goldstein. "This worked perfectly. I wonder . . ." She hesitated and tilted her head, thinking. "Hey," she said softly. "If we had more of these, couldn't we use them on the other soldiers?"

Dr. Goldstein looked sharply at her. "You mean to turn them back to normal and stop them from being so powerful?" He tapped his lips. "That's a terrific idea."

"We've figured out how to change someone without their original DNA," said Dr. Sharma, growing excited at the thought of stopping Prowl from ripping her to shreds. "So the hard part is finished. We would just need to make more devices."

"Even a few could help," said Nubia. "We could reload them with the reversal formula in a pinch."

Dr. Goldstein nodded and slipped the device into his shirt pocket. "I'll reload this one as well."

"That's such a genius plan," said Mac. "There won't be any hybrids or chimeras left to worry about."

"That's what I'm hoping," said Dr. Sharma. "Maybe you won't have to fight at all."

"I'm not so sure it'll be that easy," said Dr. Jakande with a laugh. "But you three start on those, and I'll get back to fixing Maria's device. Now that Cyke is heading to Gray's location with the remaining soldiers, I suspect he's almost done narrowing down the options for his ultimate chimera. Once he's got that formula made, he'll be able to replicate it quickly. And if he's planning to affect a large number of people almost at once, all he has to do is release it in the air or water." She paused. "I wonder if he somehow fixed the machine."

"Either way, we've got to stop him," said Charlie emphatically.

"All of them," said Maria. "The soldiers too. And especially Kelly."

Dr. Jakande flinched. "Kelly's in a tight spot," she said. "I know what it's like to be in her shoes."

Maria glanced at her. "What do you mean?"

"Well, switching sides," said Dr. Jakande lightly. "I imagine she's regretting it right about now."

Charlie looked up. "Why would you say that? Are *you* regretting it too?"

Mr. Wilde gave Charlie a stern look. "Charlie," he said, sounding disappointed in her.

"I'm just wondering what she meant," Charlie protested.

Dr. Jakande turned to her solemnly. "No, Charlie," she said. "I'm not regretting it. But I switched to the *right* side."

* * *

"I don't think Kelly's regretting anything," said Mac a little later from the pool in his backyard. "Or else she'd stop hurting people." He took a run across the surface, practicing, then slowed down to see how long he could stand still without sinking.

"Maybe she was attacked," said Maria. "It could have been self-defense."

Charlie was thoughtful. "If Kelly regretted anything, she'd have texted you by now."

"True," said Maria. "I've given her enough opportunities. She doesn't even read my texts anymore."

Mac looked at Charlie. "Did you ever test out your starfish abilities?"

"Yes," said Charlie. "At the beach in Puerto Rico. And it's just as we expected. Makes sense, though. My dad only wanted the very best feature from each animal, and he told me the *Linckia diplax* starfish is the best at healing. If he'd been looking for a swimming feature, he'd have picked a different animal for that." Charlie was glad her dad hadn't wasted an ability on swimming, though. She hadn't needed something like that in any of the situations she'd ever been in. It would have been a waste.

When they got out of the pool they saw that Ms. Sabbith had texted to let them know that the white van had stopped traveling and was stationary in a city several hours outside of Guadalajara, Mexico. She believed the entire team was together now. Only time would tell when they'd be ready to make a move, and Dr.

Gray probably wasn't going to risk uprooting everyone and being recognized if they were finding success hiding where they were. Everyone needed to be in place and ready for Gray whenever he decided to act.

"Time to alert the parents that we'll be leaving soon," Charlie told her friends as they toweled off. Mac and Maria nodded. They talked about what to pack so that they'd be ready in a hurry.

Once again the scientists worked late into the evening to get things done. Dr. Jakande finished the tweaks on Maria's device. Dr. Sharma was doing something mysterious with the Mark Five that she didn't want to talk about yet. And Dr. Goldstein and Dr. Wilde replicated as many of Nubia's DNA reversal bracelets as possible, and packed up the remaining formula so they could refill them if necessary.

In the morning when Maria arrived, the Mark Two was waiting for her to test.

Maria didn't hesitate to put it on. She clicked it shut, then tapped the screen, going into monkey mode first. Then, with a deep breath, she tried to switch over to the alligator like she'd done in Puerto Rico. This time all the monkey fur disappeared. And going into alligator mode, Maria barely changed shape. She stayed upright on her legs. Her body turned scaly. She grew an alligator tail and extremely sharp teeth and claws.

"Wow!" cried Mac.

"That's more like it!" said Charlie.

Maria ran to the bathroom to look herself over. Mac and Charlie ran after her. "That's what I'm talking about," Maria said, pleased. She turned and snapped her jaw at Mac for fun, and he jumped and nearly tripped over Charlie trying to get away.

Maria switched back to monkey mode, then immediately into alligator mode to see how fast she could transform. The transition was physically much easier now that she remained upright. All she needed to do now was test out her alligator abilities in this new mode.

"Do you have a Turbo alligator like you have a Turbo monkey?" asked Mac, looking at her device screen.

"Don't think I need it," said Maria with a laugh. "This is just perfect the way it is." Gingerly she felt her pointy teeth. "Hope I don't hurt myself," she said, but she seemed happy with her new chompers. She and the others went to the lab, where all four scientists were working. Mrs. Wilde was there too.

"It's great!" Maria told Dr. Jakande.

The woman looked up with a warm smile. "Wonderful." She told Maria to turn around so they could see her tail. "That looks a hundred percent better. Let me know if you think it needs anything else."

"I will," said Maria, turning to look at her alligator tail trailing behind her and helping her balance. She tried not to knock anything down with it. "This is going to take a little getting used to," said Maria.

"Now all three of you are set," said Mr. Wilde.

"Just in time," said Dr. Goldstein. They glanced at each other, and Charlie's dad nodded at Dr. Goldstein to speak. "Remember what Ms. Sabbith said about trying to convince Captain Zimmerman in Washington that we're looking at a real threat?"

The kids nodded.

"Well, she thought it might help to get some video of you three in action so she can present it to her. Show her what we've had to do to fight."

The kids looked at one another. "Sure," said Charlie. Mac and Maria agreed. "I need to train a little bit anyway," said Maria.

"I'm off work today," said Charlie's mom, "so I can take you three to the mountains to train like we did before. Maybe this time we can go to Canyon Lake and rent a boat. Take it out where nobody else can see us. I can shoot some video."

"That would be perfect," said Mr. Wilde.

"That sounds good to me," said Mac. The others nodded.

"Can I come along this time?" asked Andy.

"Sure," said Charlie. "It'll be hot, though. It's going to be a hundred and twelve today."

Andy shrugged. "I don't mind, especially if I can go swimming. It's not like *I'm* going to be training for anything."

"I'll swim with you," said Charlie. "I can try out my viper vision underwater."

"Cool," said Andy.

They left before it got too hot. On the way up into the mountains, Mrs. Wilde stopped at an overlook area. They were high above Canyon Lake. Smooth rock walls led to the water glistening below. The children leaned over the railing, looking down.

"Dad would freak if he were here," said Andy.

"Why?" asked Maria. "Does he get sick driving in the mountains? My stepdad does."

"No, he's afraid of heights," said Andy.

Charlie nodded. "He'd take one look over this railing and go straight back to the car."

"He wouldn't even get this close," said Mrs. Wilde.

"How's he going to handle that gecko ability in the Mark Five?" Mac wondered.

Charlie shrugged. "I guess we'll see soon enough."

At the lake, Mac and Maria got in a couple hours of practice with their water abilities. Mac ran circles around the others. Maria's swimming was smooth and sleek in alligator mode. She jokingly stalked the others down in the water, slithering just below the surface.

Charlie discovered that her heat vision worked underwater, too. Then, while her mother filmed, she shimmied up the rocky mountainside using her gecko ability.

Back on land they stopped at a trailhead and switched abilities to give Ms. Sabbith more footage. Charlie lifted a boulder the size of a refrigerator and held it high in the air, then threw it, making the ground shake. Then she ran at cheetah speed down the trail. Mac used his pangolin claws to crack a giant stone in half. Maria jumped and swung among the rocks and trees in monkey mode.

By the time they were done, they were feeling good about their training. And that the video would be more than convincing.

Ms. Sabbith was there when they got home, packing up her elec-tronics. She looked up when they came in. "Were you able to get any video?"

"I'll send you the file right now," Mrs. Wilde told her.

"Perfect," said Ms. Sabbith. "Fingers crossed. I've almost got Zimmerman to believe me. Here's hoping this'll help put her over the edge."

"Are you going back to Chicago again?" asked Charlie. It was hard to keep track of her whereabouts.

"Nope," said the woman. She zipped up a duffel bag and slung it over her shoulder. "I'm heading to Mexico."

"To go after Dr. Gray?" asked Maria.

"By myself? No thanks. I'm going to set up our new spy head-quarters and figure out how close they are to doing something stupid."

Mac looked wistfully at the duffel. "Good-bye, cool electron-ics," he said. "Hey, do you need an assistant, Ms. Sabbith?"

Ms. Sabbith smiled. "I think that might make your parents a little suspicious, don't you?"

"Probably," agreed Mac.

"Ahem," said Dr. Goldstein pointedly from across the room.

Mac grinned. "And I guess I'm already busy."

"I'll hold your assistant position open until you get there," Ms. Sabbith promised. "In case things go south with you and Goldstein. The bugs will love working with you again."

Mac cringed, because bugs. "Yeah, thanks," he said, not quite as enthusiastically. Though controlling the cameras wasn't the worst thing he could be doing. He loved that part.

"Once I get there and assess Gray's progress, I'll be calling to give you an idea of how quickly you all need to get down there."

"Sounds good," said Charlie's mom. "Thanks."

"Safe travels," said Charlie.

"Safe travels," echoed Maria and Mac.

A black car arrived in the driveway to take Ms. Sabbith to the airport. The kids waved, then returned to the lab to see how things were going.

Charlie went up to Dr. Sharma, who was hunched over Charlie's old device and using a delicate tool. "What are you trying to do with the Mark Five?" Charlie asked her.

Dr. Sharma glanced up. She was wearing magnifying safety glasses that made her eyes look huge. She lifted them and propped them on top of her head. "I'm trying to change this device so that the abilities are not tied to your father's DNA anymore."

"Why?"

"Because we want to be able to use it for anyone who needs it—thinking especially of the healing part, here, but the other attributes as well. We got lucky last time with Andy after Kelly stuck him with her platypus spike, because he shares part of your father's DNA. But if the same thing happens this time to Mac or Maria or any of us . . . well, we need to have a plan in place."

"Oh," said Charlie. "But isn't that dangerous? What if someone takes it?"

"They'll need a code to activate it, like the others. That ought to protect it."

"Since you're untying all the abilities, maybe you scientists can share it," suggested Mac. "Take turns fighting the bad dudes."

Dr. Goldstein laughed. "I'm afraid this old body isn't quite up to the kind of fighting you kids can do."

"But wouldn't the healing ability help you feel better?" asked Mac.

"It might—that's not a bad idea. But I don't think it can make me young again."

"I'm not interested in fighting either," said Dr. Sharma vehemently. "I'll be stationed with Erica, keeping an eye on you all. And Charlie's mom will be on emergency duty to help with any injuries that aren't healing automatically."

"Like my dislocated shoulder," said Charlie, remembering the fight with Prowl that had left her in excruciating pain. Her mother had had to pop her shoulder back in before it could heal.

"Don't worry. I'll be fighting alongside you, kids," said Nubia. "My new werepanther device is almost done."

"And I'm up for the challenge, too," said Charlie's dad, though he didn't seem enthusiastic about it. "The Mark Five will still be my primary device. Quinn's just making it more versatile and helpful. We're up against a strong enemy."

"Have you trained with your bracelet yet, Charles?" asked Dr. Jakande. She raised an eyebrow at him, like she already knew the answer.

"Uh, not yet."

Charlie rolled her eyes. "Oh, boy. There's a learning curve, I'm warning you. But hopefully Dr. Gray and the soldiers won't even see us coming and you won't need to do much," said Charlie, thinking of Ms. Sabbith spying on the bad guys. Would this be a total sneak attack?

"We're all crossing our fingers for that," said Dr. Sharma. "With any luck, we'll have more help from the government by then too. I still hold out hope that we'll be able to stop Gray without having to fight at all."

CHAPTER 31

A Costly Mistake

A few rainy days after Cyke, Morph, and Fang arrived and Dr. Gray was reunited with his lab equipment and his growing catalog of DNA samples, Kelly slipped out of the house. Technically she wasn't supposed to go out. Even though her face hadn't been clear on any of the security footage that had been shown on local news channels—only her long blond hair from the back—Dr. Gray had gotten increasingly paranoid and forbade her from leaving.

But that seemed stupid, and Kelly really needed a breather. She scoffed at the scientist's rules and put on a knit hat to cover her hair. Then she started down the street toward the lake that she'd just barely been able to see from her upstairs window.

It was a relief to go outside and take in fresh air, despite the weather. And get away from everyone. It was still intense in the house. Prowl and Miko were being a little too obvious about their unhappiness, though Dr. Gray seemed oblivious for the most part.

The scientist had been working an insane number of hours since they'd been here. He'd finalized the shark treatment for Mega that morning, and they were planning to administer it to her later in the day. Kelly would make sure to return in time to see that.

Gray had also had been working on the other samples Kelly had gotten for him, including the ones from her most recent zoo trip—the electric eel, which would be for Prowl. And the Komodo dragon that Cyke had seemed to want. Kelly had even managed to snag the tiny jellyfish that had been so elusive. Dr. Gray had been very pleased with her lately. But he mentioned in front of the other soldiers how great she was doing, which didn't seem to endear her to them. She wished he hadn't said anything. She didn't want Miko and Prowl to think she was enjoying this.

Kelly stopped when she got to the lake. She could see the island rising tall in the middle of it. It had houses all over the side on various levels, almost all the way up. At the top was a huge statue of some sort. Apparently Dr. Gray had been researching it—he'd told her so on their way to the zoo. He said it was so big and tall that there were a lot of shops and museums inside it. You could climb all the way to the top and stand on the observation deck and see for miles. It sounded cool, but Kelly didn't hold out hope for actually getting to explore the area.

In the distance, storm clouds were rising like they'd done several times that week. As in Arizona, the summer storms here were predictable. Back home Kelly could see the clouds building up over the Superstition Mountains all afternoon, and they would produce wind- and rainstorms around dinnertime. It was much cooler here, though—Prowl had mentioned they were at something like seven thousand feet above sea level. That was higher than the top of the

Superstition Mountains. Seven thousand—that was more like going up into the mountains of northern Arizona, where she and her parents had gone skiing all those winters before the divorce.

Kelly closed her eyes, squeezing them tight when a painful pang went through her chest. That feeling was all too familiar lately. Despite knowing she didn't have a home to go back to, Kelly was still freaked out that she wasn't able to leave here. Even if she escaped, she didn't have any money to get anywhere. Even if she *had* money *and* could find where Gray was keeping her passport, *and* she made it back to the Guadalajara airport, she wouldn't be able to get a plane ticket without a parent.

Kelly sighed. What good would going home be, anyway? Her parents didn't know her. She'd never be able to convince her friends that she was a decent person after what she'd done. Things were bleak. Was there any way to get her old life back? It didn't seem like there was.

She watched a few birds squawking at each other near a marina at the lake's edge. To the right, some ducks waddled around in a deserted park. A police officer strolled a couple blocks away. What would happen if she asked for help? If she told him everything? Would she go to jail for stabbing that customs officer? A wave of fear made her knees weak. She turned and swiftly walked back to the house.

As she sneaked up the walkway to the side door, a tiny ladybug flew across the road toward her. It landed on her hat, unnoticed, and crawled into a fold to hide.

Inside, Dr. Gray was calling everyone to come to the lab and witness Mega's transformation. Kelly sidled up to Miko and glanced at her uneasily. The two were still friendly, but Miko seemed to have distanced herself even more from Kelly the last few days, since Dr. Gray had praised her. It made her feel bad, but Kelly didn't know how to fix it, other than to try to explain to Miko that she didn't like what Gray was doing. The woman didn't seem to believe her, though she usually blamed the situation on Prowl. Miko didn't want him to see her talking to Kelly because if he did, he might stop disclosing things he'd been learning by watching Dr. Gray all day.

The distance was easy enough for Kelly to get used to, even if it hurt. That was the story of her life.

Mega sat in front of the mist machine with her helmet off. Dr. Gray poured formula into the chamber and turned it on. Mist welled up and swirled around on the inside of the glass. Mega placed her chin on the bar and fastened the oxygen mask to her face, then began to take in deep breaths. They all waited to see Mega's shark features appear.

"When the chamber is empty," Dr. Gray told her, "and you feel tingling in your body, you can take that off."

The rhino woman snorted and kept breathing until the mist was gone.

After a moment she sat back. "My face is prickly," she

announced. And then her body began to transform. Her nose and her mouth spread out and grew, flattening her nostrils, though the rhino horn still stood out. A single row of sharp-looking teeth populated her mouth. Gills appeared on her neck and began to waver. A fin pushed out.

"Wow," said Prowl, impressed. "That's frightening."

The others agreed. Mega smiled with her new huge mouth. But after a moment her smile faded. She began to make more snorting noises. She grasped her mouth and nose, feeling all around, and then gasped, "I can't breathe!"

She pushed back from the table and stumbled over to Braun. "Help me!" she rasped. "Do something!"

Dr. Gray followed her, trying to figure out what was wrong.

"Why can't she breathe?" asked Miko, alarmed.

The scientist seemed completely befuddled and unsure what to do. He looked her over frantically, helplessly. He had no answers.

Kelly was confused. Her dolphin ability hadn't given her this problem—she could switch it on and be just fine. Then she noticed Mega's gills flapping. She pushed past Cyke. "Water!" she cried. "Mega needs to be in water!"

"Quick!" said Miko, springing into action. "Let's get her to the bathroom!"

Mega staggered. Braun and Cyke picked her up by the arms and dragged her into the bathroom. Dr. Gray rushed in after them, with Miko right behind. Immediately Mega went for the toilet and stuck her head into the bowl.

"The toilet water isn't deep enough!" said Miko, hopping over to the bathtub and flipping the handles. "Prowl, find a bucket!" she called, plugging the drain. "Fill it up from the kitchen and pour it over Mega. Cyke, get her in here!"

Prowl ran for a bucket. Cyke and Braun picked up Mega and dumped her into the bathtub. She flopped and splashed as the water inched up, her protruding new shark jaw stopping her from flattening her face to the tub floor. The water wasn't high enough to cover her gills.

"Splash her neck!" yelled Kelly from outside the cramped room, standing on her tiptoes to see what was happening. On her hat, the ladybug emerged from the fold.

Cyke slipped outside the room and joined Kelly, trying to stay out of the way. Prowl came back with a bucket of water. He poured it on Mega, then went to the sink to fill it up again.

After a few agonizing minutes, the water was finally deep enough for Mega's head and neck to be submerged. The gills moved like a real shark's. Mega stopped flailing and floated more calmly as the water continued to pour over her head. She turned once and gave Braun a pitiful glance.

Braun tried to reassure her. "We'll figure this out," he said. "Won't we, Dr. Gray?"

Dr. Gray stared at Mega in dazed silence and didn't respond to Braun. It was as if he hadn't heard his question. And now that the immediate danger had passed for Mega, everybody began to throw looks around the room. What had gone wrong? What were they going to do? Would Mega be forced to live in the bathtub—forever?

"I don't know what happened," murmured Dr. Gray. His eyes focused. "She wasn't supposed to get the gills. . . . I—I don't know how to fix this right now. And I need to finish the others and continue working on my ultimate formula. We're so close. Incredibly close. I'm finalizing my plans as we speak."

Miko and Prowl looked at Dr. Gray like he'd lost his mind—indeed, they already believed he had. "So," said Prowl, "you're going to just leave her in the bathtub indefinitely?"

"What about when we have to . . . you know . . . *go?*" said Braun, indicating the toilet.

"We could draw the shower curtain closed," suggested Cyke.

"Guys!" said Miko with disgust. "Please! There are more important things to worry about than that. Sheesh. You're a bunch of animals."

Kelly spoke up. "What about the lake? It . . . it isn't far," she said. "I, uh, saw it out the car window when Dr. Gray and I went to the zoo the other day." The others turned toward her, listening. Kelly continued. "Remember, the bull sharks can live in both salt water and freshwater. Maybe Mega would be more comfortable there. At least until Dr. Gray can figure out how to fix her."

"I can hear you, you know," said Mega, sounding garbled

and slightly put out. Bubbles floated to the surface of the tub. She didn't seem excited about the prospect, but there weren't any other ideas on the table. "I guess that's better than nothing."

"How are we going to get her there?" asked Prowl. "Her head and neck are too big to fit inside any bucket I've seen around here."

Kelly's brow furrowed. How did other people transport fish? She'd won a goldfish before, when she was in third grade—it had come in a plastic bag full of water. "How about a giant trash bag?" she said. "She could climb in and . . ."

"She's too big to fit inside a trash bag," said Braun, "especially if you expect to fill it up with water high enough to cover her gills."

"We could fill a bag with water and put her head in so she's upside down," said Miko, "then tie it around her torso. And carry her that way."

"That won't look suspicious," muttered Prowl. "Besides, the rest of us can't be seen or we'll be discovered."

"We can do it after dark," said Miko. "And we've got the van now. We'll do what Kelly suggested—sneak her into the back of the van, drive to the lake, then back up to the edge of the water and shove her out."

Mega didn't have much of a choice. It was either live in the bathtub or in the lake. At least in the lake she could move around. And she wouldn't have to be present when Braun had to go to the bathroom.

It was settled. That night, almost the whole team set out to release Mega. Only Dr. Gray stayed behind, working frantically on his next animal formula and checking the other concoctions he had going simultaneously. He still liked the idea of including features from the shark for his ultimate chimera, but he'd have to figure out how to fix the gill problem. Fixing Mega? Well, that was at the bottom of his list. He was getting close to choosing the final list. With the DNA he'd stored from all of his soldiers' previous transformations, and all the new samples from their missions, he had quite a library of options. Just a few more animals to test. And now that he had the machine working so beautifully, things would be going much faster.

CHAPTER 32

Time to Make a Move

Dr. Sharma pulled her ringing phone from her pocket. "It's Erica," she announced to the other scientists and the kids before swiping to answer. "What's the status?" she said in greeting, and put the woman on speakerphone so all could hear.

"Ladybug just got an eyeful of something strange going down," said Ms. Sabbith. "If only she had a microphone, I'd have gotten quite a scoop. Unfortunately I don't have the miked insects in place yet."

"What did you see?" asked Dr. Sharma.

"Someone in the bathtub, for one thing. And everyone else standing around, water splashing all over the place."

"This is reminding me of when you destroyed the school bathroom," Maria whispered to Charlie.

Charlie frowned and poked her with her elbow.

"*Part* of the bathroom," Mac whispered, because somebody had to say it. Charlie caught his eye and they bumped fists.

Ms. Sabbith continued. "By process of elimination, the one in the tub was either Mega or Morph. I couldn't get a good view, though, because I didn't want to move the ladybug too much and risk being seen. Then later I saw one of them with a plastic trash bag over her head all bent over weirdly, and some of the others carrying her upside down like that. I'm dying to know what went wrong. A bunch of them left the house after dark. I had the ladybug stay behind, because I didn't see Dr. Gray going along with the others. I brought her into the lab, so she's in a good spot watching Dr. Gray. He's all alone and he's surrounded by beakers full of formulas. Some have labels dating back almost ten years."

"Wow," said Dr. Sharma. "I'm not sure what to think. It does sound like something went wrong, though. And those old formulas might be ones he used on his soldiers."

"Oh, yes," said Dr. Jakande. "He kept what was left of all of ours. So we can expect to see some of those animals in his ultimate chimera somehow. I only wish I knew which ones."

"Prowl's and yours for sure, I'd say," said Mac.

"I hope to be able to figure out which soldier had the bathtub incident eventually," said Ms. Sabbith.

"Did you notice anything new?" asked Dr. Goldstein.

"I noticed that Nubia was right on about her hunch—Miko has wings. And Braun has porcupine quills. Those are the only new things I've seen. But looking at what Gray is doing with multiple samples and notes and charts, and him working on a few different concoctions at the same time, I think he'll be ready soon with more animals to test out on his other soldiers."

"How is he administering it?" asked Dr. Wilde. "Injection? We smashed the machine we made him."

"Well, he managed to put it back together, because it's there and in use."

Dr. Wilde looked alarmed. "I guess we should have expected as much, but that's a setback."

"Any indication of what animals he's favoring?" asked Dr. Sharma.

"I'll try to get the ladybug over to his notes when he goes to bed," said Ms. Sabbith. "And I'd better go now, so I can get the miked spies in place." She hesitated. "But I think you'd better plan on coming soon. Grab tickets for next week. Gray's got a sense of urgency that we haven't seen before. And the manhunt down here is going strong—it's on the news all the time. He knows his days are numbered."

Dr. Sharma glanced at the other scientists. Charlie looked at them too. Their faces were serious, their expressions stern. "We can do that," said Charlie's dad. "We'll finish up a few more of these DNA reversal devices and make some more formula to bring with us—we don't want to leave a single hybrid out there when this is over."

"I've finished the work on the Mark Five," Dr. Sharma reported. "Now any of us can use it."

"And the kids have been training," said Dr. Jakande. "They're ready."

"Great," said Ms. Sabbith. "I'll monitor things until you get here."

Charlie leaned closer to Dr. Sharma's phone. "Did you happen to see Kelly?" she asked.

"Kelly is the one who inadvertently let the ladybug into the house," said Ms. Sabbith. "Got a ride in on her beanie."

Charlie and Maria exchanged a pained look. "How does she . . . seem?"

"Honestly, kids, the ladybug has been on Kelly's hat almost the whole time, until she took it off, so I haven't been able to see much of her. But I'll try to capture some footage so you can see your friend, if you like."

"Thanks, but she's not our friend anymore," said Maria.

Charlie nodded in agreement. "Make sure you're watching what she's doing, Ms. Sabbith, in case Dr. Gray gives her a new ability too. She's dangerous."

Ms. Sabbith was quiet for a long moment. "I'll watch her," she said finally. "And I'll be in touch with anything new."

"We'll plan on seeing you soon." Dr. Sharma waited a beat, then hung up the phone. There was a moment of quiet in the room. And then everybody went back to work with a new sense of purpose to rival that of Dr. Victor Gray.

CHAPTER 33

The Countdown Begins

The final days before their trip flew by for Charlie and her friends. They'd be starting seventh grade soon, but they basically had to save the world before that could happen. They increased their workouts and practiced with their new abilities. They took to the streets after dark so Charlie could practice spotting creatures with her viper vision. Luckily, with the new Mark Six, Charlie could turn off the bat echolocation ability so she didn't chirp all the time in darkness unless she chose to.

Charlie's backyard became a training center. They built an obstacle course for Mac so he could work on his agility with his basilisk lizard feature. They created enemy dummies made of old pillows and burlap, dressing them in scary Halloween costumes they found in Charlie's garage. Maria practiced attacking and tearing them apart so she could gauge the power of her alligator strength and teeth.

Charlie's mom took care of buying the plane tickets and writing up the details for the other parents. And she arranged for Andy to spend the duration of their trip at Juan's house, which would be more fun for him, and safer, too.

By the time the day of their flight arrived, the scientists had packed up everything they needed. And the Wildes' pets had been delivered to a sitter. Mac and Maria arrived at Charlie's house ready with their devices and their luggage in hand. Before everyone left for the airport, Dr. Sharma FaceTimed with Ms. Sabbith, who filled them in on the latest developments.

"Prowl has his second ability," she announced. "It's some sort of electrical shock. He tried it out on Cyke and Cyke popped him one, so it appears to be effective."

"Oh boy," murmured Dr. Jakande. "Prowl probably should have known better—Cyke is a react-first, think-later kind of guy." She smiled, as if remembering other incidents. "And have you gotten a closer look at Braun's porcupine quills?"

"Yeah, he's forgone most of his bodysuit because of them. So nobody likes standing next to him. The sharp quills will stick in you if he bumps you hard enough."

"Yikes," said Dr. Goldstein. He glanced at Mac. "You're going to have to take him on."

Mac nodded.

"What about Kelly?" asked Charlie. "Anything new?"

"Not that I can see, but her features have never been visible like the soldiers' are. I haven't noticed Dr. Gray working on her device at all. Apparently Kelly was using it to capture some elusive, very specific kind of jellyfish. It's a water creature so maybe that's for her."

"A jellyfish?" muttered Mr. Wilde. "That's interesting. I'll do some research on the plane. Anything else?"

"Cyke seems different today. He's . . . thicker, I guess. And something's changed in his face. I'm assuming he's been given a second animal now too, but I haven't had a chance to review video footage of the lab yet. It's hard to keep up without my assistants." She gave a tired smile. Charlie, Maria, and Mac elbowed one another and grinned back.

"Have you figured out who the soldier was from the bathtub?" asked Dr. Sharma.

"Yes—that was definitely Mega. She hasn't returned to their hideout."

"Oh, dear," said Dr. Jakande. "I wonder what happened to her!"

Charlie glanced at the woman, feeling her old suspicions creeping up again when Dr. Jakande spoke like she cared about the soldiers. She had so much history with them. But Charlie clamped down on her worry. Nubia was on their side, she assured herself. Just as much as Kelly was on the other.

"I'm not sure where they took Mega," Ms. Sabbith was saying. "I didn't have ears in the place until the next day, so I missed all immediate talk about it. Nobody's brought her up in detail that I've been able to pick up since then, other than a brief mention from someone wondering how Mega was doing. It sounds like they may have brought her to a hospital, but that would give them away for sure. It must have been serious."

Dr. Jakande pursed her lips and nodded. She glanced around the room, finding Charlie staring at her, and tried to smile. "One fewer soldier to fight," she said. "That's a good thing."

Charlie nodded and relaxed a bit.

"You mentioned multiple formulas in the works," said Dr. Sharma. "Do you know what they are?"

"No. But he's been building two specific formulas very carefully and secretly. He won't even let the soldiers near them anymore."

"How close is he to finishing?"

Ms. Sabbith shrugged. "I really can't tell without knowing what he's doing. I think you can make a better guess at that once you have a chance to observe."

They talked some more about the details of their arrival, which would happen late that evening, hopefully without anyone in Dr. Gray's house noticing.

Soon it was time to go to the airport. The trip to Mexico was becoming a reality.

CHAPTER 34

Exploring Options

Dr. Gray had grown more and more reclusive since the incident at the airport. The threat of being discovered was great. He worked as though his life depended on it, and in a way, it did. One wrong move and everything could be destroyed. There was so much at stake—he'd never felt such pressure to finish. Unfortunately, it meant he'd taken a few shortcuts and had accidentally messed up Mega's formula.

Sure, he didn't want to do something like that again. And he felt badly about it. But she was a willing test subject. She was getting paid a handsome amount to be part of his experiments. Things like this happened sometimes. And obviously Victor would fix her when he could. Just . . . not right now.

The formula for his ultimate chimera had to come first. And it had to come fast. Gray spent countless hours alone in the lab, locking himself inside the room to keep the soldiers from distracting him. And to keep the ones he no longer fully trusted away from his work. He even took to sleeping in there, not wanting to leave for more than a few moments at a time. He looked ragged and old, yet he doggedly continued at a pace that didn't seem sustainable.

He also grew more and more paranoid. "Did you see the police drive by?" he'd asked Prowl a couple of times a day. "Are they closing in?"

"No," said Prowl, eyeing the man. "There's nothing unusual that I can see."

"Are you watching *very* carefully?" Gray asked, narrowing his gaze. "You have to be on high alert! You have to wonder about every move anyone makes out there!"

Prowl tamped down a growl. "Of *courrrse* I'm being alert. There's really nothing going on."

"If you're lying to me," Dr. Gray said icily, "I'll turn you in. They're looking for you soldiers, you know."

Prowl stared at the man. Had he really just said that? After all the years of dedication he and the others had given Victor, he had just threatened to give them up. Prowl looked away in disgust. "I know they're looking for us," he said quietly. "We're all over the news, thanks to you. But I'm not lying. We're all very devoted, remember?"

Dr. Gray was too exhausted to reprimand him any further. Prowl stared a moment longer, then threw up his hands and went outside, where Miko was practicing flying low under the cover of tall trees and a wall that surrounded the backyard.

Gray went to the window and watched them warily for a moment, then looked up and down the street for any sign of suspicious activity. Seeing none, he went back to his work, no doubt planning to ask the same questions of the next soldier guarding the door.

Kelly had caught some of the conversation as she sneaked around the house in camo mode. Dr. Gray was not himself, and that was unsettling. Scary, even. After Prowl stormed off, Kelly went back to her bedroom and into the closet, where Miko's suits hung. She stood next to one, hesitating, then reached for the control. It was already tuned to Zed.

She pressed the button to speak. "Zed," she said. Her throat caught, and she closed her eyes tightly. "It's me, Kelly. Again."

There was no answer.

Kelly lost her nerve. She stepped away and closed the closet door, then went back downstairs to the kitchen. She paused at the doorway. Prowl had returned. He and Miko were standing by the sink talking quietly.

"He'll turn on us if he feels threatened," said Prowl. "And you know as well as I do that the police are looking for those of us who look different."

"What if we just . . . walk away?" whispered Miko.

Kelly's eyes widened. Did Miko want to escape from this nightmare too?

Prowl's nostrils flared and he glanced sharply at Kelly, detecting her presence.

Kelly hurriedly looked down and wished she'd been using her camouflage ability. "Hi," she said. She swallowed hard. Perhaps she could get them to trust her again. All Kelly knew was that things were growing scarier, and she needed somebody to talk to. Whether they wanted her around or not.

Prowl studied Kelly for a moment, then took pity on the girl and waved her to come in. He continued cautiously. "We need to do what he says for now. I'm afraid he's about to crack."

"Me too," said Miko.

Kelly took a few steps toward them but hung back, keeping her head lowered and trying not to cry. The soldiers' words were serious and frightening.

"Come over here," said Miko, seeing Kelly's face. "Are you doing okay, kiddo?"

The endearing term caught Kelly off guard and left her without her voice. She shrugged and stood with them, cautious and careful not to mess up —if she said the wrong thing, they likely wouldn't forgive her again. "I think he's terrible," Kelly finally said. "I want to go home. I'm sorry about what I said before."

The two soldiers exchanged looks, and Prowl nodded slightly. Then Miko put her hand on Kelly's shoulder. "Maybe when he's distracted, we can find our way out of here somehow."

Kelly's eyes threatened to flood, and she nodded. But there wasn't time for more conversation, because Braun came bumbling in.

"Kelly!" Braun said with a snort. He ruffled his quills and eyed Prowl, then continued. "Dr. Gray wants you to go with him."

"With him?" said Kelly, trying not to show the despair she was feeling. "Where?"

"Not back to the zoo again," muttered Miko. "Will he ever stop?"

"Not the zoo," said Braun. "He said something about the marina."

Kelly frowned. "Maybe he wants me to check on Mega," she said.

"Yeah—you could swim out to find her," said Miko. She paused, then gave Kelly's hand a subtle squeeze and said wistfully, "I wish I could leave the house. Have fun."

Braun eyed Miko. "If you wear your street clothes nobody will recognize you."

Miko stared at the porcupine-bull man as if he'd lost his mind. "Um . . . I don't think that's wise," she said sarcastically, indicating the wings and her hairy body. "I know I've done it before and all, but I'm sure we don't want to risk drawing attention right now."

"Cyke and I have gone out a few times after dark."

"Really?" asked Miko.

"I've seen you," said Prowl. "Does Dr. Gray know?" He seemed surprised that Braun would defy the scientist.

"He told me he doesn't care anymore. He said the people will have to get used to folks looking different real soon, so we might as well break them in. But maybe he just feels that way about Cyke and me. I'm not sure if he'd allow you two to do it." Braun looked hard at Prowl and Miko.

Prowl lifted his chin. "Why not?"

Braun shrugged and turned to go. "Maybe he's worried you might try to escape or something."

Miko and Prowl exchanged a nervous glance. "Interesting," said Miko. She glanced back at her wings. "I wouldn't want to get caught anyway."

Kelly wasn't sure what to think. And now she had to spend time with the increasingly paranoid doctor without anyone else around. She gave Miko and Prowl a grim smile and went to get a sweatshirt and her hat. While she was in the closet, she eyed Miko's bodysuits again.

"Kelly!" shouted Dr. Gray from the bottom of the stairs.

"Coming!" she said. She grabbed one of Miko's suits and detached the communication device from it, then stuffed that in her waist pack. If anything weird happened with Dr. Gray, she could at least contact Prowl through it.

Kelly closed her pack and clicked it around her waist. She zipped downstairs, slipping the sweatshirt over her head and cramming the hat on her head to hide her hair. Dr. Gray locked up the lab and they exited, leaving Cyke to keep watch.

The two went wordlessly down the street toward the lake. "What are we doing?" Kelly whispered eventually.

"We're sightseeing," said Dr. Gray, heading to a ferry. "I've been curious about that big island in the lake, haven't you?"

"I guess," said Kelly. She hadn't given it much thought after Dr. Gray had told her about the enormous statue. But it seemed extremely odd for Dr. Gray to suddenly want to leave his work and go visit.

Kelly knew she needed to pretend like everything was normal, like Prowl had said in the kitchen. She searched for something to say that would make her sound loyal. "So," she said, "are you still planning to give me an extra . . . you know what?" It was about the last thing Kelly wanted at this point. But Kelly was an actor, and she faked it well.

Dr. Gray's face flickered. "You'll have your answer soon enough."

"So that's a . . . yes?"

Dr. Gray sighed. "Yes. Soon."

"Okay, okay," said Kelly. "Thanks. I'm excited."

The paranoid man glanced at her, suspicious, but Kelly's expression seemed honest. "Good," he said.

Kelly quietly let out a held breath.

The ferry took them to a commercial dock on the island. The pair disembarked and followed signs to a taxi stand, where they caught a ride to the statue at the center of the island. Once there, Dr. Gray and Kelly went with a crowd of tourists going inside the statue. They avoided the museums and shops on the various lower floors, and instead focused on climbing up the endless flights of winding stairs through the body of the statue. It was an exhausting climb, but it made Kelly feel good to get some exercise again after being stuck in the house for so long. Dr. Gray, as tired as he'd seemed in the lab, appeared to be reenergized by this place.

At the top, they went under an archway and out a door to the observation deck. As they caught their breath after the climb, Dr. Gray strolled around the space, looking out over the island and water. "Lovely," he said. "Very interesting."

Kelly looked around. It was cool being all the way up here, with the breeze on her cheeks. She could see for miles, and for the first time in a while she felt like she was free, even though Dr. Gray was right there. It would be so sweet to soar out over the world without any worries. It made her think of Miko and her wings.

Kelly's eyes widened. *Miko has wings.* She could fly herself across the border back home. She didn't need Prowl or her or any of them. Had she already thought of this? Sure, the US was far away, but Miko had a way out of here and nobody could catch her if she tried it. It made Kelly's stomach twist a little, thinking about it. Would Miko ever leave them if things got too bad? She'd certainly been practicing her flying a lot lately.

Then Kelly's thoughts turned to herself. With a start she wondered if *she* could escape somehow using her camouflage and hypnotism. Could she get past airport security? Sneak onto a plane without a ticket? It gave her a stomachache to think about. Maybe she could swim to freedom. . . .

Dr. Gray motioned to Kelly that it was time to go back to their

hideout. Wordlessly Kelly followed, still thinking about Miko. They went down in the elevator this time, stuck with a crowd of tourists, then caught a taxi back to the ferry.

As they cruised across the lake to the mainland, Kelly hung over the railing and looked around for signs of Mega, but she didn't see her. She turned to Dr. Gray. "I wonder how Mega's doing. I thought maybe that's why you brought me along? To check on her?"

Dr. Gray started. "What? No. I just wanted to make sure you were nearby in case I was in need of your talents. . . . And I thought it might do you well to get away from the soldiers for a while." The man shrugged and turned to look back at the island. "I can't worry about Mega right now."

Kelly couldn't stop her face from wrinkling in disgust as she stared at the back of Dr. Gray's head. What a horrible thing to say about someone who had given so much of her life to help him. If Kelly had had any sympathy left for the doctor, it was gone now. He was a disgusting monster.

Back at the house, Dr. Gray nodded to Cyke in greeting. "Let's have you and Prowl face off in the backyard so I can evaluate your new abilities. Komodo dragon versus electric eel."

Cyke nodded and went to find Prowl.

A few minutes later the two were fighting viciously, attacking and rolling around and yelping and yowling, while Dr. Gray observed intently and took notes.

Later he returned to his lab with a spring in his step that hadn't been present in weeks. He closed the door and locked it, then went to his lab station, where beakers filled with various formulas stood in a line. He studied them, then pushed a few aside and drew the rest around a larger empty one.

He hesitated, frowned, then moved the beakers he'd pushed aside back to their original places with the others. "Don't second-guess," he muttered. His fingers shook slightly. "You've had years to decide on some of these. It's time."

With a deep breath, the biologist measured and poured a tiny amount of the first beaker into the empty one. Then he added the next. And so on, until he'd transferred them all. He mixed them, then held the compound up to the light. "Just about ready."

Victor went to a locked cabinet and opened it, then pulled out a vial containing a small amount of liquid. He brought it to the table and poured it into the mixture.

With a startling laugh, he brought the new formula to the mist machine and went to pour it into the chamber, but then he hesitated. He slowly set the beaker down, frowning. "Timing, timing," he muttered. "Let's not rush this. Think it through."

He put a stopper on the beaker and slid it, along with a syringe, into his lab coat pocket for later. He paused, thinking, then went back to the line of beakers. He pulled a large, empty container from the sterilization cabinet and set it on the counter, then began to pour all the remaining liquids into it, except for the one he'd kept locked away. "There," he muttered. He mixed it, then sealed the container and set it on the edge of the table near the door. He rubbed his eyes and shook his head as if he were arguing with himself. "A bit of sleep first might help. This must go perfectly."

While his back was turned, a ladybug flew off the table and hid in the corner of a windowsill, and a dragonfly slowly backed into the lab sink drain until it was safe to come out again. They had recorded everything.

CHAPTER 35

A Reason to Panic

At the Phoenix airport, the team of doctors and children waited near the gate for their flight to board. Most of them were seated and either reading or working on their phones or tablets. Only Dr. Jakande paced the aisle, going to the window occasionally to peer anxiously for their plane to arrive. She glanced at her new device, similar to Maria's, which would turn her into a werepanther and allow her to look human when she needed to. After so many years as a hybrid, she sometimes felt a bit odd having human skin again—it almost seemed like she was missing part of herself without her fur and bodysuit. She brought the suit in her carry-on for when she'd need it. It doubled as a security blanket in a way. She could use the extra layer as protection, but perhaps she'd also grown used to hiding behind it.

But Nubia was getting used to being her old self again, and liking the freedom of it. She glanced at the time and frowned, then returned to the group. "Our plane isn't here yet," she muttered to Dr. Goldstein.

He grunted and looked up from his work. "What's that?"

"The plane," she said, stabbing her thumb in that direction. "It isn't here yet. We're supposed to be boarding."

Jack looked out the window. "Maybe it's late. I'll check." He typed something into his tablet and pulled up details on the inbound plane. "Hmm," he said. "Delayed. Which means we'll be delayed too."

Charlie looked over, having overheard the conversation. "How late will it be?" They had a bus to catch once they got to Guadalajara, and it was a long ride. Hours, her mom had told her.

Dr. Sharma seemed about to speak, but her phone began to buzz. "It's Erica," she told the others, and answered it. "Hi. Our plane's running late. What's going on?" Dr. Sharma listened for a long moment, at times her eyes widening.

"What is it?" asked Charlie's mom.

Dr. Sharma held a finger up and kept listening. Finally she said into the phone, "Keep us posted. I'll let you know when we're about to take off. We're coming as fast as we can."

Just then the airline representative came on the loudspeaker. "Guadalajara passengers, flight 975 has been delayed. The new boarding time is four p.m."

A murmur spread through the waiting area as people expressed their dissatisfaction.

"That's almost two hours," said Mac to Maria and Charlie. "We're definitely going to miss our bus."

Mrs. Wilde was up like a shot and heading to the counter to get more information. The rest of the group gathered around Dr.

Goldstein, who was looking online for other flights. Dr. Sharma's conversation with Ms. Sabbith was momentarily forgotten while they assessed how this delay would affect their plans.

Charlie's mom returned a moment later. "There's nothing they can do," she said. "No other nonstop flights go out today. This is still our fastest option. I think we just wait it out." She sighed, annoyed. "I'll see what I can do about the bus."

"I'll help you," said Dr. Goldstein, already typing. "Maybe we could hire a passenger van."

Mr. Wilde agreed. "That might be faster than waiting for the next bus."

The adults got to work trying to figure out the best way for them to proceed, while Mac, Maria, and Charlie looked fearfully at one another. Finally, Maria tapped Dr. Sharma on the shoulder. "What did Ms. Sabbith say?"

Dr. Sharma looked up, harried. "Oh! Sorry. She said Dr. Gray is further along than we expected." Her expression turned grim. "He just put together two formulas. A small batch that appears to be only for himself, but he hasn't used it yet. The other is much larger. We don't need to guess what that's for."

Dr. Sharma continued. "Since he's got our vapor machine working again, it probably wouldn't take much work to modify it to work on a larger scale. He'd be able to release it as mist into the air and infect a lot of people at once."

"And he's ready to go?" Charlie asked, looking terrified.

"Like, now? Before we get there?"

"He seems ready," Dr. Sharma confirmed. "The formulas are done. He just needs to decide where and when to release them. Sabbith said he went out somewhere with Kelly this morning."

Dr. Jakande leaned forward. "Is Erica sure that one of the formulas is for himself? I never expected him to undergo the transformation—he's never done it in the past. I always thought he would be too cowardly."

"That's what she's assuming."

"Maybe he ran out of soldiers to test things on," said Maria.

"It's interesting," said Dr. Sharma. "Erica said he added something to his dose that's not in the larger formula."

Mr. Wilde looked sharply over at them. "He added something to it? More DNA?"

"I don't know," said Dr. Sharma. "He kept it in a locked cabinet."

Mr. Wilde tapped a finger on his chin, eyes narrowed. "He hasn't used that jellyfish on anyone, has he?"

"Not that we know of."

"He sure wanted it badly, though, didn't he?"

"He went out multiple times in search of it," said Dr. Sharma slowly, thinking hard.

Charlie piped up. "They were looking for it all the way back when we saw them at SeaWorld."

Mr. Wilde glanced at his daughter, then turned abruptly back to his tablet and began typing. "Jellyfish. Jellyfish. I remember . . . something . . ." Just as abruptly his fingers stopped typing and he stared at the screen. "The *Turritopsis dohrnii*," he said under his breath. "Just as I thought."

Charlie and the others exchanged uneasy looks.

Mr. Wilde's gaze flitted down the screen as he speed-read the article. After a moment, he looked up. "When I was researching animal healing properties years ago, I came across something that tempted me, but ultimately I passed on it for obvious reasons."

"Charles," said Dr. Sharma, "what are you talking about?"

Mr. Wilde blew out a breath and looked up. "I think I know exactly what Victor is planning. I bet he gave himself DNA from the immortal jellyfish. He wants to live forever."

CHAPTER 36

A Race to Stop Dr. Gray

As the plane drew up to the gate, Mac, Maria, and Charlie read about the immortal jellyfish. They studied the details, looking slightly horrified. After a minute, Mac set his tablet down. "I guess, unlike most animals, it doesn't grow old and die," he said. "It, uh, becomes an adult, and then it decides to just go back to being a kid and starts its, um, life cycle, all over again. And it can keep doing that forever?"

"That," said Maria, sitting back, "is crazy. So, Dr. Gray *wants* to be a kid again? He's been hanging out with Kelly too long."

Charlie nodded. "Really glad Dad didn't put *that* in my bracelet. One time going through puberty is enough, thank you very much."

"You said it," said Mac.

With this new revelation churning through their thoughts, Charlie and her friends finally boarded the plane and took off for Mexico. The flight felt immortal too—like it lasted forever.

Once they got to Guadalajara, their hired driver was waiting to take them to the address Ms. Sabbith had given them. It was a long trip, and by the time they got to the town, it was well past midnight. Bored, and with their laptop and tablet batteries dead, Charlie, Mac, and Maria messed around with their bracelets. Charlie kept accidentally activating her night vision and chirping, making everyone cranky. And Mac inadvertently clicked into pangolin mode, smashing the girls into their windows. Thankfully it was dark and Mac was able to change back before the driver noticed.

At last they arrived at the house. Ms. Sabbith came out to greet them as they unloaded their equipment and luggage.

"Anything new happening?" Dr. Sharma asked anxiously.

"Not yet." Ms. Sabbith looked exhausted. She'd slept fewer hours than Dr. Gray had, since she was alone and constantly monitoring what he was doing. When he was sleeping, she'd had to double-check the other cameras to make sure she hadn't missed something important. It was a tough job to perform solo.

Once inside, Ms. Sabbith showed everyone the setup. According to the insect cameras, the lab was currently unlocked and the door to the room was standing open. "This hasn't happened since I arrived," said Ms. Sabbith. "Victor spoke secretly to Cyke, Braun, Fang, and Morph. Then he took the two formulas and went to his bedroom."

Prowl stood guard by the front door. As they watched him, they could see Braun and Cyke come inside.

"None of them are wearing their masks," said Maria. "That's strange."

"They haven't been," said Ms. Sabbith. "Miko gave up her suit entirely. When Braun and Cyke go out, they wear street clothes. Braun covers up his quills, but not his face. Either they're feeling emboldened by what Dr. Gray is planning, or they think they are less likely to be apprehended because the news has the photos of them in their full bodysuits."

"Where's Kelly?" asked Mac.

"She shares a bedroom with Miko upstairs. As far as I know, she's sleeping."

"Speaking of sleep," said Mr. Wilde, "we should all try to get some."

Ms. Sabbith pulled herself away from the screens and showed everyone where they could put their things. Dr. Sharma insisted Ms. Sabbith get some rest, too. "I'll watch Gray's place for a while. Don't worry."

Ms. Sabbith gave her a grateful look. "I appreciate it. Wake me if anything happens."

"I will."

Charlie, Maria, and Mac found a room with two sets of bunk beds. They collapsed in them, not even arguing over who got the top. They fell asleep fast and slept hard.

At the surveillance table, Dr. Sharma monitored the screens until her eyes dried out. She rubbed them, then got up and paced the floor in order to keep herself awake. Nearing dawn, with nothing happening in Dr. Gray's house, she convinced herself she could take a short nap just so she could be refreshed enough to take action in the morning if they needed her. She set an alarm and nodded off.

When it eventually went off, startling her awake, Dr. Sharma turned immediately to the recordings to see if she'd missed anything.

The footage caught Dr. Gray leaving his bedroom. Without fanfare, he carried the mist machine and the large cylinder of liquid past Prowl and outside. Braun and Cyke followed. Then Morph and Fang.

"Where is everybody going?" Prowl asked the last two. "What's happening?"

Fang stopped and looked coldly at him. "Dr. Gray didn't tell you?"

Prowl shook his head.

"I guess you're not meant to know, then. I had a feeling he didn't trust you anymore."

Prowl's eyes widened and his new electric claws came out sparking. But he seemed too stunned to do anything. Fang shrugged and went out the door, closing it behind him.

The leopard man waited a beat, then looked around uncertainly, like he wasn't sure what to do. Eventually he sneaked out the door after them.

Dr. Sharma's eyes widened. The cameras didn't pick up what happened next. She fast-forwarded.

Prowl returned to the house, striding with purpose up the stairs. Several minutes later he came back down with Miko and Kelly behind him. The three were talking heatedly. "They're heading toward the marina," Prowl said. "They've got the formula."

With that revelation, Dr. Sharma shot up and ran to wake Ms. Sabbith. If that happened while she was asleep, what could be going on now? Was it already too late to stop them?

Charlie roused with a start when she heard footsteps pounding down the hallway. She woke up Mac and Maria, and the three of them peered around the corner into the surveillance area. They saw Ms. Sabbith, hair disheveled, rapidly working the computer with Dr. Sharma looking over her shoulder.

"Come on," said Mac. "Something's happening." He ran up to the screen. The girls followed.

Ms. Sabbith rewound the video. They watched Dr. Gray leave with the machine and the formula, then Cyke and Braun. She zoomed in on Prowl's face, showing his confusion, and they heard the conversation Prowl had with Fang.

"Can that be true?" whispered Dr. Sharma. "Is Prowl no longer trusted?"

"It can't be," muttered Ms. Sabbith. "Why would he be guarding the door if Dr. Gray didn't trust him? Fang is just trying to get under Prowl's skin. He probably doesn't like it that Prowl is one of Gray's favorites."

"That makes more sense," said Dr. Sharma.

They quieted and fast-forwarded through the part where Prowl left the house, and the part where he went upstairs. Then Ms. Sabbith slowed the video again where he came back down with Miko and Kelly.

"All of them," Prowl was saying. "Everyone but us three."

"But where are they going?" asked Miko. "Was Gray carrying the formula?"

"Yes. And he had the mist machine."

"So . . . ," said Miko, "he's going somewhere to somehow spray that stuff? And then everyone around will change into chimeras?" She shook her head in disbelief.

"Why the marina?" demanded Kelly.

"Let's go find out," muttered Miko. She said a few other things under her breath, but the insect microphones weren't able to pick them up.

Watching everything, Charlie was confused. Why weren't these three a part of this? Had they done something to make Dr. Gray mad? What was going on?

"Kids," said Ms. Sabbith, "go get ready. Right away. I'm going to see if I can find out where they're heading. And with any luck, our little ladybug here is going to find them and tag along."

CHAPTER 37

The Chase Is On

"Let's not forget these." Dr. Sharma handed the kids their earpieces for the new communication system. They inserted them and performed a quick test. Everything appeared to be working.

By now Ms. Sabbith had guided the ladybug drone onto Prowl's shoulder. She turned on the GPS system, which showed the bug's location. "Got it," she said. Three more dots appeared, representing Mac, Maria, and Charlie. "Quinn, can you wake up the others? I don't know exactly what is happening, but it's time to act."

"I'm not sure why Dr. Gray left without Prowl, Miko, and Kelly," said Maria, "but we should take them out while we have the chance. While they're separated from the others."

"Great idea," said Charlie grimly. She peered out the window and down the street, seeing it in daylight for the first time. "Where are we? Which way are they going?"

"They're going toward the lake, which is down the hill," said Ms. Sabbith. She pointed at the map and showed everyone where their house was, where Dr. Gray's house was, and a few other various landmarks to help them navigate in the unfamiliar place. "You can't get lost. We're between the park and the marina, up the hill past the shops."

"Okay," said Charlie. "We should go right now. What are we waiting for?"

"Don't we need Dr. Jakande and your dad?" asked Mac.

Charlie shook her head impatiently. "It's just the three of them. We can handle them. Dad and Dr. J. can follow us when they're ready. This is our chance to stop them before they catch up to Dr. Gray."

Ms. Sabbith and Dr. Sharma glanced at each other, and then Dr. Sharma nodded. "Okay, you can go. But only engage them if you know you can beat them. Otherwise wait and follow."

"And stay in touch," said Ms. Sabbith. "I know you're not used to talking into your bracelets, but we need to hear from you when you can manage it. We'll let you know if we see a way to help you from here. And if you get lost, I'll guide you. Just remember what I told you before and you'll be fine. We believe in you."

"Got it," said Charlie. She took off toward the door, but a second later Dr. Jakande appeared, looking sleepy and disheveled. "Charlie, wait!" she called. "What are you doing?"

"We can handle it, Dr. Jakande. I promise. It's just Miko, Prowl, and Kelly. We've got to go now so we don't lose track of them."

"Are you sure?"

Charlie nodded.

"Okay. But hold on just one more second." Dr. Jakande disappeared inside her room.

"What is it?" said Charlie, impatient to get going.

The woman reappeared and held out her body suit. "Here. Wear this. It'll help protect you, at least a little."

Charlie stared. "What about them?"

"Mac has his pangolin suit. Maria's alligator scales will help her. But you don't have anything. I meant to make you one, but I ran out of time. Take it. Please."

Charlie hesitated a second more, then took the suit, yelling, "Thanks!" as she ran into the bathroom to put it on. A minute later she was out the door and in the driveway, connecting the mask to the suit but leaving it hanging down her back for now.

Maria and Mac followed right behind. Mac took a preventative hit on his inhaler, then the three of them started jogging downhill, anxious to locate the soldiers and Kelly. It was barely light out, and very few people were up and about around them.

"It's weird not having a clue where we are," said Maria. She lifted her wrist to her mouth and tried out her microphone to make sure Ms. Sabbith could still hear her.

"I've got you loud and clear," the woman told them all through their earpieces. "You're heading in the right direction. The ladybug cam has been stationary near the marina for a while now, like they're waiting for something. You're just a couple blocks behind them."

"Thanks, Ms. Sabbith," said Charlie into her device. They sped up.

A few minutes of jogging had them in sight of the lake, too. The early morning sun shone a sparkling white path from the water's edge to a quarter of the way out. The kids could see a big island in the middle of the lake. Near the shore a few blocks to their right was the park Ms. Sabbith had mentioned. To the left was the marina with several boats and a public ferry. A few fishermen were up and moving around the wharf.

Charlie thought she caught a glimpse of three people moving. She pointed. "Is that them?" she asked.

"I think so," said Maria. She looked around carefully.

"The ladybug cam is still near the marina," said Ms. Sabbith in their ears.

"That's them all right," said Mac. He pressed to talk. "Thanks, Ms. Sabbith. We see them."

"Ten-four. Remember, call me if you need me."

Mac glanced around to see if there were any onlookers, then engaged his device, switching on the basilisk lizard to help him move faster and more easily.

"What are you doing?" asked Charlie, whirling around. "People could see you."

"Eh," said Mac with a shrug. "Maybe they'll think it's a costume. I don't think we can care about that at the moment. Plus, I can move way faster this way without getting winded."

Charlie raised an eyebrow, but his reasoning made sense.

Maria pressed her lips together, then clicked on her device too, becoming a weremonkey. "Being seen in public doesn't matter anymore with so much at stake," she said. "Besides, Prowl and Miko look pretty weird too. Maybe people will think we're in a parade or going to a costume party."

"Early morning costume parties are all the rage," muttered Charlie. But she didn't blame her friends. She had all her abilities activated too, only she didn't have to worry about anybody noticing. "Let's go with the parade idea if anybody questions us."

They rounded the corner and suddenly Prowl, Miko, and Kelly were within spitting range, standing in the road and arguing. Prowl had left his mask off and Miko was full-fledged animal with her hairy chimp body and enormous wings. "Watch out," whispered Charlie. She hid behind a parked car and peered over the hood. Kelly and the soldiers were now looking everywhere, like they'd lost something.

Maria and Mac knelt behind Charlie. "How are we going to do this?" said Maria, glancing around the street and spotting things she could potentially use to jump off of or swing around.

"I'm thinking," said Charlie. She inched forward.

In their ears, Ms. Sabbith spoke up. "Charles and Nubia leaving shortly."

The kids didn't respond. Charlie glanced at the others, took a deep breath, and then double-checked that her speed, strength,

293

and climbing abilities were on. As long Kelly stayed visible, Charlie didn't need the infrared vision. She weighed options, trying to decide the best way for the three to attack. "I'll go after Prowl," she whispered. "Maria, take Miko. Mac . . . can you take on Kelly?"

Mac frowned. Fighting against Kelly seemed weird, but somebody had to do it—she was an enemy now. He nodded to Charlie. Staying crouched, he awkwardly switched to his pangolin armor to protect himself from Kelly's spikes. That would give him his claws to fight back . . . or maybe even just rip her bracelet off. He didn't have to hurt her, he realized with relief. He just had to capture her and remove the device.

"Okay," whispered Charlie. "Everybody do your thing. Let's go." Charlie sprang up and charged, speeding across the street. Maria and Mac followed. Charlie went straight at Prowl, grabbing him around the torso before he knew what was happening and picking him up high in the air so he couldn't reach her face with his claws. He yowled and swiped at her, missing, then sliced her forearm.

"Ouch!" Charlie cried as blood surfaced and poured out of the wound. Furious, she threw Prowl as far as she could, sending him half a block up the hill and landing hard. Charlie chased after him.

Maria bounded up the side of a different parked car and jumped on Miko. The chimp woman hit the sidewalk, but her wings broke her fall. She grabbed Maria's shoulders and rolled her over. Then she hopped up, spread her wings, and took flight, staying low in the air and trying to attack Maria from above. She swooped low and reached out, grabbing the girl by her tail and carrying her up in the air. Maria shrieked, twisting and turning as she swung her fists, and tried to get free or get Miko to go down to ground level.

By the time Mac got to Kelly, she'd realized what was happening. Quickly she activated her device and looked to see who was coming at her. Mac slowed, uncertain. It was *really* weird taking on Kelly, especially now that she was right in front of him. He wasn't sure what to do. At least she couldn't hurt him. Maybe he could just let her attack him for a while, like the pangolin does with a lion. It might tire her out, at least. He stood there, waiting for her to make a move.

Kelly rushed at him. "Oh my gosh! Mac!" she said. "What are you doing here? Did you come to rescue me? Can you help me get home?"

"What?" said Mac, taken aback. Was she trying to throw him off guard? Of course she was. She was the sneakiest person he'd ever known. Mac stared at the girl, growing angry. "Nice try, Kelly. Surprise, you're still horrible."

He thought of all the awful things she'd done to them. She'd lied about using the Mark Four. She'd left them to go be with Dr. Gray after all they'd done to protect her. After all they'd tried to do for her. She'd hypnotized her own parents into forgetting her. And she'd attacked at least four people with her extremely dangerous platypus spikes—including Andy and that freaking government official who was in a coma. Kelly was bad news.

Kelly stopped. Now she looked confused. "How did you find us?"

Mac's eyes narrowed. Another ploy. He was ready to look away in an instant if she decided to try that little hypnotism trick on him. He didn't trust her for a second. He didn't care what she said. She was an actor. Always playing a part. This person in front of him wasn't the real Kelly he used to know. The one who'd given him money to buy a new iPad when his had been stolen by the same people she was fighting alongside now. This Kelly was someone trying to manipulate him. Someone trying to get him to let down his guard. And Mac was not having any more of Kelly Parker.

"Mac?" she said, her eyes pleading. "You . . . you remember me, right? It's me. Kelly."

Mac remembered all right. Everything about her was making him angry. "I sure do." Without another thought, he wound up and slugged Kelly in the face with his pangolin claws. She hit the ground, stunned and unmoving. Mac scrambled to take the device off her wrist. But like the others, it was locked on. In the confusion of getting there and their scramble out the door, they'd forgotten to get the code from Dr. Sharma. Could he rip it off without taking her hand with it?

Maria screamed overhead. Mac looked up and he let Kelly's arm drop. Miko was swinging Maria around by the tip of her tail, flying uncomfortably high. Maria was trying desperately to grab on to one of Miko's legs, but failing to reach them. One lurch and Maria could be trying to fly, too.

Leaving Kelly on the side of the road, Mac switched to basilisk lizard mode so he could run properly. He stayed below Maria in case the flying monkey decided to drop her. If she did, he'd be there to catch her. "Let go of her!" he shouted. "Go back to Oz, you flying monkey!"

Kelly rolled to her side, then gingerly felt her throbbing jaw and hoped nothing was broken. Her face clouded. Clearly Mac and the others hadn't come here to rescue her. Maybe Dr. Gray had been telling the truth about them—maybe they were the bad guys after all. Everything was so confusing.

With Mac distracted, Kelly turned her camouflage ability on and staggered to her feet. She limped down the dock to the ferry and leaned up against the side of it to catch her breath. People trickled aboard for a ride to the island. Kelly watched them for a moment, listening to them talk about the landmarks. And then she slowly turned to look at the island in the distance: the houses dotted prettily all the way up. The giant statue rising above all of them. "Oh," she said softly. "So that's where he went."

CHAPTER 38

A Dangerous Turn

Charlie kicked at Prowl, but he rolled and she missed. He hopped up and they ran at each other in the street, the leopard man trying at every turn to sink his claws into Charlie—he knew how much she hated that. The two had fought multiple times in the past, but this time Prowl had a little surprise for his old enemy. When she twisted away and ran at him again, he slammed his claws into her shoulders and sent a bolt of electricity through her.

Charlie screamed. Dr. Jakande's suit didn't seem to help in this case. A few locals heard her cries and came out of their shops and houses to see what was happening. Three of them started toward the fight, shouting in Spanish. But Charlie, furious at the electric cat, grabbed Prowl by the ankles and flipped him backward, high in the air. He landed, cracking his skull on the ground, and groaned. Charlie picked him up again and swung him around and around in a circle, clearing the area and sending the people running for cover. She let the man fly and he went wriggling through the air, trying to turn himself so he'd land on his feet. He failed and skidded into the side of a pottery shop, breaking its showcase window and knocking a sign down. It landed on his head.

Charlie gripped her aching shoulders and took the moment to look around for the others. Kelly was nowhere in sight, which wasn't surprising. Maria was being flown around by Miko, with Mac running dutifully below. Maria reached out whenever she saw something she could grab on to, but Miko always kept her just outside of reach.

"Use Turbo!" Charlie hollered at her friend, in case Maria hadn't thought of it. "Or switch to alligator!"

"I need to stay a monkey in case she drops me!" Maria hollered back.

Prowl was getting up and pulling glass shards out of his shoulders. Charlie turned her attention back to him. He started heading up the street away from the water, trying to get away from her, which seemed odd.

Charlie followed, wondering uneasily what had happened to Kelly—maybe Mac had clobbered her. Or maybe Prowl was leading her into a trap and the girl was waiting for her. Charlie activated her viper vision and swept her gaze around, just in case. Nothing. Just as she was catching up to Prowl, he turned and came at her with his electric claws again. Charlie stopped. She had to avoid those at all costs—they'd been a real shocker. And even though her starfish ability had kicked in, Charlie was still sore and shaky from it. It was a powerful ability. Too powerful. "Dang it, Prowl," she muttered.

Above the shops, Maria went into Turbo monkey mode, and

her arms, legs, and tail grew four inches. Not realizing it, Miko flew too close to a church roof. Maria's arm shot out and caught the tip of the steeple spire. She yanked herself loose from Miko's grasp and slid down to the belfry, then went inside the opening where the bell hung. She climbed down and disappeared. Mac stood at the base of the church, looking up.

"Mac!" shouted Charlie. "Help me with Prowl! His claws are electric now!"

Seeing Charlie's fear, the leopard man came at her. Mac switched to basilisk lizard and ran toward them. Charlie darted out of Prowl's reach, then jumped and stuck to the side of a building. She crawled up, then leaped on top of Prowl's head, knocking him down. Swiftly she pinned his arms to the ground. He struggled under her.

Mac caught up and switched back to pangolin.

"Sit on him until the others come," said Charlie. "And chop him up into little pieces if he tries to move." She looked around again and saw Maria exiting the church doors and coming toward them. "Now, where's Miko?"

Mac obeyed. Prowl yowled and flailed and tried to squeeze out from under Mac, swiping at him with his sharp claws, but they clanged and sparked off Mac's armor. When Mac had had enough of the soldier's squirming, he cracked his pangolin claws down onto Prowl's forearms, pinning them. He looked around to make sure nobody else was coming for him, and saw Miko swooping down toward Maria and Charlie.

"Look out!" Mac shouted, but he was too late. Miko plowed into both girls, knocking them flat, then soared up again out of reach.

Charlie flipped over and scrambled up, then helped Maria to her feet. They chased after Miko. "When she flies back at us, climb up onto this truck and grab her," Charlie whispered to Maria. They waited, then both bounded up on top of the truck parked along the street. Before Miko could swerve, the girls jumped at her, grabbing onto her legs.

"Hang on!" cried Maria.

Miko shrieked. Her wings weren't strong enough to hold two of them. The three crashed to the ground and rolled. Maria got the wind knocked out of her and couldn't move. But Charlie twisted Miko's leg hard behind her and knelt on it. Miko hollered and flapped her wings wildly, trying to get Charlie off her. Charlie nearly lost her balance but lunged forward onto Miko's back, slamming the soldier's face into the pavement. She gave a muffled shout. Quickly Charlie scrambled up and stepped on the back of Miko's neck. Miko flopped but couldn't get away.

"Maria!" Charlie called out. "Are you okay?"

Maria rolled over slowly. "I'm okay," she said, her voice shaky. She tried to get up.

Just then they heard a long, angry buzzing sound. Mac screamed. They looked over to see smoke rising from Mac's suit, and he fell limp on top of Prowl. Prowl cackled, then slithered out from under him.

"Mac!" Charlie couldn't make sense of what had happened. Mac's pangolin suit was supposed to protect him from everything.

Maria staggered to her feet. "Leave him alone!" she screamed at Prowl. She switched to alligator mode and ran at him, teeth gleaming. Surprised, Prowl stared. Maria attacked, trying to take a bite out of his shoulder, and they hit the road hard. He sliced Maria with his electric claws. and she screamed and stiffened, momentarily paralyzed by the shock. Her alligator scales were as useless as Charlie's suit against electricity.

Frustrated and knowing Mac needed help, Charlie picked up Miko and threw her hard against the church wall. The woman crumpled to the ground and didn't move. Charlie checked her to see that she was breathing but unconscious. She left her there and went after Prowl. "Go see if Mac's okay!" Charlie called to Maria.

Maria went over to Mac, trying to get his helmet off so she could see his face. "Mac!" she cried out. "Mac, answer me!"

Mac didn't answer. He didn't move.

"It smells like something's burning!" said Maria, fear in her voice.

Charlie couldn't inspect him now. She dodged Prowl's claws and slammed her head into his stomach, hoping to do double damage to an already injured part of him. The cat man howled and hissed, claws fully extended. He managed to clip Charlie's cheek, sending another shock all the way down her body.

"Ahh! Dang it!" she said. Blazing with anger, she gave an uppercut to Prowl's jaw, sending him soaring into the air and slamming down onto the pavement. He rolled to one side and stopped, unconscious.

From up the hill, Charlie's father and Dr. Jakande came running onto the scene. Dr. Jakande was transformed into a werepanther, and Dr. Wilde was wearing the Mark Five and moving pretty fast for a dad.

"We found you," said Dr. Wilde. He hesitated, looking at Prowl lying still on the ground. "What can we do?"

Dr. Jakande looked aghast at Prowl. Then she noticed her old friend Miko unconscious alongside the church and blew out a breath. She turned away. "Where's Kelly?"

"We don't know," said Charlie, staggering to her feet. "Can you go help Mac? He's over there with Maria. Somehow Prowl knocked him unconscious. He's got that electric eel ability now, so be careful. Maria said she smelled something burning." She bent down, then hoisted Prowl up over her shoulders.

Dr. Jakande rushed over to Mac and Maria. Charlie followed with the unconscious electricat. Nubia quickly tapped the device on Mac's wrist. The suit turned to liquid and shimmered back into his bracelet.

"Charles, we're going to need your device over here for Mac," said Dr. Jakande in a low voice. "Hurry."

"What's wrong with him?" asked Charlie, alarmed.

"I think he was electrocuted."

"How is that possible?" asked Charlie. She and Maria exchanged a horrified glance.

Dr. Wilde ran over. "Take off his device!" he said. Dr. Jakande keyed in the passcode and took off Mac's device. Dr. Wilde removed the Mark Five from his wrist and slapped it onto Mac's in place of the other.

"Why did you take his off?" asked Maria, frightened.

"I'm not sure what wearing two bracelets could do to him," said Dr. Jakande. "It's already risky with all the DNA in the Mark Five."

Maria held Mac's other hand. "Is the healing ability lit up?" she asked.

"Yes," said Dr. Jakande, leaning over Mac. After a moment, she sighed with relief. "He's doing better."

Charlie, relieved, and seeing she couldn't do anything to help, dropped Prowl roughly to the sidewalk. She spotted a large metal rack with room for six bikes bolted to the sidewalk. She went over to it and yanked it out, sending the bolts flying. Then she bent the rack in half until it snapped into two equal pieces. She took one half and slid it over Prowl's body, trapping his arms at his sides. Then she lifted him up and set him on the side of the road and went to get Miko.

With the other half of the rack Charlie secured Miko, squishing the woman's wings and arms inside the metal makeshift trap. She placed Miko next to Prowl on the side of the road and returned to where her father and Dr. Jakande were hunched over Mac. Mac's eyes were open and he seemed to be talking.

"He's okay," Maria told her with relief in her voice.

"I'm fine," said Mac, struggling to sit up. "At least, I'll be okay in a bit. Go find Kelly!"

"Did you get her bracelet?" asked Charlie.

"No, it needs a code, remember? I don't know what it is."

Charlie stared blankly. They'd forgotten all about it. "Dang it. Why didn't we get that from Dr. Sharma? Did you ask her for it?" asked Charlie.

"I didn't think of that," Mac admitted. "I was worried about Maria."

"It's okay. I'll take care of it." She looked at her father. "Thanks for helping with Prowl. You didn't get to use the device for very long."

Dr. Wilde waved her off. "I'm really okay with that. I think I pulled a muscle already."

"Take care of those two," Charlie said, pointing to Prowl and Miko. "Don't let them go."

Her father nodded. "Nubia and I will carry them back to the house."

"Once we get there we can use the reversal devices to take away their powers," said Dr. Jakande. "Oh, and some good news, finally. Captain Zimmerman got in touch with Erica as we were leaving the house. She watched your videos. That, combined with what Gray and the soldiers have done, was enough to convince her. She put a team together and they're on their way."

Dr. Wilde nodded. "Hopefully they make it here in time to help."

Charlie let out a breath and swept the area with her infrared vision. "That's great news. Too bad they didn't get here yesterday. We could use the help now." She didn't see anything suspicious. "In more urgent news, we need to find Kelly. Mac, what happened?"

"She asked me if we were here to rescue her. I almost wimped out, but I knew she had to be lying like she always does. So I punched her with my pangolin claws. She went down, but then she disappeared when I went to help Maria." He paused. "She didn't hurt me. Prowl, on the other hand . . . I think the electricity went through my entire suit."

"The metallic alloy of your suit conducts electricity," said Dr. Jakande. "I'm glad you're okay. That could have been a lot worse without the Mark Five."

Maria, still worried, squeezed Mac's hand. He pulled it away, but then smiled sheepishly at his friend. "I'm fine," he insisted. "I'll probably be ready to help in, like, ten minutes or less. I'll find you. Just don't let Kelly get away."

Maria smiled back and turned to Charlie. "I'll go with you, Chuck," she said. "Let's get her."

Maria switched off her device so she wouldn't attract further attention, as more people were coming outside on this beautiful morning. Charlie kept her infrared viper vision on and the two girls set off.

As they walked, Maria checked in with Ms. Sabbith. She let her know what had happened so far. "Also, can you ask Dr. Sharma if she remembers the code for Kelly's device in case we get another shot at disarming her?"

Ms. Sabbith got it and gave it to her. "I'll send Mrs. Wilde to the scene to check Mac over."

Charlie and Maria combed the streets, Maria looking for signs of anything or anyone out of the ordinary, and Charlie looking for hot spots. They went all the way down to the water, then came back up the next street over, weaving in and out, looking behind trash bins and food stands and into alleyways.

"Do you suppose she's scared?" asked Maria after a while.

"With poisonous spikes?" scoffed Charlie. "Not even a little. She's probably lying in wait, thinking she can spring out and attack us both before we can figure out what's happening."

Maria looked troubled, but she nodded. "Probably."

When they found themselves in front of the marina, Maria stopped. "Hey," she said, tugging at Charlie's arm. "What if she, like, sneaked onto a boat?"

"Or escaped on the ferry," said Charlie. She pointed to a sign, trying to make sense of the Spanish words. She knew a few of them, but out of context they didn't make sense. "What does the sign say?"

"It says the ferry runs every hour starting at nine a.m. until six p.m. in the summer. It returns on the half hour. It costs eighty pesos each way."

"Whoa. That sounds like a lot."

"It's not," said Maria. "I looked up the exchange rate—it's less than five dollars. My mom got me some money from the bank before we left in case we need it."

"That was smart," said Charlie. She knew her parents had exchanged money at the airport, but they hadn't gotten around to giving her any yet. She used her viper vision to scan the ferry, which was about to take its ten a.m. voyage. Every red spot had a visible human behind it. "She's not here."

As they turned to go up the next street, Charlie heard a crackle near her ear. But it wasn't her earpiece from Ms. Sabbith. It was the one connected to Dr. Jakande's suit. Charlie froze as Kelly's voice came through, sounding pitiful. "Zed? Are you there? It's Kelly . . . Kelly Parker. Please answer. I'm in big trouble. And I . . . I just want to go home."

CHAPTER 39

The Only Way to Win

Kelly had watched with horror as Prowl and Miko had been captured. Scared, even though she was camouflaged, she fled, not quite sure where she was going. She ran downhill toward the lake and pressed up against the buildings, where she could blend in with the environment and keep away from other pedestrians who might bump into her. Desperate, she'd tried Zed again, even though the woman never answered her—she held out the tiniest hope that Zed could hear her, even if she couldn't or wouldn't respond.

There was no answer this time either. But Kelly wasn't going to give up easily—how could she? Charlie, Maria, Mac, and the scientists were her ticket out of here. But if she approached them, would they ever believe how sorry she was? Mac, of all people, had punched her lights out. Was it too late for her?

If Zed didn't answer, Kelly had no other choice but to try to convince her old friends. With Miko and Prowl captured, she was on her own. And out of options.

A friendly cat came up and rubbed against her leg, which probably would look strange to anyone passing by. Kelly nudged it away with her foot and soon it moved on. When no one was in sight, she pulled Miko's communication device out of her pack. She held the mouthpiece close and whispered into it. "Zed, I know where Dr. Gray is. Please . . . I can help you. I'm by the waterfront."

Suddenly Charlie and Maria rounded the corner a block away and came swiftly up the street. Kelly dropped the communicator. It seemed like they were looking for her. But was it to fight? Mac had made it all too clear they weren't there to rescue her, but maybe he'd told them what she'd said about needing help. Should she go up to them? Charlie was so powerful—she could kick her can to Sunday if she made the wrong move. Quickly she picked up the communication device and shoved it into her pack so it wouldn't be visible. She held as still as she could, trying to figure out what to do.

It was obvious that Mac hadn't believed her. He'd treated her like a villain—Kelly knew that's what she was now. She knew Dr. Gray had lied to her. He'd turned her against her old friends. And Kelly certainly didn't expect Charlie to help her.

But what about Maria? Had she turned totally against her, too? It didn't seem possible. Maria had a generous heart. Maybe there was a way back into it. Perhaps if Kelly could hear what she and Charlie were talking about, she could get an idea of their motives.

Staying camouflaged, Kelly crept toward them as they stopped near the dock to the ferry. Charlie was peering all around. When they turned around and started walking by the shore, Kelly slid along the buildings parallel to them.

Charlie turned sharply.

Kelly froze. Her former friend seemed to be looking right at her. She glanced down—had her camo turned off unexpectedly? Clearly it hadn't. She blended into the blue of the building she was standing against.

Charlie and Maria started walking toward her, but they were talking and looking at each other, not at her. Kelly relaxed a little. She'd wait until they passed her, and then she'd follow them to eavesdrop.

As the two approached, Kelly flattened herself against the building and her heart began to pound. If they continued in the same direction, they'd walk within ten feet of her. She had this great camo ability, but it didn't make her completely invisible. If someone were looking hard, they'd be able to see a slight outline of her—at least that's what Miko had told her once. Kelly held her breath and waited for the girls to pass.

She could almost hear them. And then they stopped right in front of her. That's when Kelly realized with a start that Charlie wasn't wearing just any bodysuit. She was wearing Zed's.

Charlie raced at Kelly. Before Kelly could slide away, Charlie was grasping the air and easily found her arm. Her grip was deadly and Kelly squealed in pain. She tried to click on her spikes, but every time she reached for her device, Charlie yanked her arm away.

"Get her device!" said Maria, who couldn't see it.

"No!" cried Kelly. "Wait! Can you just let me—Ouch!"

Charlie fumbled for the Mark Four and tried to key in the code, but Kelly jerked her arm. Then she started concentrating hard. She began pulsing. If they wouldn't listen to her normally, maybe she could convince them . . . this way.

"Aw, crud," said Maria. "Don't look at her! She's doing that thing!"

"Knock it off, Kelly!" Charlie looked away and dragged Kelly to the park along the lake, away from the activities of the neighborhood, so she could clobber Kelly in private.

"You don't understand!" Kelly said, squirming. "I want to go home! I want to work with you."

"She's trying to hypnotize us into believing her," Charlie told Maria. "Ignore."

"I'm not!" said Kelly. "I mean, I wasn't—I really mean it! Please don't hurt me."

"Please," said Charlie with disdain. "We know you've been talking to Dr. Jakande, too. Pretty sneaky."

"Who?" said Kelly. "You mean Zed? She never answers."

"I'll bet she told you to say that." Charlie shoved Kelly to the grass, making her skid for several feet.

"Hey!" The impact broke Kelly's concentration and she stopped pulsating. She blended into the grass. Quickly she activated her platypus spikes before Charlie could go after her device again. It was clear they didn't believe her. And it was also clear that Kelly didn't have much of a chance to beat the two of them in a fight.

She got to her feet and tried to run, but Charlie caught her before she could go very far.

"What the—how?" Kelly couldn't figure out how Charlie could see her so easily, but the girl lifted Kelly off the ground. Kelly swung her arms and legs around, trying to get free. "I'm trying to explain something!" Kelly cried. "Will you please listen?"

"Stay back, Maria," Charlie shouted. "I'll bet she's got her spikes out."

Maria wisely stayed away and let Charlie handle this fight that would no doubt soon be over.

Kelly landed a hard punch to Charlie's jaw, causing Charlie to stagger backward and lose her balance. She shoved Kelly skyward and let go, sending her sailing into the air. Kelly tumbled on the grass, falling almost gracefully, like she'd learned in acting class, and rolled back up to her feet. She eyed the water. That would be her last resort.

Charlie kept coming at her.

"How can you see me?" Kelly shouted. She was winded. And she knew this was her fight to lose. If she surrendered, would they finally listen?

She powered down and was no longer camouflaged or armed with her platypus spikes. She held her hands out so Maria and Charlie could see she wasn't going to do anything. "I know where

Dr. Gray is," she said. "I was trying to tell Zed. I didn't know you were wearing her suit until I saw you. It's the truth. I really do know where he is—or I'm pretty sure, anyway. And I know what he's going to do. So you'd better not hurt me if you want me to tell you."

Charlie hesitated. "Where is he?" she demanded.

Kelly backed away a few steps. "I'll tell you if you promise not to hurt me."

"She's lying," said Maria.

Kelly's lips parted. Maria didn't believe her either.

"I know she's lying," said Charlie.

"Girls, please!" Kelly begged. But she could tell they weren't softening. In despair, she clicked on her platypus spikes, knowing it was a mistake but also needing something to protect herself with. "I'm not lying. I'm so sorry about everything. I really mean it!"

"Says the liar," quipped Maria. "Look—she just brought out the spikes, Charlie."

"That doesn't seem like something a sorry person would do," said Charlie.

"Maria," said Kelly in a quiet voice. "You know me better than that. Please. We've been friends forever."

"We used to be friends," Maria agreed, "but you betrayed us so many times, you're beyond forgiveness."

The words hit Kelly hard. "Wow." She faltered and looked at Maria. Tears pricked the corners of her eyes.

"I'm coming!" cried Mac from far up the hill.

Charlie pounced. Kelly screamed. She rolled and kicked and punched, trying to get away. One of her platypus spikes connected, and Kelly sprang away, then jumped into the water with a splash. Her dolphin ability activated and she swam, eyes closed tightly. Sobbing angrily in the water.

She hated Charlie and Maria. They didn't understand her. They didn't believe her. They wouldn't even let her explain anything. She had to get away. Or at least get to a place where she could win a battle against them.

When Kelly surfaced, she heard Charlie groaning in pain on the shore. Kelly had done it again. Her heart sank. She dived down again, tempted to go back. But she hardened against that idea. If they weren't going to forgive her before, they certainly wouldn't now. Kelly had just blown her chances of getting back home. Again. Because of the stupid platypus spikes. And now she had nobody.

"Get more help!" came Charlie's muffled cry.

"I'm going!" said Maria.

A second later there was a splash that didn't come from Kelly. Kelly froze, looking around the murky water. Charlie had entered the lake and was coming toward her. Then she looked up and saw the strangest sight. Mac, wearing a weird green suit, was running on the surface above her.

CHAPTER 40

In Over Her Head

Charlie surfaced and wiped the water from her eyes.

"She's right below me!" cried Mac, running in circles on the lake to keep from sinking. He shaded his eyes and peered at the water, then moved a little farther out. "I'll stay with her as long as I can!"

Charlie floundered, dropping back under, her ankle throbbing sharply with pain from where Kelly had spiked her with poison. Luckily, Dr. Jakande's suit had stopped it from sinking in too far. Charlie righted herself and floated back up for a breath, trying to ignore the stinging and keep her leg moving. She had to stop Kelly. And she had to find Dr. Gray before he did something awful. She dived down again, hoping her healing ability would soon take care of the injury.

She was a good swimmer, and she was used to swimming in lakes. She'd grown up near a huge one, Lake Michigan, and she and Andy had spent their summers there and at the Y, swimming all the time. But she was no dolphin. As Charlie swam for a short distance above the surface, she could tell her strength ability was helping her move a little faster and more easily through the water.

That was something, at least, but it was nothing like moving on land. She swam onward, peering through the water. She could hear a faint beeping and she realized her bat vision had kicked on in the murkiness underwater. The rocks on the floor of the lake shimmered silver around her. Mac's shadow circled the area above her, and soon she could see a silver-and-red Kelly gliding around long strands of seaweeds. Charlie's abilities were double-dipping, and that wasn't a bad thing.

Charlie eyed the weeds, then impulsively yanked some of them out of the bottom and draped them around her neck. They might come in handy, though she wasn't quite sure how yet. She surfaced for a few breaths. "You're doing great, Mac!" She sped up in pursuit of Kelly. When she found the familiar shimmer again, she pushed off a rock with all her strength, trying to find a way to speed up underwater. But her abilities were greatly hindered in this environment. There was no speed of a cheetah down here. She'd have to use her strength to power her forward. Too bad she had to breathe a lot more often than Kelly did.

Kelly had turned her camo on. But Charlie's infrared viper vision kept the girl easily in sight. Charlie surfaced.

"I can't see her anymore," said Mac, huffing and looking weak.

"I can," said Charlie. "I'm going to grab her and drag her to shore if I can. I think you can go back there for now, and just be ready to help once I've got a hold."

"Got it!" Mac, whose breath was sounding quite ragged by now from running, gladly went back to the shore.

Charlie took a deep breath, and with all the force she could gather, dived through the water and swam at Kelly. Kelly darted away, but Charlie caught her by the leg and hung on, careful not to get pricked by one of her platypus spurs. She pulled the weeds from around her neck and tried tying Kelly's legs together to keep the dangerous spurs in one place.

Kelly squirmed. "Let go of me!" she shouted, her voice gurgling in the water. She dropped to the lake's bottom and tried to shake Charlie off or kick her with her spurs. Charlie pinched Kelly's leg hard, then carefully grabbed on to the base of one of the spikes. She grunted and bent the spike, trying to crack it off, but it wouldn't. Kelly screamed in pain and twisted around, one leg slipping out of Charlie's grasp.

Charlie dodged Kelly's heel. Again in need of air, she pushed off the sandy bottom with Kelly in tow, dragging her to the surface and letting go before Kelly could kick her. She gasped for breath and Kelly managed to get some air, too.

"Leave me alone!" Kelly screamed.

"Where is Dr. Gray?" Charlie demanded. "What's he doing?" She tightened her grip around Kelly's leg.

"Stop squeezing me!" said Kelly, bending forward and slamming her fist into Charlie's ear.

Charlie grabbed it, wincing, and twisted Kelly's arm hard. She squealed and thrashed. Soon they were both back under, rolling and tussling.

Kelly slammed her heel back again, this time into Charlie's thigh. Charlie scream and sucked in water, making her choke. She floundered and let go of Kelly, then surfaced and floated on her back for a moment, coughing and moaning and clutching at her leg. The pain pulsed through her. Her leg felt paralyzed. Kelly had gotten her good with that one. She was having trouble staying afloat.

"Come *on*," Charlie muttered to herself. "Heal!" But there was no rushing the healing power, and no handling this kind of pain. Unable to see where Kelly was, she started to panic. She looked at the shore, realizing she and Kelly had been pulled farther and farther out by the waves. Mac stood anxiously on the beach. Maria was nowhere to be found. Was she still getting help?

Then Charlie saw movement in the water coming toward her from the shore. She looked closer and realized it was Maria, as a werealligator, gliding through the waves. Thank goodness! Finally! Maybe Maria could chomp down on Kelly to convince her to tell them where Gray was. But Maria couldn't chomp unless she could see Kelly. How could they turn off her cuttlefish camouflage?

Charlie groaned with pain. She tried to kick but one leg felt like lead. She took a deep breath and went underwater to see where

Kelly was. When she came back up and looked out toward the island, she saw something in the water that she never expected to see.

Charlie's eyes widened as a triangular fin cut through the waves at a high speed, coming straight at her. "What the . . . ," she muttered. And then it swam past her, heading for Maria.

CHAPTER 41

Shark vs. Alligator

Maria saw Mega, the rhino-shark soldier, about two seconds before the monster attacked. It was just long enough for her to gather her wits and open her mouth, exposing her row of sharp teeth. She struck out with her claws and tail, too. But the shark mouth with the rhino horn slammed into her, tossing her up out of the water like she was a toy.

Maria splashed back down, twisted, and chomped at the soldier's nose, hoping to at least hit her in a sensitive spot, but missed. She rolled and struck out at Mega's neck, and finally connected. She bit down hard. The shark pulled her sandpapery skin away, leaving Maria's face scratched and bloody. But Maria had left a few bite marks in Mega's neck and shoulder that the woman wouldn't soon forget. The soldier circled and charged again. This time she bit down around Maria's middle.

Maria screamed in pain and cracked her elbow into Mega's ear. The rhino-shark pushed the girl through the water, not letting go. Maria waved her claws and snapped her alligator jaws, trying to catch anything, but the shark woman had a solid grip on the girl. "Help!" Maria cried out. Mega pulled her underwater.

Forgetting Kelly, Charlie started paddling toward Maria, her useless leg trailing in the water behind her. "Maria!" she cried.

From the shore, Mac came running on top of the water, but there wasn't much he could do. If he switched to pangolin mode, he'd sink like a rock and drown. But he didn't have any way to protect himself in lizard mode. "Come back to shore!" he shouted weakly, knowing that it was easier said than done.

Mega tossed Maria up into the air again. Maria swiveled and twisted, then clawed the water as she came down, catching Mega in the face and leaving four bloody cuts across her cheek. Mega was furious. But before she could grab Maria again, Maria clamped down on the woman's shoulder and started shaking her.

Mega squealed in pain. She broke free, ripping out two of Maria's alligator teeth, which remained embedded in Mega's shoulder. Maria's blood clouded the water. Mega circled. Frenzied and angry, she went in for the kill. She clamped down on Maria's head, lifted her up so her tail was out of the water, and shook her like a dog shakes a stuffed toy. Maria's yells went silent.

"Maria!" Charlie screamed. She reached them, but there wasn't much she could do but watch in horror.

Mega dragged Maria through the water and shook her again, then whirled around and tossed her at Mac, hitting him in the chest and knocking him down. He splashed and went under. Maria sank too. Mac resurfaced, looking wildly around for his friend, then dived down to find her. He grabbed her by the alligator tail and pulled her up, taking her under the arms and keeping her bleeding head above water. Treading water with Maria in tow, he carefully removed Maria's device and pulled the Mark Five from his pocket. He slapped it on her and put her Mark Two in his pocket.

Barely able to move in the water, Charlie was a sitting duck, and her arms burned, trying to keep herself afloat. When Mega turned on her, all Charlie could think of to do was to try to pry Mega's mouth open and keep it that way. She dived down, her leg barely beginning to work again, and searched for a rock or a piece of driftwood. Not that it would hold the shark long, since she had human arms to pull out whatever Charlie managed to put in there. She came back up empty-handed, and barely had time to take a breath before Mega attacked.

Charlie grabbed the shark's mouth and pulled it open, holding it as wide as she could. She clamped her good leg around the woman's body and squeezed. The two slipped under the water, Mega flailing with her mouth forced open and Charlie attached to her torso. Her strength was solid, and she had a strong grip with her gecko ability. But her injured leg wasn't helping. And Charlie knew she'd have to let go eventually to get air.

Mega lurched and her jaw snapped shut, catching Charlie's arm inside. Charlie's eyes widened. She screamed into the water. Mega stayed low, dragging the girl around as Charlie tried placing hard kicks into Mega's stomach with her good leg.

The kicks didn't seem to faze the crazed shark. Before long

Charlie's lungs began to burn. She needed air. She twisted and tried to wrench her arm away, growing desperate, then weak, but the shark held fast. Charlie's vision began to go dark.

Just before Charlie faded into unconsciousness, she saw an infrared spot moving toward her through the water.

CHAPTER 42

One More Chance

Mega had come out of nowhere. Kelly had watched in horror as the rhino-shark woman practically shredded Maria and tossed her aside. Then she'd turned on Charlie and was trying to drown her. Charlie had little to fight back with in this setting. Not to mention she was still probably dealing with the platypus venom. It wasn't a fair fight by any means.

And Mega was out of control. It was like the blood in the water affected her like it would a real shark. And now all Mega wanted to do was kill.

Kelly stayed in camo mode. She crept closer, not wanting Mega to turn on her in her crazed attack. She thought about trying to hypnotize Mega like she'd done in the past for fun, but decided that Mega was too frantic to be caught by her pulsing. She swam closer and saw that Mega's teeth dug deep into Charlie's upper arm. She saw Charlie panicking, flailing. Drowning. She saw her head loll forward as she lost consciousness.

Kelly felt her heart hit her throat. This wasn't right. It wasn't okay. She pushed forward, staying camouflaged, and swam around Mega, slipping under her as she floated near the bottom.

Mega didn't see her. Kelly made a V with her legs around Mega's protruding belly. And then she cringed and slammed both heels into the woman and held them there.

Mega's body recoiled in shock. She released Charlie's arm, letting the girl float away, and screamed, twisting and turning until full paralysis set in. After what seemed like an eternity, Kelly yanked her spikes out, then swam quickly to Charlie's limp body. She grabbed the girl around the waist and streamed through the water toward the shore. She raised Charlie's head above the surface, not knowing what to do to get her to start breathing again—all she could do was hope Charlie's healing power was up to this kind of challenge.

Seeing people standing in the shallow water, Kelly reached for the bottom, found it, and started running, dragging Charlie with her.

"Kelly!" said Mac. "What did you do to her?" He ran at Kelly, furious, and tried to yank Charlie away.

"It was Mega," Kelly said, breathing hard. "Hurry—does anyone know how to get her to breathe?" She looked up and saw Charlie's mom running toward them with her emergency kit. Kelly and Mac climbed the bank and laid Charlie on the ground as residents of the area came to see what was happening.

"Tell me what happened," said Dr. Wilde in a serious but calm voice. She checked Charlie's airways and started CPR as Kelly explained everything.

Maria was nearby, back in her normal body and nursing her wounds. She still had the Mark Five on her wrist. Every now and then as Kelly told what happened, Maria nodded.

Dr. Wilde continued CPR on Charlie, pumping her chest until finally Charlie choked and coughed up a bunch of water. She lifted her head and puked on Kelly's leg, and then she groaned. Her left arm was limp and full of ugly tooth punctures and cuts. Her suit had a puncture hole in the thigh. Dr. Wilde slit Charlie's sleeve and the bottom half of her pant leg and checked the wounds. She looked at Kelly.

Kelly looked down. She didn't try to justify it. "That's from a platypus spike. I hit her somewhere else, too—more like a glancing hit, not a direct stab."

"My ankle," said Charlie weakly. "That one doesn't hurt anymore. The suit helped." She sat up on one elbow. "Where's Maria? Is she okay?"

"She's resting over there under that tree by Dr. Sharma," said her mom. "She's healing nicely. Mac got the Mark Five on her and brought her to shore just as I was coming to help."

Charlie looked at Kelly. "I saw you swimming toward me when . . . when I almost . . . when Mega had me trapped." Her voice wavered. "What happened? I blacked out."

"I stayed camouflaged and attacked Mega," said Kelly quietly. "Then I grabbed you. She's probably still stuck at the bottom of the lake, paralyzed. I stabbed her in two places. She's going to hurt for a while."

Charlie's expression flickered. "Why did you rescue me?"

Kelly pressed her lips together, then spoke carefully. "Because you're my friend. I meant what I told you guys earlier. I know you have no reason to believe me. I was terrible to you. But I really want to go . . . home. . . ." She started to cry and didn't try to hold back her tears. "I made a huge mistake. And I'm so sorry."

Charlie didn't know what to say. She didn't know if she could believe Kelly, even after this. Kelly was so good at acting, and she was so good at lying. But she'd saved her life. She'd said she wanted to go home when she thought she was talking to Zed.

She winced as her mother cleaned up the puncture wounds on her arm. "Tell us where Dr. Gray is."

Kelly closed her eyes and let out a breath. "He's on that island. I'm almost sure of it. Prowl said he's got a huge container full of formula that he's been working on in the lab. He's going to pour it into his mist machine thing and somehow release it into the air. It's supposed to turn everyone into chimeras." She looked sorrowful. "I didn't know he was going to do that—not until we got here. He . . . he told me he was doing good things. That he was working for the government and wanted to help people. And . . ." she looked at the ground. "He said you were the bad guys for trying to stop him." She took in a shuddering breath. "I was sad and lonely and I believed him. And now it's too late for me to escape. I don't know if I'll ever be able to go home because of what I did."

"Ugh, Kelly," said Mac. "Just . . . why?"

Maria laid a hand on Mac's arm and shook her head slightly.

"We'll talk about that later," said Charlie's mom firmly to Kelly. She sat back and looked sternly at her. "Just like always, we'll do what we can to help you. It's going to be okay."

Kelly hung her head. "I hope so."

"But now we have to stop a madman," said Charlie. "Who's with him?"

"Cyke, Braun, Fang, and Morph," said Kelly. "Are you going to try to go after him now?"

"Absolutely," said Charlie. She tested her leg, finding she could move it again, though it still hurt. She struggled to stand. "We don't have a choice. We need to stop him before he destroys people's lives. He could turn on that machine at any second." She looked up as she realized Dr. Sharma had finished with Maria. "Are you all ready?" Charlie asked. "We can heal up on the way."

Maria and Mac looked at each other and nodded.

Dr. Wilde looked like she was going to object, but then she just sighed and seemed like she wasn't going to fight it. "You're right. Let's go," she said. "Quinn, can you let Erica know what's up? And tell Nubia we need her at the ferry dock. Where's Charles?"

"He's coming," said Dr. Sharma. "Jack's staying behind with

Erica to keep an eye on the prisoners and wait for the government people to show up."

Charlie turned to Kelly and studied her for a long moment. The girl had fought her. But she'd also saved her life. Maybe she could find a way to give her one more chance. "It's hard to believe in you. You know?"

Kelly bit her lip and her eyes welled up. She looked at the ground. "I know."

"But right now we could really use your help."

Kelly looked up at Charlie. "You mean it?"

Charlie nodded and reached out a hand to help Kelly stand. "Come on."

CHAPTER 43

A Moment Too Late

They rode the ferry to the island, the kids standing anxiously on the deck with the wind in their faces. Dr. Jakande and Mr. Wilde joined the other adults a few paces away.

"I want to apologize about Andy," Kelly said.

Charlie glanced at the girl. "Okay," she prompted when Kelly didn't actually apologize. "Go for it."

Kelly seemed momentarily flustered. "I'm . . . I'm sorry. I never meant to hit him. I felt terrible. These spikes . . ." She trailed off and looked down, though the ability wasn't activated. Tears welled up in her eyes again. "They've caused me a lot of trouble."

"No kidding," Mac said sarcastically. "Maybe you should, you know, stop using them."

"I want to." Kelly turned away, stinging. "Once I'm out of this mess with Dr. Gray . . . this device is going back home with Dr. Sharma. I don't want it." A tear slipped down her cheek. She wiped it away hastily. "Is Andy okay?" she asked.

Charlie's expression softened slightly. "He's fine. We were able to—" She stopped herself, not quite ready to give Kelly any information she could use against them, just in case. "He's fine." She hesitated. "Thanks for asking."

Kelly nodded.

"So," said Maria after an awkward silence, "what else can you tell us?"

Kelly took a deep breath and let it out. "A lot, actually." She looked up, catching Dr. Jakande's eye, and beckoned the adults to come. The scientists, who'd given the kids some privacy to talk through their personal issues, gathered around.

Kelly told them everything she could think of about what they'd been doing since she'd seen them last. She talked them through the new DNA that Cyke and Braun had received—the Komodo dragon for Cyke, which gave him more strength and a venomous bite, and the porcupine for Braun.

"Are porcupine quills poisonous?" asked Maria warily.

"No," said Kelly. "But they'll stick in your skin and they hurt like crazy." She told them Cyke's Komodo dragon venom was sure to be very dangerous, as it could kill prey in a short amount of time. "His fangs are pretty far back in his mouth, between his teeth. He looks different now too. You'll see."

Charlie, Mac, and Maria listened carefully. Charlie took everything Kelly said with a bit of skepticism—she'd learned her lesson with Kelly too many times. Occasionally, as the boat took them farther and farther from the mainland, Charlie felt a tinge of worry. Was Kelly tricking them all right now into a trap on this island? Or was she luring them away from the real action? Charlie didn't think so. Kelly seemed sincere in a different way this time—it was hard to explain. But Charlie kept her guard up.

Kelly went on to tell them what to expect on the island—how they'd need to get to the statue at the top of the hill, which she believed was where Dr. Gray intended to disperse the formula into the air.

"So he's definitely introducing an aerosol," murmured Dr. Sharma. "Starting with a test group—the inhabitants and visitors of the island." She glanced at it looming before them. "I wonder how many people live here? Looking at the houses, I'd guess a couple hundred." She scratched her head, then turned sharply toward Charlie's mom. "Diana, do you have any face masks in your medical kit?"

Mrs. Wilde searched through her kit and triumphantly pulled out a sealed package. "You never know when you're going to run across an infectious disease," she said with an anxious laugh. "There are only three masks in this pack, though."

"We'll have to make do for the rest of us," said Dr. Sharma. "We can use strips of cloth or whatever we can find to keep ourselves from breathing it in."

As the ferry neared the dock, Mrs. Wilde did a quick check of Charlie's and Maria's wounds. "Are you sure you two are up to this?"

The girls nodded. The starfish powers were healing them. Maria took off the Mark Five and handed it to Charlie's dad. "I'm good now," she said. "Thanks." She got her Mark Two from Mac and put it back on her wrist.

The ferry workers tied up the boat. The team filed off. They took three taxis to the center of the island, where the statue entrance was. As they drove up to the attraction, Charlie stared out the window. Dozens of people were milling around, waiting to go up to the top of the statue.

"That's odd," said Kelly, peering past her from the middle seat. "What are they waiting for? The other day we went right up."

At the base of the stairway, something caught Charlie's eye. "Look," she said quietly. "Bottom of the steps. It's Morph."

"And Braun is in front of the elevator. Next to the stairs," said Kelly, pointing him out. She shuddered, feeling suddenly sick. What would they do to her when they found out she was with Charlie again?

"Maybe they're stopping people from going up," said Mr. Wilde, who was with them. Kelly looked closer. "People are taking pictures of them like they're part of the attraction!"

It was true. Neither soldier wore a mask, and Braun's porcupine quills served as his shirt.

Dr. Wilde muttered something under his breath.

"We need to get up there *now*," said Charlie, pressing her face against the window and craning to see the top of the statue. But it was a long way up. She glanced at her father, remembering his fear of heights. Mr. Wilde's face was ashen.

"You okay, Dad?"

He waved off her concern and tried to smile.

By the time the taxi came to a stop Charlie had unbuckled her seat belt and opened the door. She ran out, dodging to stay hidden behind tourists so Braun and Morph wouldn't see her. Kelly and Dr. Wilde ran after her. Maria and Mac and Dr. Jakande followed from the next taxi. The other adults brought up the rear.

Moments later they convened under the covered roof near the entrance, behind a large column so the soldiers wouldn't be able to see them.

"We think they're stopping people from going up," Charlie told the others. "So we'll have to overpower them without causing all of these tourists to freak out."

"We're taking the elevator, right?" asked Mac, peeking around the column.

"I don't think that's a good idea," said Kelly. "It opens up in plain sight of the balcony. We could be caught the second the door opens. It'll take longer, but I'll bet they won't be watching the stairs."

While the team discussed options for overtaking the soldiers, Mrs. Wilde doled out the surgical masks and some cloth bandage wraps from her kit so everyone could cover their noses and mouths in case Dr. Gray unleashed his formula into the air.

Kelly refused to take anything. "I won't be able to use my camouflage with something like that on." She pointed to her waist bag.

"I can hold this to my face in a pinch—it works like the suit."

Mrs. Wilde nodded.

Kelly glanced at the soldiers. "They're still in the same places. Do you want me to try to hypnotize them to let us through? People might think I'm weird but it shouldn't cause alarm." She seemed anxious to do something else that would prove she could be trusted. Charlie thought that was a good sign.

"Don't they already know about that ability?" asked Maria. "Won't they just look away like Charlie and I did? Seems like it works better when people don't expect it."

"Yeah, good point," said Kelly, frowning. "They don't know I'm with you now, though. I'm sure I can convince them that Dr. Gray is expecting me. They'll let me through."

"But there are two more soldiers somewhere—and Dr. Gray," said Charlie, trying to be patient, but feeling her suspicions rise up yet again. "You can't stop them alone. Besides . . . why weren't you in on this plan? Why weren't you here with them already?"

Kelly looked away. "I'm not sure," she admitted. "Dr. Gray suspected Miko, Prowl, and I weren't quite buying into it anymore. I mean, he tricked us. His real plan was completely different from what he'd told them all these years."

"Wait," said Dr. Jakande. "Those two are suspicious of Gray too?" She gave Kelly a hard look. "That's important to know."

"Yeah, we three are against all of this," said Kelly. "I tried to tell Charlie earlier. We don't think it's right. Maybe one of the others overheard us grumbling about it and told Dr. Gray." She thought back to the conversation in the kitchen, when Braun had come in. That was probably it.

Dr. Jakande turned abruptly and whispered to Ms. Sabbith on her communication device, letting her know what they'd just found out about the two prisoners. "Question them," she said. "Maybe they can help us."

Dr. Sharma regarded Kelly thoughtfully. "And maybe Gray is feeling so confident that he didn't think he needed you for this. It wouldn't be hard to just walk up and start the mist going without anybody noticing." She hesitated, then said sharply, "Does Gray have any idea we're in the area?"

"I don't think so," said Kelly. "None of us had a clue. I still have no idea how you found us when the police haven't. Yet."

"Anyway," said Charlie, impatient to make a move, "we're going to have to get messy here, I think, and worry about the tourists' feelings later. Hopefully we can scare some of them back to the mainland where they'll be safer." She paused, then looked at the team. "Here's what I think we should do: Kelly, you'll go over there first and distract the guards. Dr. Jakande, Maria, and my dad can all climb up this post and get inside the statue through a second-floor window. Once they're up, Mac and I will join Kelly and take out Braun and Morph." She narrowed her eyes at Kelly. "And you'd better not mess this up on purpose, or all bets are off on us helping you get out of here."

Kelly nodded. "I know," she said quietly.

Charlie continued. "Mom, you and Dr. Sharma stay down here and try to get the people to clear the area. Keep them from coming upstairs." She looked around. "Does that sound okay with everybody?"

They all nodded. Dr. Jakande put her hand up to her earpiece and listened. Then she slid around the column and started taking photos of the soldiers.

"What are you doing?" asked Charlie.

"Sabbith just told me to—she wants evidence for Zimmerman in case we need to use the reversal devices before the team arrives."

"Oh. That's smart." Charlie glanced at her father, who looked even queasier than before in the taxi. "Are you going to make it, Dad? It's just one floor up. You trained for this, right?"

"I didn't exactly have a lot of time," he said weakly. "Or desire to use the gecko ability. I'm good with the others, but I'm just not sure about the whole climbing thing."

"Okay," Charlie muttered, feeling bad for her father and a little annoyed. "If you're more comfortable helping us with the goons down here, that's cool."

"That feels better," said Mr. Wilde, his fingers trembling slightly as he turned on his abilities. When he started making a strange chirping sound, Charlie reached over and turned off his night-vision ability. "Take your sunglasses off," she said, shaking her head in mock disgust.

Dr. Jakande hid a smile and refrained from comment, but she gave Maria a sly side-eye. Maria grinned back. Dr. Wilde put his glasses away.

"Okay," Charlie said. "Let's get moving. We don't have much time. Kelly, you're up first. Get the guards to turn their backs to us and we'll be there in a flash. Don't try anything funny."

"I won't," said Kelly, who was trying not to get irritated. What more could she do to prove herself? "I promise."

"Dr. Jakande and Maria, once you're inside, just run up a few more floors—I'll catch up to you."

"Got it," said the two.

"Ready, everyone?" whispered Charlie.

They all nodded.

"Go."

Kelly turned without a word and slipped through the crowd to the bottom of the stairs, where the soldiers stood. She ran up to them, feigning breathlessness. "Hi, guys," she said. "Sorry I'm late. Dr. Gray wants me stationed upstairs, I think." She smiled and pushed past them, going up a few steps.

Morph turned and stopped her. "He didn't tell us you were coming," she said suspiciously.

From behind the pillar, Charlie signaled to the climbers. Maria changed into monkey form and Dr. Jakande switched into panther mode, and before the tourists could react to that strange sight, they leaped up and climbed the column. Reaching the overhang, they pulled themselves on top of it.

People began to point and murmur. "Let's go," said Charlie.

Mac clicked on his pangolin ability. Charlie charged out with Mac and her father behind her, pushing through the crowd toward Kelly. Both soldiers had their backs to them, talking to Kelly a couple steps above them. Kelly saw them coming.

Charlie crashed into Morph, and the woman's superclaw shot out in defense. Mac threw himself in the way to protect Charlie, taking the hit and falling to the floor hard but unhurt. Mr. Wilde flew head first into Morph's stomach, throwing her off balance and pushing her into Braun's quills. "Yeowch!" cried Morph.

"Hey!" Braun shouted, confused. He grabbed Kelly's arm, unsure if she was friend or foe. Kelly twisted and slammed her platypus spike into Braun, getting several of his quills stuck in her leg. She stifled a swear and yanked them out. Braun screamed in agony and let go of Kelly, then stumbled and turned his wrath on Mr. Wilde, who dodged. Charlie plowed into Morph again, while Mac got up and pushed Braun away from Kelly and Mr. Wilde. The spiky soldier stumbled and grabbed the railing for support. Mac pinned him there.

Morph slipped into camouflage and tried to slink away. Charlie clicked on her infrared viper sensor and followed. She grabbed Morph's deadly claw arm and pinned it down. Then Charlie lifted the camouflaged woman over her head. "Duck, Mac!" Charlie cried out, and he did. She spun Morph around and threw her hard at Braun, who couldn't see her coming. Braun flipped over the stairway railing, and Morph landed on top of him, stuck fast. The woman yelled in pain, her camouflage fading fast. Braun's quills were buried into her.

Charlie rushed to the railing and looked down at them, cringing. The two would be tied up for a while.

"Dad!" said Charlie, turning to see that he was fine and getting up. "Stay here and keep an eye on them. Tie them up if you can. If anybody else gets away from us and comes down the steps, clobber them!"

Mr. Wilde looked energized now. "Got it!" He ran down the stairs and hopped over a short railing, landing next to the soldiers. Most of the crowd had scattered, but a few remained and were calling the police or getting the scene on video.

Out on the walkway Dr. Sharma and Mrs. Wilde were trying to direct people to the ferries, but they were having trouble controlling the visitors, especially since they didn't know enough Spanish to explain things.

Charlie didn't care about the police showing up this time. Or about videos surfacing. She and her team were going to take Dr. Gray down once and for all. If the police showed up, she'd take any help she could get.

"Come on, Mac!" Charlie rushed up the stairs with Mac behind. He transformed into basilisk lizard at the first landing, but there was no keeping up with Charlie. Kelly, free of quills and ignoring the pain they'd caused, sprinted past Mac, but heard his labored breathing. She slowed down and looked back uncertainly, then waited and stuck with him while Charlie went on ahead.

As Charlie ran up a few floors, she realized the statue was a little bit like a mall, only vertical rather than long and sprawling. It had shops on the lower floors and art everywhere and little balconies and lookout spots in between. It would be a fun place to explore . . . if she weren't trying to stop the evilest person alive.

She spotted Maria and Dr. Jakande and caught up to them. "Mac and Kelly are right behind. My dad is keeping the soldiers in check downstairs."

"We might need him later," said Dr. Jakande. "All right if I tell him to disarm the bad guys with reversal devices and hand them over to the cops so he can join us?"

Charlie frowned. "Do you think just having photos of them is enough, or should we leave them as physical proof for the government people?"

"Erica decided to keep Miko and Prowl in chimera form as evidence," said Dr. Jakande, "since those two are totally harmless and immobile after your bike rack hack. So we've got them as proof. Plus, Erica just told me they're cooperating." She caught her breath and added, "If it means anything to you, they told Sabbith that Kelly is legitimately on the right side of this."

"Well, that's a relief," said Charlie. "Unless they're lying too."

"Charlie," said Dr. Jakande, "I know you've had lots of doubts.

About Kelly . . . and even about me. And you've had good reason to. But I think it's time to trust her." She paused, then put her hand on Charlie's arm. "People change. I'm proof of that. I think . . . I think she wants to do the right thing, now that she's figured out what it is."

Charlie frowned. "Maybe."

Dr. Jakande dropped her hand. "Anyway, back to your dad. I'd like to diffuse the situation down there for his sake. If those two recover, they could hurt him pretty badly."

"You're right," Charlie admitted. "I hadn't thought about that." She was grateful for Dr. Jakande's help, and for her words.

"I'll talk to him." Dr. Jakande spoke through her device, updating Dr. Wilde on the change of plans.

As she did so, Mac and Kelly rounded the staircase. They paused for breath. Then they all ascended the next few flights together, until it became clear that Mac needed more rest. "Go on without me," he said. "I'll catch up."

"I can . . . carry you," said Charlie, cringing.

"Uh, no thanks," said Mac. "We tried that once, remember? It didn't go well."

"I'm staying with Mac," said Maria. "Charlie, go see what's happening!"

Charlie looked distressed, but there was no time to waste. "All right. Do your best—you're doing fine. I'm going on ahead." She bounded up the next flights at top speed.

Kelly and Dr. Jakande stayed together, tailing Charlie the best they could.

Alone, Charlie neared the top. She stayed low and crept up the last flight. With each step she could see a little more of the vast upper floor. It was like a ballroom with marble floors and extravagant chandeliers. The ornate elevator stood closed on the left wall, and a few hallways branched off beyond it. Across the room Charlie could see a huge balcony outside glass doors. There was no one in sight. Then, on the balcony, Charlie spied Dr. Gray setting up a tripod. Next to him on the deck was the mist machine, a large cylinder of formula, and a small tube containing something similarly colored in it. Beside that were a small generator and a toolbox.

Charlie checked the area for soldiers. Seeing none, she crossed the threshold of the top step and crept to the far side of the room, hoping to get a better look at what Gray was doing. Getting to her feet, she skittered across the open space and darted behind a sculpture near the door.

Dr. Gray lifted the mist machine onto the tripod. He tightened the fasteners, then slid his fingers down the machine's electrical cord and plugged it into the generator. Once he seemed satisfied with the placement of everything, he picked up the large cylinder of formula and began pouring it into a chamber.

"Oh no," muttered Charlie, her heart sinking. Serious emergency. Where was everyone? She couldn't stop him alone. She glanced at her device, remembering what Ms. Sabbith had said.

This was definitely an emergency—she needed help. She held her finger poised over the button, then pressed it, holding it down. She hoped it had worked.

"Hearing you loud and clear, Charlie," came Ms. Sabbith's calm voice in her ear. "The others are nearby and I'm telling them you need help."

Charlie didn't dare to make a sound. A moment later she heard a scuffling sound from across the room, but when she looked, no one was there. Wishful thinking, perhaps. She was still alone.

When the large cylinder was empty, Dr. Gray set it down. He picked up the small beaker and put it in his lab coat pocket. Then he opened the toolbox and removed a remote control device. Leaving the mist machine in place, he slipped inside the glass door and stood just a few dozen feet from Charlie.

The man turned to look at the contraption. The liquid inside shimmered in the sunlight. When the door closed, he lifted the remote and clicked it.

Charlie gasped. What was he doing? The generator roared. The machine's fan engaged. Then the mist began to siphon out through a makeshift tube. It shot high into the air, the tiny particles arching and flying with the wind.

It was the ultimate chimera formula. And it was being dispersed into the air, like a flu virus, over the island. People wouldn't know what was happening. But they'd be feeling some changes. Soon.

"Nooo!" cried Charlie, abandoning her hiding place and

running at the man. She had to stop the machine! Before Dr. Gray could turn around, Cyke and Fang appeared from one of the hallways. Seeing Charlie running at the doctor, they tore after her. But Charlie was faster.

Feeling desperate, she dived at the man, knocking him to the floor. But before she could grab his remote control, Fang shot out in front of her, teeth bared. Suddenly the two soldiers were on her, pinning her to the cold floor. Then they picked her up by the arms. Her legs swung forward and she hung in the air between them. Fang hissed, his yellow irises glowing as he stared into her eyes.

And still no one came.

CHAPTER 44

Island of Chaos

"You again," said Cyke. He sounded disgusted to see Charlie. His voice had taken on a strange high-pitched howl at the end of his sentences, and Charlie thought she caught a glimpse of a few needlelike fangs inside his mouth. "You're a little too late."

"And a little too weak," said Fang. His tongue flickered.

Cyke looked at Fang like he could barely tolerate him, but said nothing to him. "Are you okay, Dr. Gray?"

"I think so." Dr. Gray got to his feet and dusted off his pants. He checked his pockets and all seemed to be to his liking. Then he lifted his gaze to the intruder.

Charlie struggled, trying to use her strength to escape, but dangling between them with their iron grip on her arms made it impossible to get any traction.

"Just this one?" said Dr. Gray, stepping back slightly in disdain. He turned to check his masterpiece. "No doubt there are more coming." The man sighed, but seemed strangely at peace now that his formula was being spread out into the air. "I thought we were through with them, but it doesn't matter. They're too late." He turned fully to the glass door. "Come here, Charlie. I want you to see what I've done."

"You're a monster!" yelled Charlie, unable to go anywhere in the soldiers' grip. "Stop what you're doing! It's against . . . humanity!" Charlie was so impassioned she could barely find words.

"It's *for* humanity," Dr. Gray insisted. "Your father's been lying to you. And I'm not a monster yet. That's next. In fact, let's do it now before your friends come." He reached into his lab coat pocket and pulled out a syringe and the small beaker full of formula. He held it up to the light. "Concentrated," he said. "Watch this."

Charlie's eyes widened. "I don't want to watch!" she cried, though she couldn't look away. She stopped struggling and felt Cyke's grip relax a little. *Where were the others?* It had been stupid of her to rush at Dr. Gray without backup around. But seeing that chimera formula had made her throw all caution to the wind. If she could catch Cyke and Fang off guard she'd be strong enough to get loose. But she was trying to buy time so her friends would arrive. They had to be coming soon.

"Put me down!" Charlie yelled as loudly as she could, trying to warn them that something was going on. Where were they? She couldn't fight all three of these men alone. Especially if whatever was in that beaker would turn Dr. Gray into a chimera with all sorts of unknown abilities.

Dr. Gray looked lovingly at the liquid. "I've put so much into this," he said. "My whole life's work for this moment." He slipped off his lab coat and pushed the sleeve of his T-shirt up. Then he uncapped the beaker. He put the syringe inside and drew it full of the liquid.

"Don't do it!" Charlie begged.

"You can't stop me," said Dr. Gray. Then he slid the needle into his arm and pushed the plunger until the liquid was gone. "It won't be long now," he said, satisfied.

Charlie stared, half-devastated and half-dying to know what would happen. "Why didn't you just stand out in that mist and inhale that stuff?"

Dr. Gray looked at the small amount that remained in the beaker. He swirled it, shrugged, then drank it down. "Because my dose is special," he said, dabbing his lips. "Incredibly powerful. As the new world leader, I need to be . . . obeyed. Forever, so to speak." He closed his eyes. "Here it comes." He began to smile as his body lines began to waver. He started to morph . . . into what, Charlie didn't know.

Fang's jaw slacked. "This is amazing," he said.

Charlie watched in shock. Dr. Gray grew taller and bigger all around. His fingers became long, sharp claws like Prowl's. His toes pushed through the tips of his shoes; claws there, too. Wings started to grow from his back. His mouth widened and his teeth became sharpened, reminding Charlie of Mega. He turned and peered at himself in the window's reflection, and began to laugh.

Charlie wasn't sure of all the animals he'd put into his special formula, but they definitely looked powerful. And Gray was

looking eager to use them. She began to wonder if her friends had all been captured somehow. Was she alone here with these monsters? She knew she shouldn't look at the stairs, because that would give the soldiers a clue that she was expecting backup. But she couldn't help it. She glanced. There was no one there. Her heart sank.

Dr. Gray began to howl with laughter, like a wolf laughing at the moon. He was really losing it now.

Suddenly Dr. Gray's hair turned from gray to brown. His face lost its wrinkles. His hunched shoulders straightened and he became . . . almost boyish.

"What's happening to me?" he cried, his voice cracking and returning less deep than before. He looked down at himself.

"You look like a young man, sir!" said Fang. He relaxed his grip, and Charlie slowly flexed her biceps to create more room for when she planned her escape.

Dr. Gray had grown younger. "The jellyfish," Charlie muttered under her breath. He had regenerated into a youthful version of himself. "Did you mean for that to happen with the immortal jellyfish?" Charlie asked, trying to catch him off guard. "Is that why you're acting so . . . immature?"

"Be quiet." Dr. Gray growled at her and began to test out his other abilities. He hopped from one foot to another with a new spring in his step. Then he slammed his fist into a pillar and broke the tile. "Nice," he muttered.

Not nice, Charlie thought, eyes widening. Now there was really no way for her to beat all three of them.

A flash of red appeared at the top of the stairs. Charlie's viper vision picked up someone in camouflage sneaking toward them. Her heart surged. Kelly! But then she grew worried. What if it was Morph? She glanced toward the stairway again, and saw Dr. Jakande nearly flat against the steps like she was ready to pounce. When Charlie caught her eye, the woman nodded almost imperceptibly. She and Kelly were there, and hopefully Maria, too. And they were ready.

It was now or never. With a wild yell, Charlie jerked her arms loose, then rammed her elbows backward with all her strength, hitting Cyke and Fang in the stomach. Then she flipped her fists up to catch them in the face.

Fang struck out with his poisonous fangs, just grazing Charlie arm, but the suit stopped him from breaking the skin. She kicked him in the chin and whirled out of his reach, then leaped at Cyke, getting a better look at his face as they went down. Charlie could definitely see two long, thin needles inside his mouth. Two poisonous chimera soldiers at a time was two too many for Charlie.

She saw Kelly on the move, heading fast toward Fang, who was struggling to get up. Charlie stuck with fighting Cyke, throwing punches at the side of his head when he tried to get up. Then he clocked her hard in the chin and she realized he now had Komodo-dragon-like claws instead of hands. No wonder he'd had such a sharp grip on her!

Kelly, in camouflage mode and with her spikes extended, whirled around with her leg outstretched. She caught Fang in the hip. He yelped in surprise, looking all around to see what had hit him. Then he began howling in pain. He raked the air with his wolf claws, trying to find his camouflaged attacker.

Dr. Gray noticed Cyke struggling under Charlie's grasp. He came toward them with a beastly swagger.

From the stairwell, Dr. Jakande saw her opportunity. She bounded forward and pounced on Dr. Gray's back, sinking her claws into his new toughened skin. He yelled, surprised, and whirled around, slapping at her, trying to get her off him. Then he backed into a stone sculpture as hard as he could, flattening the panther woman and knocking the wind out of her. Her claws retracted and she slid to the ground, gasping. He turned around and looked at her. His face was filled with surprise, then became pained. "Zed," he said. "You . . . came back." He looked confused, then his face cleared and turned stony. "But not to help me." He shook his head at her. "You joined *them*? How could you do that to me?"

Dr. Jakande slowly got to her feet, trying to catch her breath and collect her wits so she could be prepared for whatever he'd do next. Then, impulsively, she tapped the communication button on her device so Ms. Sabbith would be able to hear the conversation. Perhaps she could get a confession from the man.

"How could you do this? Try to turn everyone *in the world* into chimeras?" she asked him. "You've taken this way too far, Victor." She hesitated. "And I think you know it, too."

"There's no such thing as going too far to save humanity," said Dr. Gray.

"When you make everyone into animals, humanity loses! It's a mistake!"

"You're wrong!" said Dr. Gray, his anger building. "If that's what you believe, why did you come with me in the first place?"

"Because back then your intentions were good." Dr. Jakande tested her leg strength and prepared to pounce again. "Or at least that's what you told us. But now . . ." She sighed, almost with regret. "Now you think you're going to rule a world of obedient beasts. You hid it from me, but I know the truth about you. Do the other soldiers?" She stepped around him slowly. "Do you, Cyke? And, Fang? Do you know how badly Victor Gray has lost his way?"

Dr. Gray exploded, tearing at the air and coming at her, ready to destroy her.

Dr. Jakande dodged him. "Where are they all, Victor? Where are Prowl and Miko?"

"They're not to be trusted!" Dr. Gray roared, unable to help himself from responding. He went after Dr. Jakande again. "They don't see the benefits of my plan. But I'll terminate them. Just like I'm about to terminate you!"

Dr. Jakande tsked. "After all they've done for you, that's how you reward them?" She glanced down to make sure her microphone was still on. Then the panther woman ran and sprang over Victor's head, jumping out of reach. She climbed the wall and leaped, grabbed on to a chandelier, then dropped on top of him again, claws extended and sinking in. He shrieked and tried to wrestle her off him, but she was stuck fast.

Finally Dr. Gray managed to get his own claws in Dr. Jakande. He ripped her off him and threw her over his head with all his new-found strength. Her body flew fast and smashed hard into the wall. She dropped to the floor, broken and still. The scientist stared at her for a moment in horror, like he couldn't believe what he'd done. But then his face hardened. He whirled around accusingly and started toward the other fights. "You are the cause of this!" he roared when he saw Charlie still struggling with Cyke. "And you won't make it out of here alive!"

Charlie glared.

Kelly, who'd just stabbed Fang again with poison, looked up and saw Dr. Gray acting crazy and going after Charlie. She left the soldier half-paralyzed and hissing, and struggled to her feet. She limped toward the doctor, checking her device as she went, and accidentally clicked off her camouflage. Kelly glanced up to see Dr. Gray staring at her. In a panic she turned her camo back on again, but it was too late. Before she could attack him, the man swung his arm out like a tree trunk and smacked it into her, sending her skittering across the room. "You're a traitor too, Kelly?" he said in disgust. "After all I did for you? I *saved* you."

Kelly cowered and stifled a cry, her head spinning and her ear and face on fire. She crawled farther away, blending into the marble floor, but his narrowed eyes followed her. "You got me stuck in Mexico," Kelly said, scrambling to think of something to say that would give her a few moments to recover. "And . . . you broke your promise. You never gave me another ability like you said you would."

"I told you I would in time!" shouted Dr. Gray. "And that time would've been now—you'd have gotten the same amazing abilities as all my lovely new chimeras. Plus, I would have let you keep your bracelet." He lowered his voice. "If only you'd been loyal. But I saw what you were doing. Braun was watching you. You and Miko whispering. Miko and Prowl sneaking around these last few weeks, talking about me behind my back. I knew at the end that I wouldn't be able to trust any of you. And now, because of what you've done, I won't give you the satisfaction of receiving these abilities I've worked my entire life to collect and refine. Because you don't deserve them. Cyke," he commanded, turning to the soldier, "this fight is to the death. Call in the others from downstairs."

Cyke blocked Charlie's fist and cringed. "I've already tried. They're not answering."

"If you've done something to my soldiers . . . ," warned Dr. Gray. Before he could say what he'd do, Maria came charging at the scientist, werealligator mode deployed. She lunged at him and grabbed his arm in her mouth, chomping down hard.

Dr. Gray howled and shook her off. He picked her up and drop kicked her down the flight of stairs. Then he turned back to Charlie.

Charlie smashed her foot into Cyke's chin, sending him reeling and flopping to the floor. "Go poison yourself!" she yelled. Then she saw Dr. Gray charging toward her. "Kelly! I need help!" Winded and bruised all over, Charlie wasn't sure she could handle Dr. Gray and Cyke at the same time. But escape was a temporary option. Fingers tingling, she sprang for the wall and stuck to it, then climbed up out of reach of Dr. Gray. She caught her breath, then moved onto the ceiling and crawled so that she was above Dr. Gray's head. She scaled down onto a chandelier and started swinging on it, then let go of one hand and foot so she was hanging, ready to kick him in the face if he got too close.

Dr. Gray sprang at her. Charlie wasn't expecting him to jump so well, and didn't pull back in time. He grabbed onto her ankle and they hung there for a moment. Then he yanked her to the floor. Charlie hit hard. She lay still.

Dr. Gray stumbled and lost his grip. He righted himself and charged at the unconscious girl.

"I don't think so!" From the stairwell, Mac appeared in full pangolin mode. He clanked toward the scuffle, sharp scales pivoted outward and claws bared. Mac plowed into the scientist and began spinning, slicing into the doctor with his sharp pangolin scales.

Maria came hopping back up the stairs, in monkey mode this time. She climbed the banister and leaped for the chandeliers. Then swung from one to the next and slammed her feet into Dr. Gray's chest, sending him reeling away from Charlie. Maria turned and headed toward Cyke.

Mac noticed Dr. Jakande still on the floor in a heap, and ran to help her. Kelly reached Charlie, who was stirring. She took Kelly's outstretched hand and pulled herself to her feet. Dr. Gray, Cyke, and Fang were all down—Fang was paralyzed by Kelly's poison and seemingly out of the game. But Dr. Gray and Cyke were stirring.

"We got this," said Charlie to the others. She spat out a mouthful of blood. "I hope my teeth grow back or my mom's gonna kill me."

"Look out," warned Mac. "Cyke's up."

"Not for long," said Charlie, stepping toward him. Cyke lunged at her and she stuck her arm out, clotheslining him. He flipped and landed on his back. Charlie cracked her elbow into his face.

"Nice one," said Mac.

But Charlie's expression turned fearful as she stood up. "Oh crud," she said, looking down at her arm. Cyke's fangs had connected and sunk into Charlie's skin. Her arm began to ache and swell. "No!" she cried as the venom pulsed through her. She kicked

Cyke in the stomach with all her strength, sending him flying into the wall. Her friends chased after him to try to keep him down.

Charlie couldn't join them. She broke out into a cold sweat and bent over, feeling dizzy. The room began spinning. She couldn't control her movements. She stumbled forward and went down to her hands and knees. She never saw Dr. Gray coming.

When the man smashed his clawed foot into the side of her head, everything went black.

Charlie lay on the floor, unable to move. Her head throbbed. Poison took over her body. In her altered state, Charlie pondered over Dr. Gray and his new abilities, still not sure what they all were. She tried to remember the one-liners and random facts that Ms. Sabbith had given them over the past few weeks about the animals they'd been seeking.

Dr. Gray was just too powerful. Too strong for them—for anyone. She realized with a sinking heart that they could fight him forever, but he'd always be able to come back. There was no way to beat him.

This battle, she realized, was useless. And it was only making Charlie and her friends weaker and more vulnerable. He was wearing them down. And they were falling into the trap.

It was in this haze between life and death, in this paralyzed, dreamlike state caused by the poison, that Charlie remembered something Dr. Jakande had said. An idea began to form.

Meanwhile, Maria, Mac, and Kelly grew weaker. They couldn't

keep up against Cyke and Dr. Gray. As if in a bubble, Charlie could hear a breathless Dr. Jakande using her communications device to summon help from the other scientists. All the while, Charlie's starfish ability began to push the poison out of her body. And after a few minutes, Charlie could think a bit more clearly again. But she held on to her idea, hoping it was just crazy enough to work.

CHAPTER 45

Explosion

Charlie opened her eyes and blinked. The noise from the fighting grew clearer. Her vision was back to normal. Her breath hitched as she realized the world hadn't stopped with her. In fact, Dr. Gray was growing stronger as he learned how to use his chimera abilities.

Charlie realized how backward the man's thinking was. He talked about saving humanity, but his only purpose here, in the top of this giant statue, was to destroy Charlie and her friends. He was a monster, way more than any of them. Even more than Mega had become. And he was unstoppable. Unless . . .

Charlie sat up and almost blacked out again. She steadied herself and looked around, seeing Maria swinging from a chandelier with her feet outstretched and speeding toward Cyke's chest. And Mac, slamming his extended blades into Dr. Gray and clawing at him with his sharp pangolin claws. The man was injured and bleeding, but he was going strong. With a start, Charlie realized her dad had arrived and was in the fight now too, trying to use his strength to keep Dr. Gray from going after Dr. Jakande, who was still hurt and moving slowly.

Dr. Gray loomed over Dr. Wilde. He jabbed at him, then snatched him up and tried tossing him down the stairwell. But Dr. Wilde grabbed onto Dr. Gray's hair, yanking out handfuls of it. Dr. Gray cried out.

Charlie couldn't sit by. Her team needed her. She staggered to her feet as Maria let out a scream of pain. Her foot had been pierced by Cyke's fangs. She dropped from the chandelier and crumpled to the ground.

"Dad! Maria needs help!" Charlie cried out. "Hurry—she's been poisoned by Cyke!"

Charlie tried to think. Fighting Dr. Gray was a lost cause unless there was a way to destroy him. But she also had to keep him from destroying her friends. She stopped short of attacking when she noticed her mom sneaking up the stairs. Charlie turned sharply and went to her, crouching down.

"What can I do?" Mrs. Wilde whispered. "How can I help?"

"Sneak out to the balcony. Turn off the machine," Charlie said, pointing to the door. "Use your mask! And . . . there's a syringe on the floor somewhere near there. You're going to need it." She whispered some more instructions to her mother, who nodded.

Dr. Gray looked furiously at Charlie. "Don't you dare turn off my machine!" he bellowed at Mrs. Wilde. He shoved Kelly into Mac's sharp scales, then ran at Charlie's mom and slammed his foot into her throat, knocking her down a few steps.

"Mom!" cried Charlie. "Are you okay?"

"I'm fine!" Mrs. Wilde said, sounding not very fine. Charlie barreled into Dr. Gray, but he was like an iron statue and went nowhere. He shoved her to the ground easily.

Charlie rebounded. She took a couple breaths, then wound up and slugged the man in the eye as hard as she could. He teetered and went down. For the moment, at least. She turned to find Cyke. Who could help her take him down? They couldn't get Gray until Cyke was out.

Maria was down with a Komodo dragon poison bite. Dr. Jakande still hadn't recovered from being thrown into the wall. Charlie's dad was helping Maria expel poison, so he didn't have a device to use. Mac was rolled up into a pangolin ball while Cyke tried to pry him open. Determined to end the battle, Charlie spied Kelly and sidled up to her. "Listen. We have to take out Cyke for good, or there's no winning this. My strength, your poison. Let's do it."

Kelly, bruised and limping, wiped blood off her face and nodded. "I'm ready. You lead."

Charlie sneaked around Cyke's back as he continued digging at Mac. Kelly followed her. Then, together, the two girls ran at him. Charlie leaped and grabbed him around the neck in a chokehold. She pulled him backward and slammed him on the ground. "Now!"

Kelly swiveled and aimed her heel at him, but Cyke blocked her leg just in time.

But he wasn't prepared for Kelly's other heel. She anticipated his block, and as she jumped up again, she switched legs in mid-air like some wild soccer goddess, and scored with her other heel, sinking it deep into his side. His fist connected with her stomach.

Kelly grunted and flopped to the ground. Cyke let out a scream. And Dr. Gray came thundering over.

Dr. Wilde looked up in alarm. He ran to get between Dr. Gray and the girls to keep the ogre from helping Cyke. Without a device, though, there wasn't much Mr. Wilde could do. "Nubia! Mac! Help me keep him away from Cyke!"

Mac peeked out of his rolled-up form, then scooted away and got up.

"One more, Kelly!" Charlie shouted. She struggled as Cyke flopped on top of her, pinning her under him. Kelly moaned and rolled to her side. Then, with supreme effort, she finished the soldier off with another poison kick to the backside.

Dr. Gray's largest soldier flattened, his body writhing until the poison halted all movement. Only his screams remained. Mac and the two doctors kept Dr. Gray at bay.

Charlie lifted the meaty soldier off herself and pushed him aside with a grunt. She staggered to her feet. "Kelly, are you okay?" The girl was still clutching her stomach.

"I just . . . need to . . . catch my breath," said Kelly.

Now the team, minus Maria, faced the lone scientist, who appeared to grow even larger and more monstrous before their eyes. Everyone was injured and exhausted. Only Dr. Gray seemed energized.

Charlie signaled to the others to hold back for a moment and catch their breath before rushing at the man as a team. She caught a glimpse of her mother, who'd stealthily slipped past the various fights, and had finally made it to the balcony. She unplugged the machine and the vaporizer fan blades stopped. Then Mrs. Wilde pulled the cylinder of formula out and crouched down next to it, using her body as a shield to hide what she was doing. She glanced over her shoulder occasionally as she worked, fear in her eyes.

A moment later Mrs. Wilde slipped something into her pocket and put the cylinder back. Then she waited by the door, peering in, and watched for the right moment to come inside. Had she at least minimized the effect of the formula on the people below? Or was it already too late?

Inside, Charlie, Mac, Kelly, and Dr. Jakande struggled to corner Dr. Gray. Finally out of danger, Mr. Wilde pulled out two reversal devices and ran over to Cyke. He slapped one on Cyke's wrist, then moved on to Fang and did the same. The two soldiers morphed back into full human form, removing all indicators of their hybrid animals.

Dr. Gray looked over the heads of his challengers and stared in shock. He wrenched away from them. "What? Charles! Stop ruining my soldiers!"

Mac, Kelly, and Dr. Jakande struggled to contain him. Charlie pushed him back against the stair railing. "Hold him down!" she cried. She looked over at her father, waiting expectantly for him to come with a reversal bracelet.

"You get this one, Charlie," said Mr. Wilde. He tossed the remaining reversal bracelet to her.

Charlie caught it. "Keep him still!" She opened the bracelet's clasp and lunged for the man's wrist. But Dr. Gray's strength overpowered the others. Before she could snap the device around his wrist, he wrenched loose and slapped it away. It flew through the air, over the stair railing, clinking and clanking until they couldn't hear it anymore. Then Dr. Gray plowed through them and went to see what had happened to his soldiers.

"Are there any more?" asked Mac.

"They're downstairs with Dr. Sharma," said Mr. Wilde.

"I'll go after it," Kelly said, panting.

Charlie leaned over the railing but it was out of sight. "No, Kelly. Don't waste your energy. He'll just fight us off again." Charlie turned away and said softly, "But there's one more thing we can try."

From where the soldiers lay, Dr. Gray muttered incoherently, furious about the state of his soldiers. He turned sharply toward Kelly and Dr. Jakande. "You've set me back. But you'll never beat me."

"You're probably right," said Charlie before the others could answer. She walked toward him. "You're invincible. Stronger than all of us put together. Right?"

Dr. Gray narrowed his eyes at Charlie and took a step toward her. "Perhaps."

The others glanced uneasily at one another but stayed put, waiting for Charlie to direct them.

"We should probably just give up right now if you've got that," Charlie said. "There's no way we can ever beat you."

Mac and Kelly exchanged a look. They could tell Charlie was bluffing. But why? What was she going to do? Was she just buying time to get stronger? Or was something else going on?

"That's the smartest thing that's ever come out of your mouth," snarled Dr. Gray.

Charlie snorted. He didn't know her. He was just trying to make her feel weak. She stayed where she was, and for the moment they were at a standoff. Charlie glanced at Maria. Was she conscious yet? They needed her. But more importantly in this moment, Charlie needed the Mark Five.

Charlie continued asking Gray questions, and he, being vain, continued to answer them. Soon Maria was sitting up. When she saw everyone standing together, she staggered over to be with them.

"I guess we're at least going to try one last time to take you down, though," Charlie finally said to the scientist. "So, maybe you could humor us."

"What? That's ridiculous. Why should I?"

"Get him!" cried Charlie. Everyone charged at him, weak though they were. But Dr. Gray wasn't weak at all. He swung his fists, knocking Charlie and her friends left and right. They couldn't get a good shot at him.

It seemed like Charlie's plans were quickly falling by the wayside. Their team had lost too much strength. And Dr. Gray was more than they could handle.

Suddenly the door to the observation deck opened.

"Not yet, Mom!" yelled Charlie, without looking. She and her team were falling. Failing. And she didn't want her mom to get clobbered too.

But Mrs. Wilde opened the doors wide. The room filled with a tremendous wind, and the sound of . . . flapping wings. Charlie whirled around and looked up to see Miko soaring in. Below her, along for the ride, was Prowl.

Miko circled in the ballroom and dropped Prowl onto the evil scientist, knocking him back. Prowl sank his claws into the man's chest and sent an electric shock through him.

"Aaah!" cried Dr. Gray. "Miko! Prowl! What are you doing? Help me!"

"Help yourself!" yelled Miko. "We heard what you said about us. Maybe it's time to terminate YOU."

Dr. Gray stared, shaking and not comprehending.

Charlie saw her chance. "Kelly," she whispered, and nodded at the man. It was time for Charlie and Kelly to team up once more.

They glanced at each other with a new understanding, and attacked together. Charlie held him down and Kelly slammed her poisonous spikes into him. He writhed and moaned, but couldn't get up. Prowl added another electric shock for good measure.

"Mom! Now!" cried Charlie.

Mrs. Wilde came running over. She held a syringe in her hand, filled with the formula Dr. Gray had created for the masses. She sank the needle into Dr. Gray's shoulder and depressed the plunger.

"What on earth, Diana?" asked Dr. Jakande, alarmed. "Why are you making him stronger?"

"She's not!" said Charlie. "She's trying to make him unstable!" Charlie knelt down. "Remember what you said that one time? Too much DNA could cause big problems. And I knew we needed a backup plan." She watched Dr. Gray carefully. He didn't seem to be any more unstable than before. "Hmm," she said, growing worried. "Maybe it's because it's made up of the same DNA he already has. Maria, where's the Mark Two?"

Mr. Wilde dug it out of his pocket and handed it over. "Smart, Charlie," he said. "Very smart. I think you're onto something."

"If not, we're in big trouble." Charlie stuck Maria's device on the man's wrist and activated it.

"We can call Dr. Sharma to bring up a reversal bracelet," said Mac.

"I don't know if we'll be able to hold him that long," muttered Charlie as Dr. Gray continued to struggle free. "Let's hope this works. Take your device off and stick it on him, Mac. Dr. Jakande, yours too!"

They both hurried to do so, immediately transforming to their normal bodies. Dr. Gray began to squirm harder. His face reddened.

"Something's happening," said Maria. "Charlie, here! Add this one!" She shoved the Mark Five at Charlie, who slapped it onto the scientist's other arm, hoping the healing power wouldn't work against them in this case.

"What about yours?" suggested Mac.

"It won't work," said Charlie, distressed. "It's tied to my DNA."

"Use mine!" cried Kelly. She removed her device and gave it to Charlie.

"Awesome," Charlie muttered. She closed the device around Dr. Gray's wrist and Kelly activated it. "Come on. Please."

Dr. Gray began groaning and shaking. His body shape started to change, turning to something like a big blobfish, but soon he took on the features of the animals from the other devices. He morphed from alligator to panther to monkey, all the while turning strange colors. Fur, claws, and tails sprouted on him, then receded.

Miko and Prowl crouched nearby, watching, unable to believe their eyes as Dr. Gray began to swell and turn red.

Suddenly Mr. Wilde shot to his feet. "Get back!" he said, waving everyone to move out of the way. "Take cover! Something's happening." He looked around the building frantically, then pointed to a wide, solid marble archway. "Stand under there and shield your heads!"

"What?" cried Charlie. "Why?" But she and the others didn't wait for an answer. They dived down the hallway under the giant arch.

"Here it comes!" shouted Mr. Wilde, joining them.

Miko spread her wings to protect them. The floor shook. Dr. Wilde's eyes widened. "I think he's going to—"

Before he could finish his sentence, a huge explosion rocked the statue. Silt and hunks of plaster and rock rained down on them.

Terrified, Charlie glanced up just as the archway began to crumble around the edges. The ceiling cracked and the posts splintered, and the wide marble arch came crashing down. Instinctively Charlie jumped up, arms outstretched, and caught it before it could crush them all.

When the noise and crumbling stopped, Charlie gently moved the arch out of their way. The team began to pick through the rubble. They could see the sky in places where the roof had caved in.

"Where's Gray?" asked Dr. Jakande anxiously, looking around the area where they'd last seen him. "He didn't escape, did he?"

"Ah, nope," said Prowl, sniffing everything. "He's . . . everywhere. Blown into a zillion pieces. Eww."

"We need to get out of here before the whole statue crumbles," said Mrs. Wilde. "Everybody take the stairs! Now!"

"I can fly a few people down," offered Miko. She looked at Maria and Mac. "How about it?"

The two eyed Miko warily. "Aren't you the bad guys?" asked Maria.

"We didn't mean to be," said Miko with a shrug.

Maria was skeptical, even though they'd helped save the day. She turned to Kelly. "Are these two all right?"

Kelly caught Miko's eye and smiled. "Yeah," she said, sounding awfully pleased to be trusted. "They're all right."

"We'll see you down there," said Charlie. She turned to Kelly. "Come on, I'll race you down." She took off running.

"Hey!" cried Kelly, about to say how unfair it was since Charlie still had her device. But Kelly could never turn down a challenge, especially one from a friend. She charged after her. And for a moment, in the midst of rubble and ruin, life felt normal again.

CHAPTER 46

The State of Things

Charlie and her team gathered a short distance from the base of the statue. Surrounding the area were US government officials and Mexican police, all trying to figure out what was going on. Ms. Sabbith and Dr. Goldstein were there, too.

Kelly stood uneasily to one side, eyeing the police. She had mixed feelings about being so close to them after what she'd done. Would she end up in jail when all of this was sorted out? At least they were busy with other things for the moment.

Beyond them, tourists and locals alike who had become chimeras wandered around confused. Some of them were freaking out at their newly changed appearance, others trying to listen to the authorities to understand what had happened to them.

Charlie's jaw dropped when she saw them. There were hundreds of people affected by the mist—with claws and fur and scales, they all looked like a tamer version of Dr. Gray. Clearly their job wasn't over yet. She left Maria, Mac, and Kelly, and went up to her father. "How many of those reversal devices do you have left?" Charlie whispered. "Did you get the ones back that you put on the soldiers upstairs before the place blew up?"

"No," he said. "But Dr. Sharma grabbed the one that Victor knocked down the stairwell, and she got the ones off Braun and Morph. Sabbith brought the rest, along with the remaining formula." He rubbed his injured jaw thoughtfully. "So it'll take a while to change everyone back—but I'm so glad we have this solution."

"Yeah, thanks to Dr. Jakande for figuring it out," said Charlie. "Without her, we'd be looking at a lot more trouble right now." She gazed perplexed as the police began rounding up all the chimeras. Some of them refused to comply, but most went willingly once they realized the police were trying to help. "Let's start changing them back so they can see it's possible," said Mr. Wilde.

"And before they realize what kind of power they have," said Charlie. "Things could get ugly really quickly."

"Dr. Sharma is talking to our government officials, trying to get permission to start," said Mr. Wilde. "I think we'll be okay." He hesitated, thinking about it, then added, "Most people are decent when you get right down to it. Just because they're infected with the chimera virus doesn't mean they'll do wrong with the new abilities. Maybe some of them would do what you and your friends did. Make things better. Use power for good. You know?"

Charlie nodded. She believed that—it was like what they'd talked about with Maria. The alligator in her didn't make her turn into something awful. She made her own choices.

And even though Charlie had seen more people being evil than good with their abilities, there were also those like Dr. Jakande and Kelly, who'd tried that and turned back to doing the right thing. And Miko and Prowl, too. Charlie would have never expected them to help save the day, especially Prowl. She rubbed her shoulder where her most recent Prowl stabbing had been. The wounds were healed.

She looked around for the two of them, but didn't see their familiar hybrid outlines in the crowd. "Where are Prowl and Miko?" she asked, feeling immediately suspicious.

"Dr. Jakande used the reversal devices on them once everyone made it out of the statue. And they, uh, *got away* before the police could get to them."

Charlie thought that seemed kind of sneaky, but she was glad after what they'd done to help put an end to Dr. Gray. Charlie hoped those two could get back to whatever they missed about their former lives. But she still had questions. "How did they escape from Ms. Sabbith? Didn't you keep them in the restraints I made?"

"We did. But Nubia was in touch with Erica several times, and they overheard Dr. Gray's confession, where he basically condemned Prowl and Miko for not being loyal and suggested he'd terminate them. That didn't go over well."

"That was smart for Dr. J. to keep her mike on during that."

"You bet it was. When we called for all hands on deck to fight, Prowl and Miko, who'd been totally cooperative since their capture, convinced Erica to let them help." He paused in thought. "I'm not sure what they said to her, because Erica is a tough, savvy person and she's great at telling when people are lying. But whatever it was, Erica let them go. She must have known they had really had a change of heart."

"Wow," said Charlie. She was quiet for a moment, thinking over the events of the day, and recalled the water fight. "Don't forget Mega is still in the lake somewhere," she said.

Her father nodded. "We'll make sure everyone involved is accounted for. Miko said that Mega would be more than willing to have her animal powers reversed. She hadn't expected to be stuck in water for the rest of her life."

"I don't blame her," said Charlie.

Charlie went back to her friends to give them the scoop. She found the three of them leaning up against one another, looking like exhaustion had set in. Maria was still nursing her wounds. Thankfully she'd healed a lot before they'd lost the Mark Five in the explosion.

Ms. Sabbith finished her conversation with the officials. She turned around abruptly and waved her hand in the air, then whistled sharply to call for silence. "Okay, scientists, we're clear to get started treating the accidental chimeras. We'll create a triage area here, and the police will oversee the line. Does anyone know where Gray's remaining formula is?"

"It got blown up with everything else," said Mac.

"We'll make sure the officials use hazmat suits when they go back in," said Ms. Sabbith. "And destroy any trace of it."

"Do you think they'll ever find our devices?" Maria asked. "I kinda miss having mine."

"Well," said Mac, "they were made of titanium, so they might have survived."

Kelly frowned. "I think I'm good without mine, but thanks."

"We'll make sure we get those back, too, if they survived the explosion," said Dr. Sharma, joining them. With her was a woman in uniform. The kids stood up, and Dr. Sharma introduced Captain Brenda Zimmerman, the one who'd been in charge of Project Chimera. The one who'd seen the footage of Charlie, Mac, and Maria, and who'd decided to act because of it. "I'm afraid we'll have to turn all of the devices over to the captain," Dr. Sharma said. "They are government property, after all." She glanced at Charlie.

Charlie looked down at the Mark Six feeling a twinge of sadness. "Can I at least finish healing first?" she asked.

"I think we can allow that," said Captain Zimmerman with a smile. She turned to the group. "I want to thank you all for your work, especially you children. I've never had to say this before in my career, but I'm thrilled to be able to say it today: You literally saved the human race. We are extremely grateful for your service."

Charlie, Mac, Maria, and Kelly exchanged grins. It was weird having Kelly back with them, but it was good, too. She seemed like a changed person. Charlie hoped it would last. She also hoped Kelly wouldn't get into too much trouble.

Captain Zimmerman continued, glancing at Kelly. "And, if there were any *issues* you might have encountered in your travels while under the direction of Dr. Gray, consider yourself fully cleared of blame."

Kelly's eyes widened. "You mean the . . ."

"Yes, that," said the captain firmly.

Kelly sank to her haunches with a huge sigh and put a hand over her eyes. Her lip quivered. "Thank you," she whispered. She blew out a breath and sniffed. When she took her hand away, her eyes were red-rimmed. "That means everything." She rose again, then looked around self-consciously.

Maria, Mac, and Charlie, exchanged looks, then they tackled Kelly, slinging their arms over her shoulders and patting her on the back. Kelly, still stunned, laughed for the first time in a long time. It felt like her smile might split her face right open.

The scientists began working on the people of the island with the remaining few reversal devices, but Captain Zimmerman lingered with the four young heroes. "We're thinking about reopening this project," she said. "Despite what happened, I can see the good in it, and with the right people in place, I believe the outcome could be very different. I'm hoping our team of scientists here will stay on—their expertise is invaluable. And," she said slyly, "perhaps you four will consider going into the sciences in college so you can help us with it someday."

Charlie blinked. She hadn't given any thought to college—that was like a million years away. But she did sometimes picture herself one day working with her dad in a lab somewhere, doing good things together to make the world a better place to live. "Yeah," she murmured. "I could see that happening." But she wasn't so sure about working on more devices like these. They seemed a little bit dangerous after everything they'd just gone through.

Maria tapped her lips thoughtfully. "Maybe after my soccer career is over." Then she shook her head. "Nah. I'll probably become a chef. Cooking is kind of like science, though, if you really think about it."

"It is," agreed the captain, who seemed delighted with the conversation.

Mac was definitely intrigued. "I love animals," he said. "So I'll probably do it."

"Well," said Kelly, "you can count me out. I'm going to be pretty busy being famous on Broadway now that my chimera internet fame is a no-go."

The woman laughed. "Whatever you decide, I hope you have some time to enjoy this beautiful city now that your work is done."

"I hope so too," said Charlie. "We've worked hard this summer! We need a nice long vacation."

"Not so fast," said Mrs. Wilde, picking up on the conversation from a few feet away. "I'm pretty sure we all have somewhere else we need to be."

Charlie looked confused, and her heart sank. "We do?" she lamented. She was tired of traveling for the first time in her life. "Now where?"

"Home," said her mother. "Seventh grade starts awfully soon. We need to get your school supplies, a new backpack, and get you some clothes that aren't riddled with leopard-claw and shark-bite holes."

Charlie smiled. Home. It sounded so . . . normal.

CHAPTER 47

Back to . . . Normal?

Not everything went smoothly.

The team stayed in Mexico a few more days, making sure absolutely everyone who was affected by the virus had been located and treated. The scientists also helped the police and US officials determine if there was anything else dangerous inside the house that Dr. Gray and his soldiers had been living in.

Cyke and Fang never made it out of the giant statue. Braun and Mega and Morph went to jail. Miko and Prowl successfully escaped. Kelly worried about them, but they didn't hear anything from the duo.

Nubia glanced up. "Charlie can try to reach Miko through the comm system in my suit," she said.

But Kelly shook her head. "Unless Miko stopped back at the house, she doesn't have a suit with her. But Prowl might."

Charlie shuddered. "I'll leave that up to you, Dr. Jakande, once I give you your suit back."

They had other things to worry about, too. Like Kelly's parents not remembering her. That was a conundrum. Without her Mark Four device, there was no way for Kelly to hypnotize her mom and dad into remembering they had an almost-thirteen-year-old daughter again. So Kelly moved in with Charlie's family temporarily — and all the scientists agreed to stay around until the problem was solved.

Going back home would be bittersweet for Kelly. Not because she loved the idea of living with Charlie, though it turned out not to be too bad—after a while it felt kind of like having a sister and brother. But going home meant she'd get stuck in the middle of her parents' fighting again. It had been nice to be away from that for a while. Maybe things had calmed down between them by now. The Wildes assured Kelly that she always had a place in their house if she needed it.

The first day of seventh grade went pretty well. Kelly had little trouble—she just told everybody she moved back. The hardest part for Kelly was talking in circles around her whole "fame" incident back in the spring, when she'd used her camouflage on live TV. She began to wish she had her Mark Four back so she could hypnotize everyone to forget it had ever happened.

But all of that trouble was worth it when she got to audition for Mr. Anderson again. She nailed her performance and Charlie told Kelly afterward that the hope on Mr. Anderson's face was magical.

After dinner that first day, everyone somehow ended up at the Wildes' house. Charlie and her friends and the scientists had

bonded so much over the summer. They'd had lots of laughs. And they'd been through so many harrowing experiences and special moments together that it just seemed right to share their stories of their first day of school like they were one big family.

When there was a lull in the conversation, something came to Charlie's mind that she'd been meaning to ask the scientists for days. "That government official," she began, "Captain Zimmerman. Remember her?"

The scientists laughed and nodded. How could they forget?

"She said something about continuing Project Chimera. Did she ever talk to you about that?"

"She did," said Dr. Sharma. "She asked us all to stay on the project."

Charlie looked concerned. "I hope you said no," she blurted out. The more she'd thought about the situation over the past week, the more she felt like it was a terrible idea.

"Yeah!" agreed Maria and Mac vehemently.

"A big fat no," said Kelly.

"What?" said Andy, crestfallen. "Before I even get my chance to be a superhero? That wouldn't be fair."

Charlie and her friends explained passionately to Andy about why it was such a bad idea.

The scientists seemed amused by the kids' strong reactions. Mr. Wilde put his hands up. "Everybody, hold on," he said. "We came up with a good idea."

The kids stopped talking and looked at the scientists. "What did you tell them?" asked Charlie.

"We convinced them that Project Chimera, as we knew it, should be shut down for all the reasons you're mentioning," said Dr. Sharma. She glanced at Mrs. Wilde, who wore a small smile and seemed to be brimming with a secret. "But there was one aspect of the project that we felt was not only redeemable, but could change the world—for the better."

Charlie looked at her mom, then back at Dr. Sharma, then at her mom again. And she thought she knew the answer.

Maria leaned forward. "What is it?"

"The healing," said Charlie. "Right?"

Mrs. Wilde nodded. "How did you guess?"

"I remember when I first told you about the healing power," Charlie said, "and you said how wonderful it would be if emergency rooms everywhere had access to that. It would change the world."

"That's right," said Mrs. Wilde. "It's been on my mind since then. So we pitched them this idea of a new project to create a device that would not only heal physical wounds like the Mark Five and Six could do, but maybe one day our scientists would come up with a way to cure diseases." Her eyes shone. "The possibilities are incredible."

"And we'd be working on our own terms," Dr. Sharma added. "Doing what we love."

As Charlie and her friends imagined what that could mean for their lives, their futures, they began to talk about how amazing it could be for the world.

"There's just one issue," said Dr. Goldstein, straight-faced.

"What is it?" Charlie asked, narrowing her eyes. Was that a hint of teasing in his voice? She couldn't tell.

"Talos Global's lab is in Chicago. You have to move back."

Charlie felt the blood drain from her face as Mac, Maria, and Kelly erupted into arguments. Then Charlie saw the gleam in Dr. Goldstein's eye. "Wait, wait, everybody wait. You're just kidding, right?"

"Yeah," he said, apologetically. "Sorry—that got a bigger reaction than I envisioned. The truth is Dr. Sharma and I are thinking it would be more fun to move the lab out here and create the southwest branch of Talos Global. Does that sound better?"

Charlie sighed deeply and the others relaxed. "Much better." She hadn't realized until this moment just how much she loved living here now. She couldn't imagine going back. "I want to be with my friends—these friends —forever. As long as I live."

"Agree!" said Maria, and she echoed, "For as long as we all live!"

"Yeah!" said Mac.

Kelly narrowed her eyes craftily. "Hey, that gives me an idea. Remember that immortal jellyfish?"

The other three and the scientists looked at her in alarm. "NO!" everyone cried in unison, then they all broke down in laughter. Being immortal was quite possibly the worst. Idea. Ever. Sometimes it seemed like animals could be just a little *too* amazing.

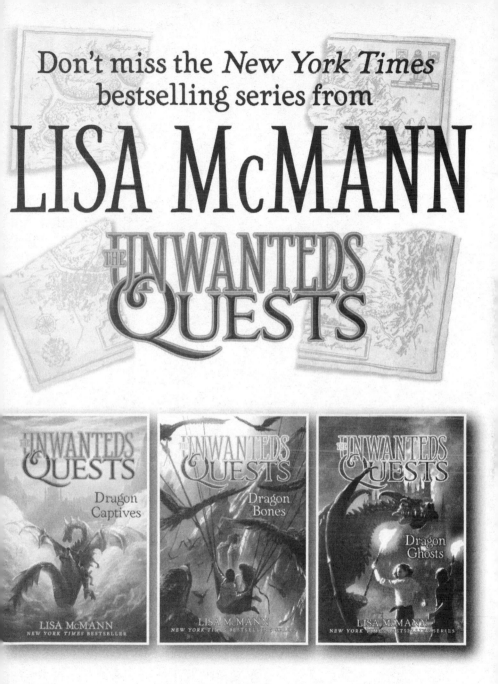